Little Creatures Everywhere

Little Creatures Everywhere

MARY BRINGLE

A CRIME CLUB BOOK

DOUBLEDAY

New York   London   Toronto   Sydney   Auckland

A CRIME CLUB BOOK

PUBLISHED BY DOUBLEDAY
a division of Bantam Doubleday Dell Publishing Group, Inc.
666 Fifth Avenue, New York, New York 10103

DOUBLEDAY and the portrayal of a man
with a gun are trademarks of Doubleday,
a division of Bantam Doubleday Dell
Publishing Group, Inc.

"Little Things" reprinted with permission of Macmillan Publishing Company from
Collected Poems by James Stephens. Copyright 1926 by Macmillan Publishing
Company, renewed 1954 by Cynthia Stephens.

Library of Congress Cataloging-in-Publication Data

Bringle, Mary.
    Little creatures everywhere / Mary Bringle. — 1st ed.
        p.   cm.
    "A Crime Club book."
    I. Title.
    PS3552.R485K55   1991
    813'.54—dc20   90-39756
                                                      CIP

ISBN 0-385-41358-0

January 1991

First Edition

For Ann, Don, Edward, Fritzi, and Phil.

Little things that run and quail
And die in silence and despair;

Little things that fight and fail
And fall on earth and sea and air;

All trapped and frightened little things,
The mouse, the coney, hear our prayer.

As we forgive those done to us,
The lamb, the linnet, and the hare,

Forgive us all our trespasses,
Little creatures everywhere.

—JAMES STEPHENS

ONE

The problem was that she was over-tired, and sleep refused to come. Lying in a strange room, without her husband beside her, and hearing no sound beyond her windows were as much novelties as needing a blanket in August.

Laura willed her muscles to relax, especially the recalcitrant ones in her neck and shoulders. She replayed the long day just passed, seeing it in a series of swiftly moving pictures, newsreel-style. There she was at Newark Airport, furious because there was no water fountain and she felt very nearly dehydrated. Most of America was simmering in unheard-of heat, and the friend who had driven her to the airport from Manhattan had no air conditioning in her ancient Chevrolet.

Wrong image: The memory of her dismay about the lack of water fountains pumped adrenaline, the last thing she needed. She'd given up and bought an overpriced diet soda at one of the clip-joint refreshment stands, and it had been so filled with nasty chips of ice it was mainly water before she'd taken three sips. Move forward, she instructed her mental camera, but a small voice was telling her not to be such a naive person. *The reason there were no water fountains was to force travelers to buy drinks at a two-hundred-percent markup.*

All right, point taken, she thought irritably. Could a person get some sleep around here? Move to the flight to Denver, the brief glimpse of the beginnings of the Rockies she'd had when switching planes, and then the tranquil and uneventful flight to Portland, Oregon.

Just as she was picturing herself in the rented car, driving out of the city and toward her romantic and remote destination, she heard a faint booming sound, rhythmic and disturbing in the unaccustomed silence. Was it her blood beating in her ears, telling her that life in New York City had made her a candidate for an early stroke?

She composed an obituary. *Thousands mourn Laura Banks McAuley, whose death, by stroke, at the untimely age of thirty-seven, has rocked the world of publishing. Ms. McAuley died in a derelict hotel on the Long Beach Peninsula in the state of Washington. It was her first and only visit to the Pacific Northwest.*

No. The worst thing she could do was to write an obituary, which was so very much like jacket copy on a book. She turned on her side, reminding herself to be grateful for the cold air in her room, and returned to her scenario. Over the amazing bridge at Astoria she drove, a bridge that seemed to go on forever over the mighty river that had deceived Lewis and Clark more than a hundred years ago. The waters on the Washington side were called "the graveyard of the Pacific," because so many ships had foundered there. She was in a world of cool, dark forests, bounded by the Pacific Ocean, that gradually gave way to the long spit of land called the Long Beach Peninsula. Twenty-eight miles of beach, but too cold to swim. Like Fire Island, in fact, if you discounted the cool temperatures and lack of trendiness. She passed through tourist centers with huge chain-saw sculptures of mermaids at their hearts. There were motels and restaurants and curio museums featuring "shells from around the world," and then long stretches of nothing but piney woods until the next village came into view.

Her destination was nearly the last settlement on the Long Beach Peninsula, so far as she could tell from the map. It lay between a tidal bay and the open Pacific, and the hotel was on the bay side.

Grey Whale Hotel, read the sign that had been dismantled and lay in the long grass at the building's front. To the north of the hotel an enormous pile of oyster shells mounted toward the sky. The long circular drive led to the kitchen door these days, and Laura had encountered the caretaker squatting anxiously at the septic tank.

Gradually, her brain informed her that the booming noise was simply the Pacific Ocean. While she had been trying for sleep, the surf had risen. She was sure it would be a lulling sound under normal circumstances, but tonight it propelled her from her bed. She drew jeans and a sweater on over her thin pajamas, combed her straight, fair hair with her fingers, and made her way out to the landing. Before she had time to wish she'd packed a flashlight, the floorboards in the hall informed her she'd be well advised to put on some woolen socks.

This time, she left the light on in her room so it could cast a feeble glow out into the dim, vast space. At least it felt vast to her; as a hotel the Grey Whale had been small in its heyday—ten bedrooms and five bathrooms—but as an almost empty space she shared with only one other person, it was formidable. She nearly missed the stairwell and would have gone past it except for a faint light from the lower floor.

Tomorrow, she told herself, she would familiarize herself thoroughly with the Grey Whale's floor plan. It had been growing dark when she'd arrived, and Jesse, the caretaker, had told her to pick any room she liked. "I have my own apartment down here," he said, and Laura thought it showed surprising delicacy. He knew she wouldn't want to select a room connected to his by a bathroom, and saved her from having to inquire.

She descended the staircase slowly, wondering where the light came from. The big lounge, with its scattered sofas and easy chairs, its out-of-tune piano, was dark. To her right, when she stood on the bottom step, was the larder, also dark, and presumably beyond it, Jesse's quarters. She stepped through into the dining room and saw the caretaker writing at one of the tables. A single light burned at what had once been a table for four, and books were stacked high at every place but the one where he sat. She was about to clear her throat, but Jesse looked up with an expression of concern. "Couldn't sleep?" he asked.

Laura shook her head. There was something about him that suggested a trapper or Indian scout. He was about her age, and although he was not tall, he was powerfully built. She thought he must have some Indian blood. His skin was fair and his longish hair brown, but in profile his handsome beaked nose cried out for a warbonnet.

"Maybe you'd like a glass of wine?" He gestured toward his own glass of red, and to the jug at his elbow. "It might make you sleep."

"Yes," said Laura gratefully. "I didn't mean to disturb you, though."

Jesse glanced at the papers and books and smiled. "I was finishing up," he said. He scraped back his chair and padded—it was the only word to describe the silent glide of a man wearing stout hiking boots —through the dining room and into the kitchen, returning with a glass.

Her first sip of wine sent warm little fingers soothingly into her bloodstream. It, and her strange surroundings, made her suddenly long for a cigarette. She had cut down to five a day and long since used up her allotment. A pack of Marlboros lay on the table, and a full ashtray. She thought it odd that Jesse, an ecologist and nature man according to her friend Claudia, smoked at all, but she was reassured.

"What are you writing?" she asked.

"Oh, I'm not writing yet. Just gathering material. Taking notes."

In New York she would have asked the nature of his research, but this was not New York. She had not come three thousand miles to play editor in a disused hotel on the edge of the Pacific.

"How long have you known Claudia and Jack?" Jesse asked with a surprising directness, although he looked not at her but at his stack of books.

"I grew up with Claudia," she said. "I met Jack when she married him twelve years ago. I was a bridesmaid." She made her voice ironic, to show that being a bridesmaid was not the usual thing. Since Jesse only smiled politely, she added, "For the first and last time."

"I only met them two months ago, when they bought the hotel."

"Were you born here?"

"No, Seattle," said Jesse, lighting a cigarette and narrowing his trapper's eyes. "A friend of theirs recommended me. So far it's worked out well."

Laura tried not to show her surprise. "I'd trust Jesse Paget with my life," Claudia had said on the phone. "Think of the Grey Whale as your home away from home, at least until we open it up for business again."

The whole point of her flight to the Pacific Northwest was to soak up some much-needed rest. The only fly in the ointment was her husband Dan's business trip to West Germany, which meant he couldn't join her in Washington for ten days. For ten whole days she'd be with Trapper Jesse and whoever else the peninsula offered up in the way of company.

"Your husband will be joining you?" Jesse said, as if reading her mind.

"Oh, yes," said Laura. "He'll be here before you know it." She looked at the red end of Jesse's cigarette and compromised herself. "I could go upstairs and get one of mine," she said.

He was quick on the uptake and shook a Marlboro out of his pack and into her waiting fingers. "The Milky Way is spectacular tonight," he offered.

Before the night was ended, she found herself out on the lawn in front of the Grey Whale Hotel, giddy with red wine and exhaustion, admiring the glorious band of light in foreign skies.

"Good night, good night," she called, climbing up the stairs with new confidence. If Jesse answered, she didn't hear him. She found her way to her room, stripped away her heavy clothes, and crawled between the covers. The booming of the Pacific surf was now a pleasing sound, and she sank quickly into a deep and dreamless sleep.

"Beautiful, isn't it?" The voice could have come from the reeds, and it made Laura jump. She turned to confront a tall, attractive woman who had apparently taken the same path she had without making a sound. Was everyone here a tracker?

"I'm Althea," the woman said. "I just dropped by to lend Jesse a book, and I saw you down here."

They were in back of the hotel, as far as you could go without wading out into Willapa Bay, and it was, as Althea had said, beautiful. The bay was bounded on the far side by heavily wooded hills, and the sunlight had turned it from the gray she had seen last night to a pure and intense blue. The golden reeds appeared as if in a children's book illustration—too intensely and prettily colored to be true. Even as she said hello to Althea, a blue heron whirred out of a concealed nest not two feet away.

"Sorry I jumped like that," she said. "I didn't hear you coming."

"Probably because you live in a city," Althea said, cocking one long leg the better to balance a large carpetbag on her hip. "In a city it's so noisy you lose the ability to differentiate sounds after a while. I hate cities."

"You're from the Peninsula?" Laura asked. In her experience people who said they hated cities could be quite tiresome, but she detected no hostility in Althea.

"From Northern California. Lived in Alaska for ten years. I like it here."

They stood in companionable silence for a while, relishing the view of the bay, and then Althea abruptly said, "Come on. I'll introduce you to some berries."

Laura had noticed the berries and wondered if they were edible. The approach to the bay was thick with them, and they looked almost like blueberries, but nothing could have induced her to try one without the local seal of approval. For years now her only acquaintance with berries had occurred at the Korean produce stalls in Manhattan. All she knew was that she had reckoned herself successful on the day she'd realized she could afford to buy raspberries.

"They're salals," Althea instructed her, scooping nimbly to strip a little bush of its treasure and depositing her take in Laura's hand. "They're in decline, so late in the season."

The berries were tart and sweet in a bewilderingly wonderful fashion, and it was with their taste in her mouth she entered the Grey Whale, feeling she'd had a magical encounter in the reeds. Althea had roared off in an ancient pickup truck, and for the moment Jesse was nowhere to be seen. She decided now was as good a time as ever to explore the hotel by daylight.

In the kitchen, two eggs were boiling on the range, so she supposed Jesse hadn't gone far. The large containers of bottled water in the larder reminded her of his warning not to drink the water that came from the pipes. She wasn't likely to forget it, after her morning bath. The water came from the taps tea-colored, and although it had no odor, and was probably not harmful, it wasn't water you wanted to put in your mouth.

She resisted the impulse to examine his pile of books in the dining room and went upstairs. After a thorough patrol of all ten rooms, she was convinced she had chosen the best. Two of the rooms were equipped with twin beds. The remaining eight were full of surprises. One very attractive corner room featured a collapsed mattress, and another adjoined a bathroom in which a sign had been neatly taped: DO NOT FLUSH THE TOILET IN THIS LAVATORY. She wondered if Jesse had been the author of this note, but it looked ancient, before his time, and she didn't think he would use the word "lavatory."

The bedside lamp in another room didn't work, which seemed a definite minus, even though the light was breathtaking, filtered as it was through the dense limbs of fir trees on the hotel's southern and western extremities. No, with dumb luck she had chosen the best room. Her mattress was reasonably firm, her bathroom worked, and she had two windows. One looked out on the bay, and the other, the one which had permitted the sounds of the surf to come in last night, afforded a view of more fir trees. She could also make out the immense mountain of oyster shells up the road, but from this distance they seemed inconsequential—a mild blot on the landscape nobody could really find distressing.

When she had familiarized herself with the upper floor, scouted out the large linen closet with its frayed sheets and towels and pillowcases, she went back downstairs. Jesse was in the kitchen, expertly slicing tomatoes, adding them to the hard-boiled egg slices and dousing the whole thing with oil. As his final gesture in this culinary exercise, he crunched a green herb between his fingers and sprinkled it over the eggs and tomatoes.

"My favorite," he said to Laura. "Plenty for you, too."

"Thanks, but I was just going to drive into town and pick up some supplies."

Jesse arched an eyebrow so minutely she might be imagining it, but of course there was reason for mirth. Driving "into town" for "supplies" was a trifle grandiose for a journey that she recalled could not be more than a quarter of a mile. They were hardly *really* isolated, as it had seemed last night. "What do we need?" she asked briskly.

At her question, Jesse stopped what he was doing and went to the large refrigerator, making a survey. Then he repeated his survey in the larder, checked on his little wire basket of onions and garlic, and said, "Nothing, really. Only what you'd want for dinner. I was planning to cook pasta."

"Right." She jingled her car keys, smiling, and went out the back door. On the clothesline were pegged three dishcloths, several pairs of socks, and two blue workshirts exactly matching the one Jesse was wearing. There was something uncomfortable in these little domestic details. *What do we need from the store, dear?* She didn't know Jesse well enough yet to feel totally at ease planning their evening meal. Should it be shared, or taken separately? What time did he eat? If she decided to go out to eat, would it be proper to invite him to join her?

She peeled out of the long, circular drive and discovered that a white truck was entering just as she left. It had DALE'S PENINSULA PLUMBING painted on the cab in bright blue, and the driver, Dale himself no doubt, nodded to her and said in a deep, Western voice, "Howdy."

She spun out into the road, heading for the landmark of the piled mountain of oyster shells, where she turned left. After no more than the equivalent of two blocks in Manhattan, she had left the woods behind and was, in fact, passing the local supermarket too quickly to turn in. She stopped her sigh of irritation before it could start. So, you missed the turn, she lectured herself. No big deal. You're not in New York, nobody's waiting for you to make a decision, nobody cares if you spend the entire afternoon cruising the two-block main drag of this tiny town.

The whole point of this vacation was for her to relax in a low-pressure atmosphere, and the Grey Whale Hotel and its environs was about as low-pressure a spot as anyone could wish for.

Besides the supermarket and garden center, there were a pharmacy, a coffee and curio shop, and three taverns, one with a restaurant attached. The main road simply stopped at the edge of some dunes, but a sign said driving was permitted on the beach, so she drove out on a path of hard-packed sand, climbed a small rise in her obedient rented car, and was suddenly rewarded with the sight of the Pacific Ocean. It filled her vision, the great mass of silvery blue, and she understood that she'd come to the end of the continent.

She stopped the car and got out, feeling amusement at the melodious notes the car gave out whenever the door was opened.

Poom, Poom, Poom sang the car's mechanism in a ladylike bid for attention. She slammed the door shut, feeling how silly technology was when you were looking at the Pacific Ocean. Today, under sunny skies, it was orderly and nonviolent, but she remembered the primordial booming noise that had invaded her bedroom the night before.

Some children were running at play far down the beach, and she could see several bright kites in the sky, but otherwise she had the ocean to herself. She sank down on the sand, feeling contentment and wonder in equal measures. Say this about water too cold for swimming, about a part of the country where the thermometer rarely rose above sixty-five, even in August: it offered a chance to look on beauty undisturbed.

When she roused herself and drove back to the supermarket, a fine mist was stealing in. The sun burned through, but she could see it concentrating over what she thought must be her end of the peninsula. Sad pictures of missing children were reproduced and hung at the porticoes of the market, along with notices of an OYSTER FESTIVAL and KITE-FLYING CONVERGENCE and CONVERTIBLE SOFA-BED FOR SALE. She studied the face of the eight-year-old who was last seen at an Indian reservation in Idaho, and instructed herself to move on.

Once inside the store she was delighted to see that Washington State law permitted the sale of wine. She selected a jug of red, to make up for the large inroads she'd made on Jesse's wine, and added two bottles of mineral water. Into her cart went cheeses and crackers and scallions, green peppers and ears of sweet corn and virgin olive oil. Something told her that Jesse was impecunious and would be glad of her purchases. She wondered what Claudia was paying him, and if —despite his frontiersman's guise—he could survive.

At the checkout counter the young girl gave her a friendly smile. She moved the items along with a dexterity Laura had forgotten supermarket clerks could possess. "I guess you'll be staying for a while," the girl said, indicating Laura's purchases. Good Lord, a checker who appeared to enjoy her work and was actually friendly! She counted out her money and handed it over, and then realized that she'd made no answer.

"Yes, for at least two weeks," she said.

The girl looked up, her pale, greenish eyes seeming to accuse Laura of shortchanging her, but it was information she required. "You staying up there?" she asked, indicating the bay side with a forward thrust of her chin.

"At the old Grey Whale," said Laura. And then, because something else seemed required, "It's very beautiful here."

"Yep," said the girl, "it sure is. You have a nice evening, now."

Imagine, Laura thought, being so accustomed to rudeness and hostility that I'm overwhelmed when a supermarket clerk speaks to me. It wasn't that the young clerks in New York were innately less nice or genetically hostile. The new ones were always cheery and full of juice at the beginning, but by the end of their first month on the job the sheer drudgery of the work turned them angry or listless, and usually both. She supposed it was a minimum-wage sort of job here, too, but clerking in a clean, uncrowded market on the peninsula had to be miles better than the same job—but a frantic and physically uncomfortable one—in New York, with a half-hour subway ride to look forward to. Half hour? No, make that forty-five minutes, Laura told herself as she drove out onto the road.

Right at the oyster shells, then down the road until she saw the low white building, the circular drive. Dale's Peninsula Plumbing had quit the premises, and there was an eerie quiet over the place when she got out of the car. The chiming mechanism seemed a violation, and she shut the door as quickly as she could after lifting out her grocery bag. It was quiet inside, too, and Jesse was not at his scholar's perch in the dining room. She put her purchases away and headed for the lounge, or sitting room.

He was kneeling on a couch at the windows facing the bay.

"Oh," she cried out, in a too-loud voice, "here you are!"

He turned and lifted a finger to his lips, motioning her to come closer. It seemed she was destined to feel a fool in this man's presence, unless rendered mildly drunk, and she tiptoed toward him. The distance seemed enormous.

A red doe and her fawn were at the bottom of the overgrown garden, nibbling industriously at the berry bushes Althea had shown her.

"The fawn's been wounded," Jesse said in the quietest of voices, but not whispering. He passed a pair of binoculars over.

"But surely that's an old wound?" Laura managed, focusing on the hard seam in the deer's flank.

"Probably a bullet wound from last year," he said.

The deer worked their way mechanically from bush to bush, and Laura positioned herself at different windows to watch their progress. They were feasting at the bushes abutting the main road when a car passed, and they bolted in a flurry of white tails and flashing limbs.

Laura, who had not had a nap in the afternoon since she'd been four years old, felt a powerful desire for one now. She started to call to Jesse that she was going to her room, but stopped herself in time. She was not accountable to Jesse, didn't have to announce her every move. Worse still, it might sound like an invitation to him. Exasperated, she walked firmly up the steps and found the peaceful little room as she had left it. From the bureau she took up a book on the

Pacific Northwest she had bought in New York once she knew she'd be going on this supposedly restorative and restful vacation. A cool breeze from the bay played through the room delightfully, lifting the hem of the nightgown she'd hung on the bedpost. The mist she had glimpsed in town had vanished, or been blown out to sea, and the sun was warm and strong, without the glaring, punishing aspect it so often presented back East.

She skipped over the chapters on Northern California and Oregon and went directly to Washington State. There were plenty of maps, and in the map of Washington the Peninsula appeared as a tiny strip, a hooked pinky finger in the extreme southwestern corner. She read the names of the touristy towns she had passed through: Ilwaco, Seaview, Long Beach, and Ocean Park. Her own town was called Nahcotta, named for a great Indian chief, and the only one farther up was Oysterville. There was a romantic name for you. Perhaps the first settlers who had dispossessed the Indians in this remote outpost named the town Oysterville to guarantee that oysters would always be plentiful. Or perhaps it had always been called Oysterville by the Indians, and the usurpers had merely translated an ancient name.

The arthritic hook of the little finger's tip was a wildlife preserve, protected by the government. Rich in bird life, it was also abundantly blessed with all sorts of berry bushes, which meant that bears padded about enjoying the smorgasbord. Laura smiled at the idea of bears not far away; it was the season for them to be searching out food. Sleepily, she thought of color prints of bears she had seen in the *National Geographic* as a child. They were always depicted with trout or salmon flapping between their jaws, or else poking their blunt snouts into hollow trees filled, inexplicably, with honey. The idea of bears browsing through berry bushes seemed wildly inappropriate. Unlike the mincing, pretty deer she'd seen, the bears surely lacked the finesse needed to separate a tiny globe from a slender stalk. And how many berries would a bear need to eat to feel satisfied?

Before she allowed herself the delicious luxury of a brief nap, Laura read about Oysterville in her book. *Vacationing families,* she read, *often came to Nahcotta by train, where the railroad ended. They proceeded overland to Oysterville, a thriving center which is now virtually a ghost town. Oysterville was, and still is, the site of awesome winter storms at sea.*

Her editor's mind took over, and she was unable to continue reading. What did the winter storms have to do with the vacationers, who presumably took their holidays in fine weather? She closed the book and lay back on the soft pillows the Grey Whale had provided. Everybody, her husband included, tried to make out that this rest was badly needed. They treated her as if she were a Type A personality, likely to explode at any minute if rest and recuperation didn't intervene.

She knew differently. She was merely tired, and for good reason. She was tired of being mistaken for that which she was not, but equally suspicious of those, like Jesse and Althea, who quite possibly disapproved of her.

What would she write about herself if compelled, at gunpoint, to describe her character? "I am a reasonably intelligent woman, one who can delegate responsibility, but not afraid of large loads of work. I have learned to make decisions without agonizing over their absolute correctness. As an editor, I acquire books of which I approve mightily—and that doesn't happen too often—in spite of the fact that the company would prefer me to purchase only money-making drivel and celebrity biographies. In doing so, I run the risk of losing my job at some point in the future, but my conscience is clearer than it would be if I toed the company line. At present I feel I do my job well, and am disturbed by those who don't. I resent having to take on the work of others—publicity, for example—when they are drawing a salary and shirking."

Instantly, the face of Jackie Brickner, the detestable Crowther and Hull employee who consistently lied about getting review copies to *Publishers Weekly* in time, swam up before her closed eyelids. "I sent the galleys on *time*," Jackie was whining, as she had at a meeting two weeks ago. Sure. And the check was in the mail.

Jackie's long, baleful face began to melt and turn into Althea's more pleasing face. "I hate cities," Althea said, and then she bolted away and Laura could see that she had a white tail. The white tail became the plumes of water in the fountain at Lincoln Center, and then the fountain revealed itself as the Pacific Ocean, and Laura hurtled into her first nap in more than thirty years.

She woke in a panic, not knowing where she was at first. A loud male voice was calling repeatedly. "Hello? Anybody here? Anybody here?"

It was still light in the room, but the mist promised earlier curled delicately at her windows. Her feet were cold, and she wondered why Jesse wasn't dealing with the caller. Her watch told her it was after five.

By the time she'd splashed brown water on her sleep-slackened face and thrust her feet into sandals, the intruder's voice was beginning to annoy her. It was a self-righteous voice, deep, like the voice of the plumber who had bid her *howdy*, but without the plumber's neutrality. When she got downstairs to confront the voice's owner, he was just striding out the front door, which had been left open.

"Here I am!" she called. "What did you want?"

The man turned, suprised. He looked at her through faded blue, Marlboro cowboy eyes, hands on his hips. He was enormous and blond, with an immaculately seamed face, and he seemed poised on some impossible peak of concealed rage.

"Where's Jesse Paget?" he asked.

"I don't know," said Laura. "He was here earlier."

The man scratched his head and shifted his weight from the left leg to the right. "I'm Ralph Henderson," he said, "from the Nahcotta town planning board. I have to tell you that this hotel is not ready to open. It is a violation of several codes to declare this place open for business." He paused and waited for her reply.

"It's not open," Laura said. "There's nobody here but Jesse and me." And then, because Ralph Henderson seemed to suggest a leer, "My husband and I are on vacation here."

"Where's your husband?" he wanted to know.

Laura sensed that to tell him her husband was in West Germany would be the wrong thing to do. "He's temporarily away on business, but he'll be here in a week."

"You see," said Ralph, "long as you don't plan to operate without the town's permission, everything is okay."

"I'm sure no one plans to operate without the proper license," Laura said in civilized tones, wishing she were more alert.

"This community depends on the oysters," Ralph said. "We can't tolerate their being jeopardized."

"Far be it from me to jeopardize your oysters, Mr. Henderson."

"Ralph. That's my name." He narrowed his eyes further and gave her the look she imagined he reserved for dunces of all stripes. "The sewage lines," he said, "the cesspit—there are problems that will have to be worked out. It will take an engineer's report. These things take time. We can't have raw sewage running into the bay."

"I should hope not, Ralph. Raw sewage contaminating the bay is not what I had in mind when I came here." She'd put enough smart-ass New York into her speech to intimidate him and get his back up, and she regretted it, for he immediately wheeled off toward the Cherokee Chief he'd left parked near the back door, under the clothesline.

Before he revved off up the driveway, he stuck his head out the window and bellowed, "Remember you said that, ma'am. Remember you said that, Mrs. Arnold."

Mrs. Arnold! He thought she was Claudia, the brand-new owner of the Grey Whale.

She sprinted down the driveway after him, calling that she was not Claudia, but Ralph Henderson, and the Cherokee Chief, drove off in righteous fury into the enveloping mist.

TWO

It just went to show you, Dorrie Geiger was thinking as she mechanically wiped down the bar, the first place is sometimes the best place. You can have everything you need, and not know it. She half expected to hear someone agreeing with her, and by the time she realized she hadn't spoken out loud it was too late. She was feeling just as aggrieved as if Katha, her daughter-in-law, had been sitting on a barstool two feet away, refusing to comment on what Dorrie had said.

She was filled with the wonder of her insight, but then a doubt crept in. Maybe the first place wasn't the best *at a certain time* in your life. Maybe she'd needed to move away from the Peninsula in order to appreciate it. It was just possible that the twenty years she'd lived down in Portland had opened her eyes to some basic things.

"The dirt, the filth, in the city," Dorrie was fond of saying. "The crime in the city is terrible. People don't realize."

It was a lonely hour at Luby's Hideaway, the hour at the very end of the afternoon. Dorrie found she was completely alone, but it didn't bother her one bit. Even if Katha *had* been sitting at the bar, as she'd momentarily imagined, the girl wouldn't have a clue. She was too young to think about anything but fast cars and shooting pool and where to get the best price on quilted Huggies for six-month-old Brigitte, Dorrie's first grandchild. Brigitte was named for that giant Scandinavian woman who'd been married to Sylvester Stallone for about a year. Katha and Eddie maintained it gave her a good start in life.

Luby's Hideaway had been on this spot, about five hundred yards from where the town ran out, since Dorrie could remember. It was a one-story structure, quite large inside, with a long bar and three pool tables. These days it also had a long shuffleboard, a basketball game where frenzied competitors were invited to sink as many baskets as they could before their coin ran out, and a jukebox that was capable of playing some very raunchy tunes. Just before Dorrie had left, she could remember "Red Sails in the Sunset" and "Cara Mia" as favorites, and even in those days the tunes had been old. People on the Peninsula never specially liked the Beatles or the Rolling Stones.

Dorrie turned to inspect her image in the murky mirror over the bar. She saw both the dark-eyed, small-nosed girl she had once been and the hefty woman in a sensible, short hairdo she had become. Both images pleased her. They blended together to form an amalgamation of the wife and mother she had been in Portland and the sturdy, grateful keeper of peace at Luby's Hideaway, now that she'd returned.

"Be nice," she told her customers when one turned nasty unexpectedly. "Act nice."

It was amazing how effective words could be, Dorrie thought. You'd think a two-hundred-pound man like Jack Happle, arms thick as posts and covered with tatoos, you'd think Jack, who sometimes turned mean when he'd drunk too much, wouldn't take any notice of Dorrie's admonitions, but he did. Only two nights back—

But her thoughts were cut short by the very unexpected arrival of a customer. The door opened to reveal a solid wall of mist, and like a trick-devil in a play, Ralph Henderson's form materialized.

"Hello there, Ralph," Dorrie said, glad of the company. Not that she liked him—she thought he was a self-righteous son of a bitch lots of times—but she was in the mood for some company.

"Howdy," said Ralph, parking himself on a stool near the door so she had to walk almost the entire length of the bar.

"I'll take a beer," he said.

Ralph Henderson drank Rainier beer, and rarely too much of it. She'd known him in high school, when he'd been a wild one, but on her return to the Peninsula she'd discovered a stern Ralph Henderson, a pillar of the community who had married a girl from Oysterville, fathered five children, and got religion.

"You know," she said, setting the bottle down before him, "before you came in I was just thinking how odd it is that a man like Jack Happle will back down real quick if I just tell him to act nice."

"Is that a fact." He made it into a statement, not a question. He tossed back his beer, the way he might have done twenty years earlier, and set the bottle back down, folding his hands around it.

"Just a few days ago, Jack was looking for trouble in here. He wanted to hear a particular song on the jukebox, 'The Rodeo Song'—"

" 'Here comes Johnny with his pecker in his hand,' " Ralph said, singing it contemptuously. He shook his head.

"Yeah, that one," said Dorrie. "Anyways, Ruth Baker was feeding quarters into the box, and we all know what kind of song Ruth likes, and Jack starts bellowing for the rodeo song. Walt Baker told him to keep it down, and Jack got this black look on his face. Next thing we knew—"

"Luby around?" Ralph asked abruptly.

That was just his style, Dorrie thought. Taking the wind out of your sails. People in Portland weren't like that, not the ones she'd known, and she had to repeat the well-worn litany—the crime, the filth, the noise—to regain her composure.

"No, he's over to Ocean Park, talking to that kite-maker," she said. "His son, Roger, is going to enter the festival this year." She deliberated, wondering if Ralph could be made to see his breach of etiquette.

"There's nobody here but me, Ralph," she said in the driest tones she could muster.

This produced immediate results. Ralph looked her straight in the eye and smiled. "Hey, Dorrie," he said, "how's Eddie and Katha?"

The inquiry after the well-being of her son and daughter-in-law failed to melt her. It was too much the sort of thing Ralph did at town planning meetings, when he knew he was in the spotlight.

"Fine," she said. "They're just fine."

"That's great," Ralph said, smiling his political smile. She waited for what might follow, but he seemed committed to hugging his bottle and looking sincere. For something to do, Dorrie emptied an ashtray and then lit up a Marlboro Light, fanning the smoke away with her hand. Ralph had given it up.

"No need to do that," he said. "I enjoy the smell."

"What did you want to speak to Luby about?" Dorrie asked.

"I'll have another beer," Ralph said, relinquishing the bottle as if he had been holding it hostage. After he'd put down a few gulping mouthfuls he smacked his lips and shook his head. "I sure don't know, Dorrie," he said in a mournful voice.

"You don't know what you wanted to talk to Luby Sorenson about?"

That made him narrow his eyes still further. Dorrie had always thought Ralph's eyes would have been really pretty if they opened wider. He had eyelashes any woman was bound to notice, and envy, and the eyes themselves were an unusual shade of washed-out blue, like faded denim.

"You always were one to sneer," he said. "Thank the Lord that for every woman who laughs at trouble, there's a man who's willing to take action."

"I didn't know either one of them activities was confined to a single sex," Dorrie said, stabbing out her cigarette with two decisive little jabs. "If you want to talk about action—"

"What would you say if I was to tell you the woman who bought the old hotel was here right now? Right here in Nahcotta, big as you please, just as sure she's welcome as you're sure you got all the answers."

Dorrie felt it was her turn to take some wind out of sails, so she said, "What does she look like, Ralph?"

"Hardly matters, does it? What matters is that Mrs. Big-city Arnold thinks she can open up the old Grey Whale without adhering to the code. You know what that could mean? If she's allowed to get away with it, it could mean the end of everything as we know it."

Dorrie let her eyes do a survey of the tavern. As always, she wanted to wince at the sign over the corridor that led to the ladies and gents. It advised patrons of Luby's Hideaway to use the carcass of a spotted owl instead of toilet paper. Luby had hand-lettered the sign himself and was very proud of it. Even though the Peninsula, at the far end, depended on oysters for its livelihood, and not timber, Luby wanted to show solidarity for the lumber mills in the rest of the state. It wasn't right, he maintained, to deprive a working man of his job because some tacky bird nobody would miss didn't have enough get up and go to find another habitat. Dorrie herself sympathized, but twenty years of living in a city had given her enough of an impression of ecology—what the environmentalists were always screaming about —to make her feel confused on the issue.

"Contamination," Ralph was repeating. "If that woman lets all the waste from her hotel seep into the bay, we can look at oyster farming as a thing of the past."

"What makes you think she's open for business?" Dorrie asked. "She'd be a fool to try something like that, before it's been approved."

"Cars have been seen coming and going," he said, putting as much drama into it as he could. "These big-city people, specially from the East, they don't understand the rules. All they know is turning a profit, and damn the consequences! It's like that Trump, in New York City, but we're not New York City here, Dorrie. We're a small, close-knit community. Hell, we went to school together, didn't we? We know the game, and how it's played. It's known as the Domino Effect, honey—you tip one over and the whole line falls down."

She wondered if Ralph Henderson, having drunk an unaccustomed two beers before his supper, should be told to act nice. What was all this raving about ruined oyster beds and pirates from New York? As far as she knew, all this Mrs. Arnold had done was to travel to her newly bought property to spend some time there. It made sense to scope out the territory if you were a decent, law-abiding citizen who had bought an old hotel in the hopes of seeing it flourish again in the future.

"It'll all be okay," she said to Ralph, unconsciously speaking in the soothing voice she had used on her former husband in Portland. "Believe me, it will. Trust me."

"There's nothing I wouldn't do to stop her," he said, draining off the rest of his beer. "Nothing." He got up from the stool and pocketed his change, leaving her with a very meager tip. "We don't need her type here, if you get my meaning. Let her make one false step, and I'll be on her like the wrath of God, and that's a promise."

"My, my," said Dorrie, under her breath, and then, just before he got to the door, "you never told me, Ralph. What does this witch look like?"

"You women," said Ralph. "She's a skinny blonde. Just what you'd expect. That satisfy you?"

"Sure," said Dorrie Geiger. "See you, Ralph."

On her second evening at the hotel, Laura felt much more at home with Jesse. She had eaten a solitary meal at a small restaurant called Richter's Kitchen. The meal had been good, plain fare, served to her by a woman who proved to be Mrs. Richter. Driving back to the hotel, Laura imagined the seat belt was ever so slightly tighter as a result of the outsized portions of everything on her plate. "You sure I can't tempt you with dessert?" Ellie Richter had wheedled. "The pies are all fresh baked. There's peach, and rhubarb-strawberry, lemon, cherry, and I think one slice of coconut cream is left."

Laura had shaken her head, smiling. It was a mannerism anyone in New York would have understood—it meant "I've already eaten more than I usually do in an entire day, thanks very much all the same," but Mrs. Richter had simply looked disappointed and written up the check.

It would have astounded Laura to know that on that very day a man had referred to her as a skinny blonde. She had been plump as a teenager, and even though the extra poundage had miraculously melted away just before she entered college, she thought of herself as someone who must be extremely careful in her eating habits. Nearly twenty years of being reasonably slender weighed as nothing com-

pared to the handful of years in which she had felt herself destined
for obese adulthood.

The twilight mist had drifted out to sea, and the sky was clear and
star-speckled as she approached the oyster shells and made her turn.
There was a time when, if she and Dan had been forced to be briefly
separated, she would have been mentally describing things to him,
storing them up for when they'd be together again. Jesse, Althea, the
deer, the view of the Pacific at the end of town, the almost comically
hostile Ralph Henderson—all these would be chronicled and filed
away to be held up for his amusement or censure. She was aware that
she had done no mental journal-writing on her husband's behalf, and
then she was forced to admit something else. Whenever, in the small
space of time she'd inhabited this strange new place, she'd missed
Dan, it was because of his *convenience* in the scheme of things. The
convenience of having Dan as a buffer between herself and Trapper
Jesse, or as protection from self-important louts like Henderson. Not
once had she missed him for his company alone, or as the one who
shared in her life's adventures.

She knew she ought to feel sad about this lack of emotion, but
sadness would not come. Her stomach might feel full, but her head
felt curiously light as she pulled into the long, curved drive to the
Grey Whale. She could see Jesse through the windows of the long
dining room, bent over his writing. Only the one lamp burned, and
the rest of the room was gloomy. Was he trying to be economical with
electricity, or was he the sort of man who didn't think what a place
looked like to anyone outside of the space he occupied? She thought
it was the latter, but she couldn't be sure.

He raised his head as she entered the shadowy kitchen, but didn't
say anything until she'd come into the dining room and stood within
five feet of his makeshift desk.

"Claudia called for you," he told her. "She wants you to call her
back."

"Is something wrong?"

"No," said Jesse. "She just wants to know how you're settling in."

Laura sat at an adjoining table rather than at the one Jesse had
appropriated. She didn't want him to imagine himself as her nurse-
maid. The one who would have to shepherd her through the night

hours, providing wine and conversation and instructive comments on the night sky in the Northwest.

She described her encounter with Ralph Henderson, and asked if Henderson's misunderstanding would mean trouble.

Jesse smiled and considered. "You never know with him," he said finally. "He's the kind of man who could *purposefully* misunderstand a situation just to stir things up. Didn't you correct him?"

"I tried, but he rode off into the mist without hearing me," said Laura.

"I'll contact him tomorrow and explain, but I wouldn't mention it to Claudia for now. Of course, if you feel you must . . ."

"Is there something I'm not getting here?" Laura asked.

"Quite possibly, but it's not your fault. How can you be expected to understand Peninsula politics in one day?"

Laura's feeling of precarious well-being vanished as quickly as it had come. "Look," she said, "there's the truth, and there's rumor, which is often not the truth. There are certain clear and distinct channels for making clear which is which."

Jesse threw her a look which seemed almost pitying, but all he said was "Maybe I'd better have a word with Claudia, after all. Then I'll turn the phone over to you." He rose and padded toward the phone at the bottom of the stairs, but before he turned the corner he looked back and said, "None of this is your fault."

She remained in her chair in the dining room, but his voice carried perfectly. She heard him outline her confrontation with Henderson, and also heard the long silences between his narrative, indicating that Claudia was plying him with questions.

When it was her turn to take the phone, Laura felt like the only member of a conspiracy who didn't understand the issues. Was she comfortable in her room, Claudia wanted to know. Didn't she find the Peninsula beautiful and oddly restful? Wasn't the view of Willapa Bay somehow like the slice of Lake Michigan both women had seen from their windows in childhood?

Yes, Laura replied to all questions. Yes, and yes.

She barely had time to return the phone to its cradle when it rang again, making her jump. The voice at the other end was not quite *right*. It seemed the voice of an unskilled actress, playing a part she wasn't advanced enough in her studies to tackle.

"I was just wondering," said the voice, "if I could make a reservation at your hotel?"

"It's not a hotel yet," Laura said firmly. "I'm only staying here as a guest of the owners."

"Oh, I see. But I was told that for the right price . . ."

Laura was beginning to feel angry. There was a smarmy, conspiratorial tone in the woman's voice, as if she were really calling about an illegal gambling club, or a back-street abortion.

"I can't imagine what you were told," she said, "but this hotel can't possibly open for at least a year. It doesn't even have a license yet. When the owners have brought everything up to standard code"— she was sure that would have pleased Ralph Henderson—"the hotel will open, and not before."

There was a stunned silence at the other end of the line, and she felt sure the woman was about to hang up. "Who shall I say called?" she inquired sweetly.

"Oh, well, it doesn't matter, does it? I mean, if I can't make a reservation."

"But Mrs. Arnold will want to know the names and addresses of everyone in the area who hopes to patronize the Grey Whale," Laura said. "She'll want to notify you when it's ready for business."

"Say Mrs. Nicholas called," said the woman, and hung up without giving an address.

"Do you know a Mrs. Nicholas?" Laura asked Jesse when she'd hung up.

"Nope," he said. "I couldn't help overhearing. She wanted to know when the hotel would be open, didn't she?"

"Well, actually, she wanted to make a reservation. She even hinted at being willing to pay extra. I think she was a fake. Someone put her up to it."

Jesse smiled. "It might interest you to know," he said, "that an old couple in a camper pulled in here when you were gone. They wanted to stay here, too. Said they'd been used to having family reunions at the Grey Whale for forty years before she closed." He sorted through the papers on his table and produced an old envelope upon which the wife of the old couple had recorded their names—Bill and Esther Stevenson—and their address in Northern Oregon.

"They sound legitimate," Laura said, "but this voice on the phone just now—it was like a kid calling for a prank, but it wasn't a kid. And she didn't give me an address, either."

"Maybe Ralph Henderson made his poor wife call up and pretend to be a potential customer. It's about the sort of thing he'd do. Low-level investigation."

Laura went to the kitchen to get some ice water for her rather parched throat. Cracking open the fridge's freezer, she saw they were running low on ice. Without thinking to turn on the lights, she took several ice-cube trays and filled them with tap water. She was in the act of sliding them into their niches when she saw, by the refrigerator's dim light, that in a few hours' time the ice cubes would emerge pond-water brown. She made a little sound of involuntary disgust and went to tip the water out, then journeyed to the pantry to find the bottled water.

Hygienically correct ice cubes in their embryonic state, her own glass of cold water clasped in one hand, she came back to the dining room feeling rather like a pioneer woman.

"I was just thinking," she told Jesse, who appeared to be, well, *smirking* at her misadventures in the kitchen. "Who was the caretaker here before you came? Someone has to have lived here during those years."

"They weren't just the caretakers," Jesse said. "They bought the place from Mrs. McClintock when she was too sick to run it. Not as a hotel, of course, but just as a place to live. They're the people your friends bought from."

"Are they still around?"

"Not three miles away. The Cottons. Wayne and Dot, they're called. A most interesting couple."

He gave a little, secret laugh at the thought of Wayne and Dot, and Laura wondered if it were a compassionate comment on local eccentricities, or the smile of a contented trapper as he bent to put his knife to use.

"Pass me a smoke," Dot called to her husband, who had risen to switch channels on their television set. The remote control no longer worked, a bone of contention between them.

"I wish you'd think about cutting down," said Wayne, as he did at least five times every day. "Smoking is, what do you call it, slow-motion suicide, Dot. It doesn't do you any good."

"Maybe not," said Dot, "but with my nerves in the condition they're in a smoke does more good than harm."

"It's your lungs I'm worried about, not your nerves," he said, giving her one of the cigarettes from her pack, reflecting that she was never likely to quit now. Women who still smoked nearly two packs a day at the age of sixty-one rarely did.

"Thanks, dear," she said, her head wreathed in smoke. He could tell she was smiling at him behind the cloud by the lilt in her voice. When the smoke drifted away, he studied his wife with concern. Beneath her carefully rouged cheeks he thought he detected a pallor, and the crepey skin beneath her eyes looked almost bruised.

"While you were happy pottering around at the shop today, I was suffering the torments of the damned," she announced.

Wayne leaned forward and smiled encouragingly. Dorothy rarely passed a day without suffering from something, and it was best to let her tell about it. Sometimes at length, very great length, and repeatedly.

"I had the beginnings of one of my nasty headaches," she said. "I went to look for the ice pack, and it wasn't where it's supposed to be, on the shelf in the linen closet. Somebody must have been *very inconsiderate* to mislay it like that, knowing how I depend on it when I get one of my nasty headaches."

"I'll have to plead guilty, dear," said Wayne, who had never used the ice pack in all the thirteen years of their marriage.

"Well, never mind. Let bygones be bygones is what I always say. Anyway, it was when I found it underneath the bathroom sink, in that cupboard—*that's* when I bent down and felt something go in my back. Oh, it was awful, Wayne. It felt as if my back wasn't *there* anymore, only a second or two later the pain came, and I can tell you it made me wish my back *wasn't* there. It felt as if twenty little devils with pitchforks were jabbing me, like those what d'you call thems, those men who stick things in bulls in Spain. Those things like hors d'oeuvre picks, and the poor bull is quite maddened—"

Wayne made a sympathetic sound and allowed his mind to wander now that she'd got into her narrative. He thought a softer hairdo might be quite becoming to her, but she wouldn't hear of it. Or, if not an actual change in style, at least a more subtle rinse. It wounded him, as a professional hairdresser, that his own wife refused to listen to his opinions. She let him do her hair, but she would brook no change.

"When I was a girl," she often said, "my hair was the color of a shining copper penny. I don't want to walk around having it look like a dirty penny, do I?"

He could have told her that a certain looseness and softness was required to project the shining copper illusion, but she preferred her hair to be rigidly waved, and then teased, to achieve what she called "volume." It was a word she had read about in one of her magazines, and it made him feel old-fashioned. Even he, without benefit of the latest terms, could have told her that a sixty-one-year-old woman rarely aspired to volume.

Still, she had retained her slender figure, and her high cheekbones, and he could still see in her the good-looking, if mature, woman he had married. If he were to throw caution to the winds and drink three rum and cokes, he might even find her beautiful.

"I had a measure of relief when I lay down, flat on my back, with pillows under my knees," she was saying. "I was just about to fall asleep, when it happened."

Wayne lifted his eyebrows.

"Do you know how it is when you think a flight of stairs has five steps, but really there are only four? You put your foot down and get the most terrible *jolt*. I must have been dreaming I was going down the stairs, because I felt that jolt all up and down my spine, and then it was as if someone was holding a blowtorch to my back."

"You seem well enough now," Wayne said.

"It could return at any moment. The slightest movement, the least little disturbance—who can predict? You can smile—you're still young—but it comes to us all. The body fails, Wayne, in the end it fails."

"I'm fifty-seven, dear," Wayne said, standing up and stretching. "In case you hadn't noticed, I'm failing, too."

"You are relatively pain-free," said his wife sternly. "You can bounce around all day with your curling tongs and mousse and never suffer for it."

"That reminds me," Wayne said, hoping to change the subject.

"Dorrie Geiger's daughter-in-law came in today. Katha, the one who's married to Eddie. She wanted me to give her a whole new look."

"Poor Katha," said Dot. "If she knew what fate had in store for her she wouldn't even bother." This was an oblique reference to "the change," and since Katha was only a young thing, Wayne rolled his eyes and tuned out again.

He had thought the little bungalow he bought when Mrs. Arnold acquired the Grey Whale would cheer Dot up. It was neat and as small a house as two people could comfortably live in—two rooms up and two down, a modernized kitchen, and what could have been a really nice garden in back. But had she been pleased? Oh, no, Dorothy now said she missed the "roomier accommodations" she had once cursed. The bungalow was three miles down the road on the bay, and she felt isolated and lonely. She didn't like to drive her little Toyota because her nerves got to her when she saw teenagers behind the wheels of pickup trucks, and as for the garden, she had first strained her back bending to inspect some clematis.

Wayne looked up and saw Dot's face crumpling as if she were about to cry. For all her nerves and her complaints, she rarely cried, and he thought he'd better tune in again.

"Sometimes I'm afraid to go to sleep in case I dream of him," she was saying. "Not him as he is now, but when he was just a little thing. Such a sweet-looking child, such curly hair, and those big brown eyes! Oh, Wayne, if only you could have seen him."

"I've seen the photos, dear," Wayne said, and then bit his lip, because the photos were never mentioned. He wondered if she looked at them secretly, when he was off at the beauty shop, and felt a sense of great pity enter him.

"I don't know why I should worry," she continued. "It's never happened. Not once. You'd think, in all these years . . ."

"I know what," Wayne said. "Come into the kitchen and I'll give you a nice shampoo." Dot used to love a relaxing shampoo, said he had the magic touch, but now she merely tightened her lips.

"At this hour?" she said.

In the end she succumbed to a back rub of the gentlest kind. "Mind you don't press too hard," she said. She had changed to her royal blue chenille bathrobe and slipped into the matching blue slippers she claimed "massaged" her feet. He sat beside her recumbent form on their bed, and noted that she really did need to change conditioners. Well, that was seen to easily enough. He switched his focus from her hair to the back beneath the robe. Yes, still had a shape to it, a hint of a waist at one end and none of that hump business the media was warning about up on her neck region. Slowly, he began to stroke the tense back, and after a few minutes she turned her head and actually smiled at him. In the glow of the rosy-shaded bedroom lamps, she looked almost like the handsome, forty-eight-year-old widow he had met when he first moved up to the Peninsula from Northern California.

"You were saying something about Katha getting a whole new look," Dot said dreamily.

"Not so very radical after all, dear. Just a relaxed perm."

"How's Dorrie?" Dot was a local. To her the barmaid at Luby's Hideaway was not Katha's mother-in-law but a kid she'd once known when she herself was poised on the brink of womanhood.

"Fine, I guess. Oh, but here's something Katha told me. Dorrie told her that Ralph Henderson said Mrs. Arnold was up to the Grey Whale. Wouldn't you think we'd have heard first?"

"Well, of all the nerve!" Dot twisted her head violently around, her eyes narrowed to slits. "That's what I call ingratitude. We were so nice and accommodating, Wayne, and then she comes skulking onto the Peninsula like a thief in the night. She ought to have called us."

"Now, now," Wayne said, feeling all his good work undone. "She only just got here, apparently. Give the girl a chance."

"Well, I suppose," said Dot doubtfully. "Still."

"Besides, you know what that Ralph is like. He just loves to stir things up. Katha said he was trying to persuade Dorrie that the Arnolds were operating illegally, without a license."

"Oh, no, I wouldn't think that's so. Claudia Arnold is too sensible to risk it, and Ralph's just a wicked person. Always has been. When he got religion it didn't fool me—not for a second."

After ten minutes of Wayne's ministrations, she pronounced herself relaxed enough to try to sleep. He lay in the bed, watching her cream her face and attend to all the many bedtime rituals she performed. He nearly fell asleep before she slipped in beside him, but a jarring image propelled him back to wakefulness. The image was that of his trimming scissors somehow sliding from his hands but continuing to snick away at a customer's hair. He had to reclaim them before the wayward scissors went too far, or jabbed her scalp.

He felt Dot's weight depress the mattress, and whispered a sleepy good night. His sleep should have been deep and untroubled, but later he recalled something that could have been a dream, and could equally have been a strange reality.

He was sure that Dot had left the bed and gone downstairs. He could hear her talking, but he was sure she wasn't talking to herself. It sounded as if she was talking on the phone, but who would she be calling so late at night?

The house was so small, and the silence in the woods outside so deep, that sound traveled with great distinctness. Very clearly, he heard Dot say:

"Tell her Mrs. Nicholas called."

THREE

Laura looked over Althea's left shoulder, not knowing where else to look. They were sitting in the dining room at a table for two, and Althea was about to lay out the Tarot cards to tell Laura's fortune. She had already announced that she insisted, absolutely insisted, and would not take no for an answer, and Laura could barely suppress a sigh. Not just Tarot cards, she thought, but *feminist* Tarot cards.

If they'd been in New York, she could have been very firm in declining, but she was in Althea's territory and didn't want to offend a woman she knew she could like, given the chance.

She saw something flashing in the long grass on the hotel's drive, and blinked. It couldn't be a car, because she'd be able to see it, but something was definitely moving toward them, and sun was reflecting off metal. For a crazy moment she thought of Ralph Henderson creeping toward them on his hands and knees, an assault rifle strapped to his broad back.

"Something's coming," she said.

"Something?" Althea looked up from the deck of cards, which she'd been clutching, willing their knowledge to flow into her before she laid them out. "I'm afraid you've broken my concentration, Laura." She looked out the window where the curving drive now seemed devoid of movement.

"There *was* something," Laura said. "Sorry about your concentration."

The asperity in her voice was not lost on Althea, who grinned and said, "It's that city living that's put you on edge. Try to loosen up a little."

Laura's eyes widened as an apparition rounded the final bend in the driveway and continued on toward them at a steady pace. It resembled a bicycle, but was much larger, and the rider did not so much pedal it as coax it forward with odd movements of his shoulders and legs. Behind it trailed a wagonlike apparatus, and behind the wagon a covered pail on wheels.

"Look again," she cried. "It's here—what on earth is it, Althea?"

Althea turned and looked at the odd tableau drawing up to the kitchen door. "It's just Teddy," she said, sweeping her cards into her large bag and standing up briskly. "Teddy Vine." She walked toward the back door, indicating that Laura should follow.

"Hello," Laura heard Teddy Vine saying, "I come bearing gifts."

He had dismounted from his vehicle, which she could now see was an immense tricycle, and stood shyly blinking in the yard. He was lean as a whippet, but the muscles of his thighs, revealed by his tattered shorts, were formidable, He wore the kind of cap she associated with sea captains, and although the face beneath it was tanned and fairly weathered, it was the sort of face, unlike Ralph Henderson's, she would not have been surprised to encounter in one of her own authors.

"Meet Laura," Althea said. "She's a friend of the new owners."

Teddy Vine seemed indifferent to this information, even as he extended a hand to Laura. "I've brought along some lettuce from my garden for Jesse," he explained.

"Jesse walked down to the library," Laura said. "He should be back before long."

Teddy was handing her a large sack of peculiar-looking greens. "Organically grown," he said. "There's a couple of fine squash at the bottom, too. We're getting a bumper crop this summer."

"I thought you were bringing salmon," said Althea in a teasing voice.

"Maybe by tomorrow." Teddy Vine nodded in a serious way. "Definitely oysters by tomorrow."

Althea nudged Laura to show they were acting out a familiar drama. "But where's the main course?" she said to Teddy.

He went to the covered pail on wheels and withdrew two small creatures with long furry ears, hanging limply over his arm. "If all else fails," he said. "I could skin them now and save Jesse the trouble."

"Are those what I think they are?" Laura said.

"Rabbit," said Teddy Vine. "Can't beat 'em for taste."

"Teddy and Fran raise rabbits," Althea said. "Have you ever tasted rabbit, Laura? It's like the tenderest young chicken. Really delicious."

Teddy seemed to notice her for the first time. "Look," he said kindly, "when you sort that lettuce out, don't throw away the little blue flowers. They're edible." He cut a tight little grin in Althea's direction, and Althea's lips curved up in answer.

Feeling like the victim of a conspiracy, Laura took the sack of greens inside and emptied it into a collander. Sure enough, there were a number of tiny, starlike flowers winking up from the lettuce—if lettuce was what it was—and they were periwinkle in hue. She picked one up and sniffed at it, but of course it had no odor. She had half expected it to be made of spun sugar, an elaborate joke.

Looking out the window, she could see Althea and Teddy deep in conversation. The positions of their bodies interested her. Althea's looked totally relaxed. Her hands were thrust deep into the pockets of her khaki pants, and her long legs performed a little weaving motion as she listened to Teddy. He was ramrod erect, his muscular thighs braced against an invisible pressure. Whatever they were discussing, it was obviously of greater concern to Teddy. They seemed to come to a decision, and then Teddy returned to his contraption, mounted it, and with a wave backward began to perambulate himself back up the way he had come. To Laura's relief, he took his rabbits with him.

When she rejoined Althea in the backyard, she became aware that Althea's truck was nowhere in sight. The woman had simply appeared at the door and Laura, accustomed in New York to visitors with no visible means of transportation, hadn't given it a second thought.

"How did you get here?" she asked.

Althea cocked her thumb in the direction of the bay. "Kayak," she said. Then, consulting her watch, "I've got to go. Walk me down to the water?"

On the path where Althea had introduced her to salal berries, Laura tried to find the right tone in which to discuss Teddy Vine. "So," she said as they descended to the bay, "tell me about Doctor Dolittle?"

Althea made a growling sound in her throat, and then erupted in laughter. "Doctor Dolittle!" she shouted, and a flock of crows flew up above their heads in alarm.

"That's who he reminded me of," Laura said, stumbling a little over a particularly large molehill.

"That's what Jesse said when he met Teddy." Althea turned and gave Laura a wry look, her dark eyes widening in mirth and then abruptly shutting down, neutral. "The thing is, Jesse said it with a certain admiration."

"Why does he ride that contraption?"

"Teddy disapproves of automobile emissions. So much so he's willing to pedal to Oregon to get his copy of *Mother Jones.*"

Laura felt a familiar nausea. "He's not a writer, is he?" she asked, dreading the answer.

"No," said Althea, "unless you count letters to local papers about environmental issues. He and Fran live in a beached tugboat just the other side of the post office. They grow all their vegetables, organically of course, and Teddy raises the rabbits and has a little oyster bed staked out."

"I don't want to eat bunnies," Laura said. "Nothing will compel me to eat bunnies, no matter how delicate and chicken-like their flavor."

Althea laughed again, this time with less volume. "Don't worry," she said. "Nobody wants to eat Teddy's rabbits, except maybe Jesse. It's a standing joke. No, he'll bring some salmon tomorrow."

They had reached the final descent, and Laura could see the kayak among the reeds. The water of the bay was less vividly blue today, and reminded her of the edible flowers in Teddy's offering. She had so many questions to ask, and no time in which to gracefully ask them. She was grateful that the Tarot reading had been aborted, but why had Althea come if not to read her cards? Where was she rushing, after Teddy's uninvited visit? Was the abandoned Grey Whale now simply the site of dinners for the local eccentrics—a sort of potluck affair where entry was insured by bringing a rabbit or an edible, periwinkle-colored flower?

"Do you know a Mrs. Nicholas?" Laura asked as Althea skinned into the kayak. She had put on a yellow oilskin parka, and sat in the claustrophobic little hole with an air of great determination.

"Should I?" she called back.

Laura shook her head, feeling obscurely defeated.

"See you tomorrow at dinner," said Althea with a wink, and then she was paddling, hand over hand, away from the shore and out from the reeds, into the bay. She reached her true course some distance away and headed north.

Laura watched until the figure became a heroic spot of yellow on the periwinkle horizon.

Grace Best opened the tiny post office promptly at noon. She was always prompt, unlike many backwater postmistresses. It was one of her many virtues. Another was that she tried very earnestly not to do what was practically her professional right: snoop. People knew it and rewarded her with their trust, which was no small prize when you lived in an isolated end of a peninsula at the edge of the continent.

Not that Grace thought of her circumstances in such dramatic terms—she had been born on the Peninsula and wasn't given to romanticizing its geographical position—but she was glad that her neighbors liked her and thought of her as sensible.

Lately she had begun to feel older than her forty-four years, and she knew it was because she'd been a widow now for almost a year. In the earliest weeks after Norm's death she had been so preoccupied by the bewilderment of grief that she'd scarcely been aware of herself as a person. Then came a long period of getting things running again—post office, oyster beds, her youngest son's graduation from high school. These activities had sapped so much of the energy she'd formerly taken for granted that she'd felt a false exhilaration. Now she was settling back into a routine unmarked by either grief or elation, and it felt bleak to her.

"What will become of me? What's going to happen to me now?" These were questions she asked herself constantly but never voiced to anyone else. When she looked in the mirror she saw a small, wiry woman with pale brown hair and unremarkable blue eyes. It was the same image she'd been seeing for years, except with more wrinkles and a perpetually chapped nose and chin no creams could smooth. The weathering came from being out on the oyster beds, especially in the colder weather, but it seemed to persist year-round. When her husband was alive, it would signify nothing to him but her valuable assistance in harvesting their crop, but now that he was gone, who could look at her and understand the geography of her face? Questions like that puzzled Grace and made her feel uneasy. Sometimes at night, just as she was about to fall asleep, she would hear strange noises coming from inside her. Thrumming, persistent noises, like the sound from the cannery when it was open all night, or the boom of surf from the sea if the tides were high.

Such familiar sounds had never disturbed her before, had in fact been her lullaby for all the years she could remember of her life, but now that she was alone they took on a sinister meaning. She could no longer tell if a dull, beating, regular sensation was occurring in the natural world outside or represented the blood trying to fight itself into the chambers of her heart. An aneuryism might be building up, as it had in Norm, and she could mistake it for the heartbeat of the cannery.

Once she had been so frightened, so convinced that her body was about to explode, she'd bolted out of bed and was halfway across the scrubby ground that separated her house and Teddy Vine's grounded tugboat before her sense was restored. Nobody about to die could hotfoot it so swiftly as to find herself darting between the rabbit hutches in her flannel nightgown! There had been a fine display of stars that night, and Grace thanked them for calming her.

Sliding open the post office windows, she reminded herself that the tide would be out tomorrow. If her son, Marty, hauled himself out of bed in time—if Marty was even in bed tomorrow morning and not off somewhere for the night—she wouldn't have to slip her skinny feet into rubber boots and squelch off over the mud flats to care for the oysters.

Almost the moment the windows were open, a fair-haired woman in expensive jeans and one of those Irish-knit sweaters walked through the door. Grace knew immediately that the woman was the one staying at the Grey Whale, but she didn't want to make her feel uncomfortable or feel that everyone had been talking about her, so she only nodded and said "Afternoon."

The woman held up her P.O. box key as if it were identification. "I'm Laura McAuley," she said, "from the old Grey Whale. I'm just picking up the mail for Jesse."

"Jesse under the weather?" Grace asked.

"Oh, no. No!" Laura shook her head. Then she did something Grace found amazing. She advanced to the window and lowered her voice conspiratorially. "Actually, I feel like a fool," she confided. "I told Jesse I'd get the mail, and he gave me this key." The key was produced again: evidence. "Even though I had the key, I thought I had to wait until noon to come here. When Jesse came back and asked if there was any mail I told him it wasn't quite noon, so I didn't know. The look he gave me was so strange. It never occurred to me the front door might be unlocked."

"Don't they have P.O. boxes where you live?" Grace asked pleasantly.

"Well, I suppose they do, of course they do, but I didn't think—"

"Why should you," Grace said. Something had unstrung Laura McAuley, and she wasn't going to pass judgment on her the way some of her neighbors might. Luckily the door opened to admit Sherry Henderson, who was carrying a package to be mailed, and Grace gave Sherry her attention. The McAuley woman went and peered into the Grey Whale's box, and finding it empty went away with a tentative wave in Grace's direction.

"That's the one who bought the Grey Whale, isn't it?" Sherry asked as soon as the door had closed.

"Now, Sherry," Grace said, "she's not the owner at all. She's a friend."

"How do you know?" Sherry Henderson's nostrils had opened wide, and Grace imagined a tiny tape recorder implanted in her nasal passages. It was a crazy image, but Ralph Henderson made a person think like that. If things were entirely up to Ralph, everyone in Nahcotta would believe that Laura McAuley was part of some sinister plot to ruin the oyster industry.

"For one thing," she said, stamping Sherry's package to Portland with the franking machine, "I've met the owner. Mrs. Arnold. That girl is just a friend, and she's here for a vacation."

Sherry bit her lip, then released it with a long, hissing sound. "I don't know about you, Grace, but I'm not exactly thrilled by the idea of people like her coming here every summer. It doesn't feel right, does it?"

"I couldn't say," said Grace. "I don't know her well enough."

Defeated, Sherry Henderson pouted and flounced out, if a woman wearing a straining T-shirt embossed with the legend I DON'T BRAKE FOR SPOTTED OWLS could ever be said to flounce.

Grace was suddenly feeling pleased. She could have told Laura McAuley that the Grey Whale had no mail today, but she'd held back, sensing that each P.O. box holder should be allowed to make the discovery on his, or her, own.

The secrets she knew! If you lined them up, end to end, they would circle the Peninsula and make her the custodian of all the lives lived there. For example, she knew it had been more than a year since poor Dot Cotton had had a letter from Walla Walla, but she would never let anyone else know. Today, regular as the tides, Wayne would come in just as she was closing and collect his and Dot's letters, mostly bills, and Grace would feel a terrible sadness for Dot.

Grace had never read *Moby Dick*, but everyone knew the basic story about the sea captain and the great white whale, even if they hadn't been to the movie version with Gregory Peck. It was just one of those things you knew about. Fran Vine had once told her that *Moby Dick* wasn't even the author's best work; Fran preferred a story about a man who'd gone nuts from working in the Dead Letters office of a P.O. Grace turned it over in her mind, recalling that Bartleby the Scrivener "preferred not to" do many of the things required of him.

She pictured herself waking tomorrow morning, her knees stiff as they so often were these days, and contemplating the clothes she would put on for her foray to the oyster beds. Marty was nowhere in the house, and it was raining. What would happen if she turned her back on the oysters, got back in bed, and covered her head with the pillow? How would people react if she told them the oysters had gone neglected because she *preferred not to?* The notion made her laugh softly to herself, so that when Teddy Vine popped in to ask her if she was coming to dinner at the hotel tomorrow evening, Grace imagined she might have seemed, at that moment, to be losing her grip.

Laura tried to lift her booted foot from the deep mud, and found she was trapped.

"Heel and toe," Jesse called to her over his shoulder. He lifted his own right foot and pantomimed what it was she must do. Laura made her bare foot in its borrowed rubber boot seesaw from heel to toe, and amazingly the boot pulled free with a rude, sucking sound. Why had she agreed last night to go on this instructive jaunt across the muddy bay, practically at the crack of dawn?

It was cold, too, even though it was August, and she wished she'd grabbed a pair of gloves from the mounds of warm outerwear heaped in the cloakroom. She turned and looked back at the shore, which was distressingly close. She thought they'd come much farther, but it was slow going, and there were places where the withdrawing tide had left little pockets of water that had to be stepped around, prolonging the journey to the oyster beds. She could see the poles that marked Claudia's claim, or rather the claim her friend had purchased from the Cottons. It was for all the world like making a safari through mud, slogging toward an unlovely destination.

Before her Jesse paced on across the bay's bed, dragging a sort of sledge filled with flat plastic forms. They were, he had told her, the baskets which served as incubators for the baby oysters.

Just before they reached the beds, he stopped and became very still. One arm slowly raised itself and pointed upward. Laura looked and saw two gray herons swooping in a circular glide toward their nest in the tall firs lining the shore. Grudgingly, she admitted that the herons were beautiful, and also that there was a sort of beauty to the mud flats on this colorless morning. She preferred the vista in its blue and gold manifestation, but if she squinted slightly everything she saw appeared etched in dull silver, like a very old engraving.

On the other hand, she could summon no enthusiasm for the oysters themselves. Jesse was bending and taking up the gray, lumpy products of the complicated harvest. With a sharp implement that looked like a short screwdriver, he probed at various fault lines, trying to pry the casement apart and see what it might yield in the way of a cash crop. He seemed surgeonlike, hefting the things in his hands, flirting with his knife, and then, with awesome decisiveness, plunging the point in and twisting until it fell apart in two or three pieces. When he found a prospering baby, he transferred it to one of the baskets already set up in the mud. Occasionally he took up an obscene-looking object, long and skinny, and threw it back onto the bay's floor. "Culls," he said. "They're useless, except for babies to attach to."

Far up the bay, Laura could see a tiny figure bending and straightening, presumably engaged in the same activity as Jesse.

"Who's that?" she asked, pointing.

"Probably Marty Best, working Norm's patch," he said. Then his trapper's eyes narrowed and he seemed to arrive at a decision. "From the movement, I'd guess it was Grace, Marty's mother," he said.

"Isn't she the postmistress?"

"Yup," said Jesse. He took one of the flat plastic forms and coaxed it into a basket shape, pegging it into the mud.

"How far under water will that be when the tide comes back in?"

"Only six feet," Jesse said. "It's only about six foot here."

Laura blew on her fingers, taking advantage of his distraction as he gazed at the far-off figure of the postmistress.

"I was wrong," he said presently. "That's Fran Vine up there."

"Does everyone here have oyster beds?"

"Better believe it," said Jesse. He scooped an oyster from its nacreous hiding place and offered it to her. "Care for one fresh from the source?"

Laura looked at the mucousy glob and shuddered, thinking of pollution and food poisoning. "No, thank you," she said in a prim voice she hated the moment she heard it escape her.

"Your loss," said Jesse, popping it into his mouth with an indecent haste. "It's not like eating bunnies, you know. Oysters don't have long, floppy ears and twitching little noses." He smiled, to take the sting from his words, and then swallowed with obvious pleasure.

They were just heading back for the shore when she heard the sound. It was flat and unmistakable, the crack of a rifle. "Someone's shooting," she said, following Jesse and his sledge. "What's in season?"

"Nothing I know of," he said comfortably.

She waited until she heard the sound repeated half a dozen times before she spoke again. "Could someone be shooting clay pigeons?"

"Wrong kind of gun," Jesse said, maneuvering around a tidal pool.

Laura resisted an impulse to throw a handful of mud at his retreating back. "Terrific," she said. "It sounds like someone's on a rampage and all you can do is trudge along and give monosyllabic answers."

Jesse turned and smiled at her. "Don't worry," he said. "That isn't the sound of mass murder you're hearing. It's probably just target practice."

"Oh, I see." Laura's boot was stuck and she felt outrage at having to perform the silly heel and toe exercise when she was so annoyed with Jesse. "I'm so relieved. I guess it's just Teddy slaughtering the bunnies."

" 'Fraid not," said Jesse as he scrambled up the bank. "He strangles them."

Laura clambered after him. "I'll ignore that for now, Jesse. What I want to know is: who's doing it and what's the target?"

"The target is surely inanimate," Jesse said. "Notice that I used a four-syllable word when I could have said the target wasn't live. As to who the shooter is—" He grew very silent, listening, and she once more saw him as an Indian scout. There were three more shots in close succession, and then he said, "I'd guess that comes from the Henderson place. Ralph's a gun enthusiast."

"Really!" She put as much sarcasm in her voice as she could manage. "What a surprise."

FOUR

The impromptu dinner party, which she'd been dreading, was turning out quite nicely. Teddy had come cycling up on his infernal machine with Fran in tow on a regular bicycle. Fran had the pinkest cheeks Laura had ever seen on an adult woman, and beautiful cornsilk hair. No rabbit carcasses were in evidence, but the promised salmon, which was a heroic-looking fish, was laid out on the kitchen table for all to admire.

"Did you catch him?" Laura asked.

"It was barter," Teddy said.

She turned quickly to Althea, before Teddy could say what the salmon had been bartered for. Althea had brought a casserole of sweet onions made from something she called Walla Walla Sweets.

The other guest turned out to be Grace, the postmistress, and Grace's presence soothed Laura, because Grace seemed the sanest person she had ever met. Grace brought several bottles of Washington State wine, and homemade cookies for dessert.

The preparation of the meal had been very communal. Jesse and Teddy had prepared the salmon for baking, while Althea warmed up her Walla Walla Sweets. Fran, standing at the large restaurant range, was kept busy stir-frying the sliced squash, while Laura set one of the long tables for six and Grace Best tossed the salad and arranged the edible flowers strategically.

When they were all seated and partaking of the feast, Laura felt all the anxiety slipping away. These were good people, her mind informed her after her third glass of wine, salt of the earth! Here she was, in a remote part of the country, eating a superb meal with new friends.

Jesse brewed some of his strong coffee to drink with Grace's cookies, and just as Laura's well-being was hitting new levels, the phone rang in the hall. Jesse went to answer it but came back at once. "It's Claudia," he said. "She wants to talk to you."

"Hi, friend," was Claudia's greeting. Laura felt her guard go up, knowing that the use of the word "friend," no matter how absolutely true it was, probably meant Claudia was going to ask her for a favor.

"We've just talked to our lawyer," Claudia went on, "and it looks like the folks out there are going to be giving us some trouble. Legally, that is."

"I'm so sorry," Laura said. "I'm not altogether surprised."

"That's why I called. I want your reaction to the people you've met. Tell me how they seem, what they think of the idea of the Grey Whale operating as a hotel again."

Laura smiled. It was so like Claudia to assume that she, Laura, had used her three days on the Peninsula to gather information. Claudia admired her professionalism as an editor, and falsely believed her old college roommate to be endowed with a vast power of observation.

"Most of the people I've met are here right now," she said.

"I can hear Teddy laughing. Who else?"

"Fran and Althea and the postmistress, Grace. And Jesse, of course. They're not the problem. I had a little run-in with a man called Ralph Henderson who seems to think you're going to open up without bringing things up to code. I think he's worried about the oyster beds."

Claudia released a little sigh of irritation. It came down the distance sounding exactly like the sighs she had once breathed before exams in Philosophy 101. "Yes, Ralph *is* hostile," she said. "I can't tell if he really thinks we're going to mess up the ecology of the Bay, or if he's using it as an excuse."

"An excuse for what, Claudie?"

"Oh, for not liking Jack and me. For not wanting the hotel to open again. Who knows?"

"I think he's a lunatic. He was doing some shooting while Jesse and I were out on the beds this morning."

"You went out with Jesse?" Claudia sounded delighted. She seemed as smitten by oysters as everyone else.

"Yes," said Laura. "I don't think I'll do it again, though. It's too much like hard work for a vacation." Something was snagging at her memory. "Do you know a Mrs. Nicholas? She called wanting a reservation."

"Nicholas," mused Claudia. "Not that I know of. Of course you explained about the hotel's status?"

"Naturally." She began to explain about how Mrs. Nicholas sounded like a fraud in any case, but Claudia cut her off with one of her great, sweeping plans.

"A party!" Claudia cried. "We'll give an open house! All the locals will meet us, and they'll be able to see for themselves that we're not a bit threatening. It'll make for goodwill, don't you think? A big open house at the Grey Whale, so they can see the kind of people Jack and I are."

Again Laura smiled. "I know what kind of people you and Jack are," she said, "but what do you expect them to see?"

"A man and woman like them. A couple who are serious about the environment, although"—she permitted herself a little chuckle— "not quite as serious as Teddy Vine. They'll see we're committed to the ecological integrity of the Peninsula. After all, what kind of hotel could we run if we despoiled the area?"

Laura heard Althea and Fran launch into a discussion of the feminist Tarot cards, then heard the slap of the cards as they hit the table. Apparently Fran was about to get a reading.

"Half the fear of the unknown can be dispelled by simply appearing in front of the locals and showing them we're perfectly nice, normal people," Claudia was saying. "I've met Ralph Henderson and his wife, but never in a situation where they were partaking of my hospitality. It makes a difference, Laura."

"No doubt about that, Claudie. When would this open house occur?"

"I think we have to move quickly," Claudia said. "We can't serve liquor, or even wine or beer, since we don't have a license. We'll have cheeses and brownies and soft drinks and tours of the place. That should do it, don't you think?"

Laura made sounds of encouragement, glad that she would not, in all probability, be around for the open house intended to show the locals how friendly and sober the Arnolds were. "Next year," she said. "Around February?"

"This weekend," Claudia said in a stern voice. "I told you we have to move quickly. "I'd appreciate it if you and Jesse could spread the word. Jack and I will fly in day after tomorrow. I'll get a flight to Portland, or Seattle. No need to pick us up—we'll rent a car. Just get the word out. 'Gala Open House to Introduce the New Owners of the Old Grey Whale.' Should be child's play for you."

"Child's play," said Laura. "Right, Claudie."

" 'Bye, friend. I really appreciate it."

Grace was looking pleased when Laura reentered the dining room. "You should have your cards read," she said. "Althea is very good."

"Yes, I am," Althea said. "The atmosphere tonight seems especially conducive."

"I already know my future," Laura said. "I'm going to be inviting people to an open house here at the weekend."

Althea laughed. "Is that how Claudia Arnold plans to win the town over?"

Jesse, who had been washing dishes in the kitchen with Fran, came in and stood with his arms folded on his chest. "She can't be serious," he said.

"Well, she is, and I get the job of letting everyone knew. How can I do that when I don't know everyone?"

"That's easy," said Grace. "Put a notice up at the library, the post office, and on the bulletin board at the supermarket. News travels fast here."

Teddy came in at the kitchen door looking beatific, and Laura realized the light from the woodshed had just gone out. The faintest smell of pot clung to him. It was unfortunate that Althea chose the moment to ask what sort of food Claudia would serve at her open house. To forestall proposals of rabbit pâté, Laura explained the extreme simplicity of her friend's plan. "And no liquor at all, because they don't have a license."

"But it's not a hotel, either," said Grace.

"Doesn't matter." Jesse looked distressed, agitated. "When it comes time for them to apply, they'll want to look clean as they can."

A pall seemed to have been cast over the pleasant evening. Fran suggested they all go out on the lawn and look for shooting stars, which were most plentiful in August, but when they found themselves gathered in front of the hotel, craning upward toward the heavens, the stars refused to oblige. Laura felt her head swim as she confronted

the constellations, the Milky Way. It was a sight of great beauty, and
as a city dweller who rarely saw the stars so naked and glorious, she
felt obliged to comment but couldn't summon up the will to do so.

One of her heels hurt where the rubber boot of that morning's
excursion to the mud flats had rubbed the skin raw, and she felt
profoundly tired. Her journey with Jesse to the oyster incubators
might have taken place a month ago and the recent, happy dinner
was only a memory. She didn't know why Claudia's call had changed
their collective mood, and wondered if something bad were moving
toward her.

"There!" shouted Teddy. "Did you see it?"

Everyone wheeled in the direction of his pointing arm, but there
was no shooting star to see.

"Darn," said Fran.

As if at some unseen signal, Teddy mounted his machine and Fran
assumed her position on her bicycle. Murmuring words of thanks,
Grace sat on the flatbed, and the three bobbed and weaved their way
up the drive.

"Why do I have the feeling that Teddy only pretended to see a
shooting star?" Laura said, more to herself than to Jesse or Althea.

Back in the hotel, Althea prepared to leave, sweeping her belong-
ings into her bag and wondering out loud if Ralph Henderson would
dare to show up at the open house.

"Your cards," Laura said. "Don't forget your Tarots."

This seemed to invigorate Althea, who said, "Before I leave, I *must*
tell your fortune."

Laura picked a card, watched as Althea laid out the complicated
structure with a wizard's determination. Her long, tanned fingers
flipped cards over, considered them with a scholarly and meditative
air, while in the kitchen they could hear the comforting sound of
Jesse scraping out the Walla Walla Sweet pan at the sink.

Althea was silent for a long time.

"Well?" Laura asked. "Does the Fool mean Ralph Henderson will
come and shoot us all?"

Althea shook her head and puckered her lips to show that Laura
wasn't to speak. Her dark eyes shuttled between the cards. The silver
earrings swung at her lobes with an almost violent motion.

Jesse came into the dining room and sat a table away, his eyes watchful and somehow wounded.

With a sudden movement, Althea swept the cards into a pile and gathered them into a little heap which she thrust into her bag.

"Something's wrong," she said.

Her white pickup was waiting in the starlight, and as she drove it away, Laura could hear the sounds of panic in the shifting of the gears.

Something's wrong might have served as a slogan for the Grey Whale during the following two days. First there'd been a call that was vaguely threatening, if unclear. "Give it up," the voice had said in Laura's ear after a thick silence. At least that's what it *appeared* to say; after she had hung up, she couldn't be sure. Then a voice sounding like that of Mrs. Nicholas phoned and asked to speak to Mrs. Arnold. "Mrs. Arnold won't be here until tomorrow," Laura had explained, whereupon the woman said she was Mrs. Cotton, and if there was going to be a party at the hotel she would appreciate a personal invitation. When Laura said there wasn't time for invitations, Mrs. Cotton said she and her husband would drop by that evening to collect theirs, sparing anyone the trouble of mailing it out.

But what disturbed her most was Althea's behavior when she saw her at the market. Althea was buying peaches and when Laura, no more than eight feet away, called hello, Althea pretended she had neither heard nor seen her, and wheeled her cart quickly away.

Laura bought stationery, most of which would go to waste, all to write out an invitation for the implacable Mrs. Cotton. She sat waiting for that lady to appear on the evening before Claudia's arrival, unsure of even Jesse's goodwill toward her. Jesse seemed more secretive than usual. Perhaps, she thought, he had been receiving menacing phone calls, too.

She was sitting in one of the lawn chairs, a glass of wine and the invitation on the little wrought-iron table before her. Jesse was inside, writing away on whatever it was that he wrote.

The evening was lovely, still warm and clear after a cloudless day. The water of the bay was a deep, patriotic blue, and the crows were calling in the trees far above her head.

Dan's secretary had called earlier to say that Mr. McAuley's plans had changed, and he would be obliged to stay on in Europe for another week. He would be calling her from Amsterdam or Geneva, and he was sorry he couldn't join her on the agreed-upon date. He had called Anne, and not Laura, because the time difference between Germany and the Pacific Coast made it more convenient to phone New York.

Laura planted Dan in the chair across from her and asked herself: would I be happier if he were here at this moment? The answer was yes and no. Certainly she would feel safer if Dan were here, that was indisputable, but something told her she would be very uncomfortable on another level. Dan would see no need for the special invitation to be proffered the Cotton woman. It would make him irritable to think that his wife was resorting to an elaborate subterfuge to salve the wounded feelings of an elderly eccentric who had once lived at the hotel. He would be bored by the prospect of meeting her, just as he would be bored by Grace and Althea, Teddy and Fran. That was an essential difference between them: Dan was only interested in people who were very like himself, whereas Laura's interest was piqued by those who were fundamentally different. It was what made him such a good corporate businessman, and it was what once had made her an excellent editor. Uneasily, she thought the two professions were now nearly indistinguishable, and her very curiosity might doom her as a top-flight player in the world of publishing.

She heard the car crunch over the gravel and stood up to welcome Mrs. Cotton and her husband. The man who emerged from the driver's side was small and sported Marc Antony bangs cut high over a worried-looking forehead. He scooted around to open the door on the passenger side, and produced a long, thin woman with a dyed, bouffant hairstyle surmounting the sort of head that required private invitations to open houses at obscure hotels.

"Greetings!" the little man called as Laura approached. "Hello!"

"Hello," said Laura, taking his outstretched hand and smiling over his shoulder at the woman she felt sure was "Mrs. Nicholas."

"Allow me to present my wife, Dorothy."

Dorothy Cotton gave Laura the tips of her fingers in greeting, like royalty, and said, "We're ever so pleased, Wayne and I, to meet you." Her face, which seemed grooved with a lifetime of successive pains, split alarmingly in a smile. "Call me Dot," she said.

"I have your invitation here," Laura said. "Would you like to sit out here on the lawn? It's such a nice evening, I thought—"

"Oh dear," sighed Dot, "much as I'd like to, those chairs would finish me. My back, you know."

"Come inside then," said Laura. "You know the way!" She'd intended the last to be a jaunty acknowledgment of Dorothy Cotton's prior right to the Grey Whale, but it came out sounding snippy.

"If you're sure," she said dubiously. Her husband took her arm and planted her on the course toward the kitchen door with a familiarity that suggested to Laura a very long period of custodianship.

It took them quite a time to settle in the living room, because Dot stopped often to examine things which were new. "Those little winking lights," she said in the kitchen. "They look for all the world like Christmas tree lights, even though they're all white."

"Claudia bought them in Seattle the last time she was here," Laura said. "She thought they'd make the kitchen look festive."

"I don't know about festive," said Dot. "I'm not sure a kitchen needs to be festive, are you Wayne? And I'm sure it can't do your nerves any good to have lights winking at you when you least expect it."

"They're not winking, dear," Wayne said.

"Well, *twinkling* then."

In the dining room she acknowledged Jesse with another huge smile. Seeing his pack of cigarettes lying on the table, she reached in her purse and withdrew her own pack. She lit up, deposited the match in Jesse's ashtray, and then gave a cry of alarm. On the longest table in the room, Claudia had placed a large ceramic fish, a bloater of some sort.

"Ooooh," Dot breathed, "what a thing like that does to the digestive tract! When I've had a nice bite to eat—and it's all too rare I enjoy my food these days—I don't want to look at 'Jaws.' "

Wayne began to make peculiar noises and Laura was afraid he was having a seizure, but Dot seemed unconcerned as she moved on to examine some potted plants in the window facing the mound of oyster shells. Jesse laughed politely, and she realized Mr. Cotton had only been trying to render the theme music from *Jaws*.

"New sofa over there," Dot said in the living room, settling into an armchair with cautious movements.

"Now, honey, we don't live here anymore," said Wayne. "It's up to Mrs. Arnold to do whatever she sees fit."

Dot inhaled deeply on her cigarette, a sharp crease of displeasure appearing between her eyebrows. "You don't have to tell me that, Wayne," she said. "A person likes to see the changes in a place where a person has spent so many happy years."

Laura asked if she could give them something to drink and Wayne brightened, but his wife announced that since they'd be having a few drinks at the open house, it was best to abstain. "I always say the occasional drink can't hurt anyone," she told Laura. "A nice glass of sherry is quite warming when it's cold and all wintry, and in the summer it can be quite beneficial to sip a gin and tonic. The important thing is *moderation.*"

So saying, she snuffed her cigarette and immediately lit another.

"Really," said Laura, "you might as well have a drink now, because we can't at the open house. Jack and Claudia don't have a liquor license yet."

"In that case, perhaps I'll have a sherry, even though it is summer," said Dot, shivering with exaggerated movements. "I'd forgotten how cold it is here."

Laura said she didn't think there was any sherry in the larder, but Jesse said there was, and he'd get it.

"Orange juice for you, Wayne?" Dot asked.

In the larder Laura watched with fascination while Jesse pushed aside a drum of cooking oil to reveal a bottle of Spanish sherry, and then poured some vodka into Wayne's orange juice. "This is how it's done when they visit," he said. "Where's the invitation?"

When Laura returned with the envelope in hand, Dot was screaming with laughter. "Oh," she cried, "that poor, nice girl! That darling Mrs. Arnold! She didn't know what she was bargaining for when she came to our Peninsula."

Laura looked to Jesse for enlightenment.

"I was only explaining," he said, "that I've been attending town meetings at Claudia's request. The first time I went I expected most of the business to center around the Arnolds' variance for the hotel and the purity of the Bay." He seemed to grow uncomfortable beneath her gaze, and he stood up and switched on a lamp.

"Of course," he added, "there's also the problem of water rights.

Althea is trying to get permission to dig a well, and all she gets for her troubles is the amount of money it would take to connect her with the town's supply."

Laura waited for what she was sure was the punch line of Jesse's experiences at town meetings.

"I was kind of surprised when the main topic of conversation turned out to be the labs," he said sheepishly.

"Labs?" Laura said, feeling confused.

"So wicked," Dot said. "So very wicked and stupid." Her face had fallen into a solemn and punitive mask which defied reasonable discussion. "They brew up drugs in these labs. Homemade drugs."

"Methamphetamine," said Jesse. "Crank. Ice."

She nodded, having read a lengthy article recently about California school kids addicted to this new form of cheap speed. "Surely not *here?*" she asked.

"Why not here?" Wayne asked with a touch of belligerence in his voice. "Trends start out here, on the West Coast, and move east. Pretty soon you'll have it in New York."

"No need to bite Mrs. McAuley's head off, dear," said Dot.

"It was all just speculation," Jesse said. "But as Wayne says, why not here? Deep off in the woods, cut off from the main part of the state? When you think of it, the Peninsula's a perfect place for a lab."

"Yes, I see." Laura moved off on the pretext of shutting the front door, which had been propped open by an amusing doorstop in the shape of a jumping frog. It was true that the warm air had vanished, and the chill of night was creeping in through the screen, but mainly she needed to occupy herself away from the three pairs of eyes at her back. Was it her imagination, or were they trying to tell her something? And why had Dot, so solemn in her condemnation of the drug labs, been howling with laughter as she came into the room?

She entertained a bizarre little fantasy while she lifted the doorstop, closed the door, and then lingered as if she were scanning the darkening sky. Dot was really a drug czar, and Wayne her henchman. Jesse had been sent to pose as a caretaker while he infiltrated town meetings and gathered intelligence for the ring. It all seemed hopelessly comical, unless she factored in the peculiar phone calls and trigger-happy Ralph Henderson. What if all the strange behavior was simply a form of playacting designed to drive her, and her friends Jack and Claudia, away from the area permanently?

"Tell us what you do in New York, dear," said Dot in a carrying voice.

Laura turned and wanted to laugh at her melodramatic scenario. Dot was leaning forward, smiling grotesquely, and Wayne was bobbing his head in encouragement. Only Jesse looked impassive, glancing away as if the question embarrassed him. The little trio was one she quickly cast as: The Hypochondriac, The Lackey, and The Indian Scout. All harmless.

"I'm an editor," she said, resuming her place in the circle.

"On a newspaper in New York?" Wayne asked, looking alarmed.

"No, with a book publishing company. Crowther and Hull."

"I suppose you mean you make sure they have their grammar right," said Dot. "You put the commas in the right place."

By all that was decent and friendly, Laura should have left matters as they were. She should have confirmed the assumed scope of her duties and hurried the conversation along, but in her slightly altered state of consciousness she felt the need to defend her job. "It's a bit more than commas and grammar," she said. "Of course, I work very closely with my writers, but I also acquire new manuscripts. It's a part of my job to find what's new and fresh and bring it to the public eye."

Jesse didn't like her explication, but wasn't about to say anything.

"Like folks being kidnapped by those UFOs?" Wayne asked.

"Closer to home," Laura said. "More real. There was a sensational murder in New York last year—do any of you recall it? A young ballet dancer was raped and thrown off a roof in Manhattan. The killer pleaded, in his defense, that she was stronger than he was, and managed to injure his self-esteem. Before she died, she managed to damage one of his eyes."

Dot didn't like this turn of events, and made her displeasure clear by openly sneering. "And what's that got to do with your job, may I ask?"

"I sensed the possibility of a very good book in the trial and subsequent publicity. Not a lurid book, but one which would really examine the intricate—" She broke off, aware that she sounded like an editor at a sales conference. "All I mean is, a good book came out of it, written by a very fine novelist turned crime reporter."

"I don't approve of that," Dot said, pressing her hands to her temples. "Raking up the muck, making innocent people relive their terrible tragedies—it's wicked."

"Now, now," Wayne said, "I'm sure Laura didn't do that, pet. You mustn't excite yourself or you'll get one of your headaches."

"Too late, I'd say. I already have one. Oh, the band around my head!"

Wayne got her to her feet, and with many apologetic shrugs and smiles, propelled her toward the back door. Laura, distressed, followed with Jesse in her wake. As Wayne was opening the car door for his wife, Laura said, "I'm so sorry, Mrs. Cotton. I didn't mean to upset you."

"Never mind," said Dot with one of her ghastly social smiles. "It's just my nerves, you know. Never mind. We'll see you at the open house. It will be such fun!"

The car went up the drive at more than the usual speed, and Laura and Jesse were left alone beneath a sky full of stars.

"There's one!" Jesse called, pointing dramatically as Teddy had done.

Laura looked and saw nothing.

"Only joking," Jesse said with a droll smile.

"What was that all about?" she asked. "What upset her so much?"

"Wouldn't worry," he said. "Almost anything can get Dot going. You must have seen what a hypochondriac she is."

"But it was something beyond illness, real or imagined. All that stuff about making innocent people relive their tragedies." She kept her face turned up, telling herself it would be a sign of good luck if she saw a falling star. One was winking, exactly as Dot had accused the little lights in the kitchen of winking, but though it brightened and dimmed with regularity, it remained in the heavens to foil her.

"Some old tragedy," Jesse said. "It happened years ago. It involved her only child."

"Well?" She felt indignant at Jesse's shorthand method of storytelling. "Could you be a little more specific?"

"Ask Claudia," he said.

Jack and Claudia arrived at the Grey Whale with a car packed full with provisions for the party. There were sacks of soft drinks, cartons

of cheeses, boxes of crackers. "The caterers in Oysterville are bringing the rest," Claudia said as they were struggling to bring everything
into the hotel.

Claudia looked radiant. For her return to the Peninsula she had
chosen to wear a long denim skirt and a Guatemalan vest, open over
a frilly Victorian blouse. Her blond hair was gathered up and held
with a clip of silver and enamel. She looked, Laura thought, almost
exactly as she had twenty years ago. It was Claudia's special blessing
to be endowed with the belief that she was eternally at the beginning
of some marvelous adventure.

"Truth," Claudia cried as they were stowing the bags and cartons
in the pantry, "Don't you love it here?"

"Well, in many ways it's very—"

"I always knew you were going to find it simpatico, Laura. You're
the first person I thought of when Jack and I saw this place."

It was the sort of thing she would not believe if anyone other than
Claudia had said it, but Claudia was obsessively truthful. Orphaned
at the age of ten, Claudia Ransom, as she'd been then, was raised by a
rich but undemonstrative grandmother, far up in some remote region
of Michigan.

By the time Laura met her they were both eighteen, and both sure
great things lay in store for them. Claudia had more reason than most
young girls to look to the future with pleasure—on her twenty-first
birthday she would inherit a great deal of money, held in trust for her
ever since her parents had died in a plane crash.

Laura understood that her friend's sometimes overbearing exuber-
ance was the natural outcome of a childhood marked by terrible loss
and continued in a sort of privileged isolation. "I always knew my
grandma loved me," she told Laura, "but I couldn't help feeling I was
in this prison while I was growing up. A benevolent prison, but who
wants to be in prison? Now I'm free. I was a model prisoner, and my
keeper was fair and now at last it's all over."

Jack came into the kitchen with a huge stack of paper plates. "I
could hear you from the other room," he said to Claudia. "Do you
realize you didn't give Laura time to answer your questions? You
steamrollered her with euphoria." He touched his wife's hair gently,
in passing.

"I'm sorry," Claudia said, putting aside the quilted book which contained her checklist for the open house and giving Laura her full attention. "It's a flaw in my character."

Laura smiled at her. She was glad to have Claudia and Jack on the premises. Much as she had begun to like Jesse at times, she needed these emissaries from her other, her *real* life, to put matters in perspective.

While Jack went in and out of the larder and conferred with Jesse, she and Claudia sat together at the kitchen table and traded information. She learned that Althea was having an on-again off-again affair with a wealthy local, and that Teddy Vine aspired to a political career on the Peninsula as an environmentalist.

"What's Mrs. Cotton's tragedy?" Laura asked.

Claudia furrowed her brows. "She's a terrible hypochondriac," she said, "but beneath it she's an old sweetie."

"Her child," Laura pressed on. "Something about her only child. I have the impression it was a daughter who got raped, something like that? I'm afraid I put my foot in it, talking about a book we did at Crowther and Hull."

Claudia bit her lip. "Oh, that," she said. "I'm afraid you have it the wrong way around. Dot's child was a boy, a son. Grace Best told me he was a real no-good, practically from the cradle. One of those kids you knew would end up bad. She was right."

Laura tried to picture Dot Cotton in the days when she had a son, and found it was an almost impossible task. "What did he do?" she asked.

Claudia moved her shoulders in an awkward gesture, as if trying to shake the Cotton boy's crime well away. "It was ugly," she said. "It was the kind of thing I can imagine Ralph Henderson doing in my wilder moments." Absentmindedly, she sliced open a pretzel bag with one sharp nail and extracted a pretzel, nibbling on it delicately. Laura remembered her in the dorms at school, resorting to vending-machine treats when reality became too harsh to bear.

"He picked up a hitchhiker on his way to Seattle," she said in a dreamy voice. "She was a teenager, and he met up with her somewhere near Chehalis. He raped her and left her for dead in a ditch. He'd strangled her, but he made a botch of it."

"She identified him?" Laura said.

"No," said Claudia, pushing the pretzels across the table. "She went into a coma and died. They later arrested Dot's son because he had all these clippings about the murder. That, and a forensic matchup with the skin they found under her fingernails. There was also a fingerprint or two. It was a sensational trial for its time."

"Where is he now?"

"At the penitentiary in Walla Walla," Claudia said. "Dot's always maintained that he's innocent. Railroaded."

"Is there a chance that could be true?"

Claudia swung her head violently. "No," she said. "That's Dot's tragedy, as you call it. She honestly believes her son is imprisoned on false pretenses."

Laura remembered how Dot had reacted to the book about the girl who'd been raped and thrown from the roof, and wished she'd never mentioned it. Poor soul, she'd make it up to her tomorrow, try to be specially nice to her. She wracked her brains to see if Crowther and Hull had any new books on their list a hypochondriac would like.

It was after dark when Jack came in from a stroll down the drive. He'd gone out in good humor, saying he liked to contemplate the hotel by starlight, but when he came back almost immediately his face was gray and strained looking. "Jesse, could I have a word with you?" he asked.

This was so unusual—Jack speaking to the caretaker in the tones of a stern headmaster—that Claudia arched her brows in alarm. "What on earth?" she said, but Jack shook his head at her and wheeled off in the direction of Jesse's rooms. Moments later the two men went off on what Jack called an errand. He said he'd explain everything when they returned.

"They're around at the front door," Laura said. Claudia got up and walked in the direction of the living room. "Stay back!" Jack shouted, hearing her footsteps. "Stay back in the kitchen."

"I never thought I'd hear my husband order me to the kitchen," Claudia said with a smile, but she was very much alarmed, and so was Laura.

"It's probably just Ralph Henderson out there in camouflage with a hunting knife," she said, and then, although she'd intended it as a joke, felt afraid.

The first thing Jack did when he came back was wash his hands very thoroughly at the big sink. Then he poured himself quite a lot of scotch, not remembering to offer a drink to anyone else. Laura thought that if Jack, normally the most courteous of men, could behave in such a fashion he must have been very badly shaken. Jesse stood near the refrigerator, looking sad.

"Sorry for all that," Jack said after he'd taken a long swig of whiskey. "I didn't want either of you to have to see what was on our doorstep. I thought the best thing was for Jesse and me to get rid of it as quickly as possible." He drank again. "It was a deer," he said. "A very young female—a fawn, Jesse?"

"Yearling."

"It had been shot," Jack said. "It was dead, and someone put it right on the front doorstep."

"It was the deer we saw," Jesse said, and Laura realized he was talking to her. "She had that little scar on her flank we saw through the binoculars."

"How cruel," said Claudia. "How unspeakably mean and ugly. Why would anyone do such a thing?" She gave a little mirthless laugh. "I guess they hate us more than we realized."

Laura felt a pang for the creature who had appeared almost as if to welcome her. "What did you do with her?" she asked.

"Carried her out into the woods beyond the outbuildings," Jesse said.

"I thought we should bury it—her—but Jesse explained we'd hit sand if we tried to dig a grave." Jack looked miserable, and Laura knew it was on Claudia's account. The hotel was her project, and she could only imagine Claudie's fervor back East, planning the open house that would make the Arnolds fast friends with their new neighbors.

"What I don't understand," Claudia said, "is how the deer got here at all. If a car or truck drove up, we would have heard, wouldn't we? Or could it have been here for a long time? We hardly ever use the front door."

"It wasn't here this afternoon," said Jesse. "Whoever put her there managed to do it between the time you arrived and the time Jack discovered the carcass."

"It's impossible," Claudia said. "I've never been in any part of this place when I didn't hear a car come up the drive. Never."

Uneasily, Laura recalled the time Althea had come by kayak. Not that she could see Althea kayaking up to the reedy landing with a dead deer as cargo. Where would there be room, in a kayak, for anything but the passenger? "They could have come by water," she said.

Claudia frowned. "It's too bizarre," she said. "I'm going to take a hot brown bath and go to bed. It's the only thing I can think to do."

Jack followed his wife up the stairs, leaving Laura and Jesse in the kitchen. "Who do you think did it?" Laura asked, but Jesse merely shrugged unhappily.

A terrible picture was taking place in her mind, but it was also funny in some deeply distasteful way. It was an image of Teddy Vine, so eager to bring rabbit meat to his hosts. She was aware, the minute the words escaped her, of how very inappropriate they were.

"Maybe," she said, "it was Teddy's way of contributing venison to the open house?"

Jesse considered her frivolous remark, and then he did something she had never seen him do before.

He laughed.

FIVE

Deer or no deer, the day of the open house began as gloriously as even Claudia might have wished. Laura, who had appropriated a large sherbet container for rinsing her hair, knelt in her tea-colored bath and poured streams of water over her pale hair. She was determined to look her best, and act her best, to buttress Claudia's plan of ingratiating herself with the locals.

While she was sitting on her bed, using the blow dryer she'd brought from New York, Claudia came tapping at her door. A vision in purest white, Claudia was wearing white trousers and a white, summer-weight cotton sweater. She, too, had washed her hair, and

she looked the very image of wholesome, golden, American innocence.

"This is going to be a wonderful day," Claudia said. "I can just feel
it." She made a kissing sound, winked, and left the room.

Downstairs, the caterers had arrived with dozens of party sand-
wiches and an enormous basket of rich, dark brownies. All alcoholic
drinks were stowed on the highest shelf in the larder, covered by
ranks of large cereal boxes so no guest would be tempted to pour a
few drops of liquor in their cola for added party spirit. Claudia, however, confessed that she was not prepared to be abstinent. When the
four of them were gathered in the kitchen, Claudia produced a large,
handsome silver flask and announced it was full to the brim with
vodka.

"Are you sure that's wise, honey?" Jack asked.

"It's not only wise, it's necessary," Claudia said. "I'm not a big
drinker, but even I couldn't get through this day without knowing
relief was at hand. If things get too awful, I intend to slip some nice,
liquid tranquilizer into my law-abiding soft drink." Her eyes were very
bright, and Laura wondered why someone expecting a wonderful day
should seem so nervous.

"Now," said Claudia, "I don't want to be selfish about this, so let's
agree on a hiding place for the flask. We all swear not to abuse it, of
course, but if the need arises—"

"It has to be someplace the other guests won't want to visit," Laura
said. "They're going to be swarming all over the place, upstairs and
down."

"We could stash it in one of the bathrooms," said Claudia, "but
there's no really good hiding place in the downstairs loos, is there?"

Jesse cleared his throat and they looked at him expectantly. "The
room where all the boots and macs are," he offered. "It's such a mess
nobody will want to stay there long."

They walked, single-file, to the cloakroom. Claudia held the flask
high, like a priestess offering a chalice to an unseen but all-powerful
deity. She spun round, reviewing the raincoats and yellow sou'westers
hanging from the hooks, the hip boots and selection of Wellingtons
lying every which way on the floor, and gave a triumphant cry. She
slid the flask down into one of the largest boots, manipulating it
down into the toe, where it was completely hidden. "In the boot of

the giant," she intoned, "we will find our deliverance." As she spoke, they heard the wheels of a big vehicle growling up the drive, and they knew the party was about to begin.

"Hi there," said the comfortable-looking woman who hopped down from the driver's seat of a blue pickup. "I'm Dorrie Geiger, from Luby's. I tend bar there."

"Welcome to the Grey Whale," Claudia said. "You're our first guest today, Dorrie. I'm Claudia Arnold, and this is my husband, Jack."

"Real nice to meet you," Dorrie said, and then, "Hi, Jesse."

"Hi," said Jesse, who to Laura's amazement had slipped into a tweed jacket at some point and was looking ruggedly presentable.

"This is Laura McAuley," Claudia said. "We've been friends forever."

Laura wanted to wince at Claudia's bright social gambits. It was clear to her that the Geiger woman was uncomfortable at being the first to arrive, and only wanted to slip into the hotel and have a look around before she loaded a paper plate with brownies.

She needn't have worried, because even as they were trooping in through the front door, where the poor murdered yearling had so recently been deposited, a cavalcade of visitors were making their way to the open house. She saw Althea's white truck in the forefront and a van with blackened windows just behind, followed by Teddy's pumping knees as he propelled himself, Fran in tow, toward the festivities.

A boy called Martin had been hired to direct the parking, and he seemed euphoric, motioning with both hands and blowing on a whistle hung around his neck. He seemed hauntingly familiar to her, and it wasn't until Grace Best arrived, on foot, that she made the connection. Martin was obviously Grace's son.

When she cornered Grace, the postmistress would only say, "You've heard of rhinestone cowboys? Martin is an oyster cowboy, and that's the truth."

Dot and Wayne Cotton made a dramatic entrance, Dot carrying a huge shoulder bag and saying, to anyone who would listen, "I have a bit of history with me. It's a gift for Mrs. Arnold." Whenever a guest inquired, politely, into the nature of the gift, Dot smiled in a far-off, hieratic manner, and said that time would only tell. She was dressed in a russet pantsuit that looked welded together at the seams, and wore amber-tinted glasses, plucking them off with an irritable frequency. Wayne was dapper in double knits. For some reason, he pressed a peppermint into Laura's hand when he greeted her, as if she had been a child.

By the time Ralph Henderson arrived, about fifty people were on the grounds, or in the hotel. It seemed half of them wanted to see the upstairs, either out of simple curiosity or, in the case of one old couple, because they had once stayed here long ago. Claudia had taken up several groups on tours, and then Laura had taken her turn, but in the end, as more people arrived, it seemed best to let them wander about at will.

Laura had been out on the back lawn, watching a group of children running and stumbling on the molehills, when Ralph's big truck hove into view. Martin Best, who had been staring longingly at the woodshed, had to turn his attention to getting Ralph parked. Laura passed by close to the shed and immediately understood Martin's interest. Cannabis perfumed the air, but when she glanced in it was not Teddy Vine toking away, but three men she didn't know. Would Henderson make a citizen's arrest? She giggled, and then composed her face in a neutral expression. She had only gone to the cloakroom once to add to her drink, but the combination of Dr Pepper and vodka was far from pleasant, and she'd tipped the drink into the sink surreptitiously. Claudia, on the other hand, seemed to go to the cloakroom quite often; the level in the large flask had been mightily reduced, and she was sure Jesse and Jack were making do with the official drinks provided.

Ralph stepped down from the cab of his truck with a huge grin. He was actually wearing cowboy boots, and she recalled Grace's reference to oyster cowboys. He wore tight, fashionably washed-out jeans and a belt with a big silver buckle. He came up toward the hotel with a self-consciously theatrical walk, swaggering, as if he fancied himself the hero of a B movie from the fifties.

"Mrs. Arnold!" he bellowed in Laura's direction while he was still twenty feet away. "Well, isn't this nice of you to come all this distance to show us hicks a good time?"

A little pocket of silence formed in her vicinity, and people fell still, waiting to see what Ralph would do. How far would he go? Was he drunk? Only the children, playing with shrill shrieks under the pines, were oblivious to the confrontation that was shaping up.

"Well, hell, what's going on here?" Ralph said. "I thought this was supposed to be a *party*." He spread his arms and threw back his prodigious neck and emitted a rebel yell. "Eeee-yoo! Yoo! *Yow!*"

"What's all that commotion?" came the voice of Dot, who was peering out the kitchen door, bereft of her tinted glasses.

"It's only Ralph, dear," said Wayne, who had positioned himself on the pathway of crushed oyster shells.

"Hello, Ralph," said Dot, but he advanced on Laura without seeming to hear Mrs. Cotton's greeting.

"I'm not a man who'd spoil a party," Ralph told his audience. "This is a truce. We're gonna have a nice afternoon at the old Grey Whale, and we're gonna forget all the issues that divide us. Right, Mrs. Arnold?"

"Exactly right!" The voice rang out from a window on the second story, and Laura saw Claudia's head thrust out. The sun made a halo of her hair, and blotted out her features. Ralph stared up in bewilderment.

A large, commanding figure came striding out between the row of vehicles and parked herself in Henderson's path. "You see?" said Dorrie Geiger. "I told you you had the wrong party all along, Ralph."

All around her, Laura felt conversations resume. Ralph's dramatic entrance had been foiled, and she could almost feel sorry for him.

Much later, he searched her out and offered his apologies.

"I'm truly sorry I talked to you the way I did," he said, cornering her in the living room, where she was trying to eat a brownie.

"Apology accepted," Laura said.

"Oh, no," said Ralph Henderson, "you're not taking me seriously. That's a mistake. I mean everything I say, and you better believe it. I'm only apologizing because I said it to the wrong person."

"Claudia's not your enemy," Laura said. "She means to do everything by the book."

Ralph arched an eyebrow in another deliberately theatrical gesture. If he had moustaches, Laura thought, he'd be twirling them. *"Whose* book?" he said. "That's the question. We'll see."

Over his shoulder she could see Fran Vine nibbling at a brownie. "Excuse me," she said to Henderson, who seemed to have lost interest in their conversation in any case, "there's someone I want to talk to."

Now he switched persona, giving an ironic little smile and half bowing. He turned smartly on his heel and walked off.

"Who does that man imagine himself to be?" she asked Fran. "He got out of his truck like something from *High Noon,* and just now he seemed to be impersonating a Gestapo officer."

Fran giggled, then grabbed a sandwich from a tray. "I don't know," she said, "but I can tell you one thing. Everyone's always saying Ralph is crazy, but I don't think he is at all. Not one bit. I figure he just wants certain people to think he's crazy. That way they won't take him seriously, and he can beat them every time."

The phrase "certain people" had not been lost on her. Presumably, Ralph was quite sane around Teddy and Fran. "But he was just *telling* me to take him seriously," she said, feeling the need of another nip from the cloakroom. "Isn't that defeating his purpose?"

"No, because we never do take people seriously when they tell us we should." Fran licked her fingers. "I'm eating far too much," she said. "I really should show some restraint, shouldn't I?"

Laura thought of all the rabbit Fran probably had to make do with, and urged her to eat as much as she liked, and then, as if reading her mind, Fran said, "The thing about the bunnies is, I get *attached* to them. They can be quite *sweet,* Laura. I could do without the strangling, quite frankly. I'd rather just raise them."

Althea was making her way toward the table, but when she saw Laura she gave a languid wave and changed course, wandering off toward the kitchen.

Laura consulted her watch and saw it was past four in the afternoon. The limits of the party had been set at one to four, but nobody ever left parties on time, apparently not even parties where there was nothing to drink of a cheering nature. It would go on for some time, even though the cries of the children had turned fretful, and the sun had disappeared, leaving a pale sky and the promise of mist. A chill was seeping in through the open doors, and she thought of going up to change into something a bit warmer than her blue cotton shirt, but a visit to the cloakroom seemed more in order. Claudia, she saw, had already wrapped a shawl around her white ensemble; Claudia was just going up the stairs as she crossed the hall.

In the cloakroom, she simply selected a flannel shirt from one of the pegs and draped it over her shoulders. Then she knelt by the boot and tipped some vodka into her glass. The flask was now almost empty. Feeling melancholy, she stood at the window and surveyed what she could see of the open house outside the hotel. Teddy was just going in to the woodshed with an expectant look, and he was followed by Grace Best's son. One of the children had mounted Teddy's contraption, and Jesse seemed to be giving him lessons on how to propel it.

Ralph Henderson was nowhere in sight, but she could see Jack talking to the Geiger woman. They had been joined by a vivid man wearing a cowboy hat in whose band flourished three long, plumy feathers.

It would be comforting, she decided, to wait in the cloakroom until all the guests had gone, but it would be rude and ungrateful, too. She decided to stand at the window, observing, for a decent period of time, and then move back out into the fraught atmosphere. When the interval had passed, she again consulted her watch and found she'd only been in her hiding place for nine minutes.

There were innumerable small calamities for the rest of the afternoon. A little boy in the downstairs loo managed to upset the shallow bowl of potpourri—meant to conquer the rather musty smell of that room—all over the floor. Another child slipped on the crushed shell path and cut her knee on an oyster's edge. Martin Best, while trying to guide a departing guest up the drive, nearly caused a collision with a jeep. Two men she had never seen before began a heated argument about oyster farming, and poor Dot Cotton, clutching her large handbag, looked ready to drop. The tinted sunglasses had disappeared.

It was past five-thirty when Laura saw Grace Best come down the stairs. She looked up and saw a pair of legs descending in a shaky, hesitant manner. Grace came into her view slowly, and when the whole woman was revealed, Laura felt a thrill of alarm gather at her spine. Grace's face was blanched, and she seemed dazed. The cords in her neck stood out, and her hands clawed at the newel post at the bottom of the stairs as if she needed assistance.

Nobody else seemed to have witnessed Grace's dramatic reentry into the spirit of the party. Laura was about to go to her when Grace strode from the hall to the dining room and, taking up a huge cake server, pounded it on the table and released a great, screaming cry.

"Call for an ambulance," she shouted. "Somebody call for an ambulance."

Claudia had been discovered, face down, in the linen closet on the second floor of the hotel. She lay with her hands outflung, as if she'd tried to prevent her fate. A large pool of blood had clotted at her scalp, and the fair hair was parted to reveal the wound. It was black and extensive, and apparently lethal.

"Don't touch her," Jesse said to the kneeling Laura. "She's dead."

Jack knelt on the other side of his wife's body, his jaw hanging open in astonishment and horror. It seemed frozen in that position. He stretched out a hand toward her in a mute, pleading gesture, but his hand trembled so violently he let it drop on his knee. The only sound in the big closet was the rasp of his ragged breathing and, in Laura's ears, the thud of her blood rushing. "Who?" she said. "What?"

It was silent down below, so silent that she heard the sound of feet mounting the stairs toward them. She glanced wildly up at Jesse, not wishing to intrude on Jack's grief. "It's okay," Jesse murmured. "That will probably be the sheriff's deputy. He was out on the lawn when Grace told us. Someone must have gone to fetch him."

"What have we got here?" a deep male voice inquired, and she looked up to see a skinny, mournful-looking man whose presence she had barely noted during the long afternoon. "If you could move aside, ma'am?"

Laura got to her feet and stepped gingerly over Claudia's head to the hall, where Jesse stood.

"Sir?" the deputy was addressing Jack, who hadn't moved. "Are you this lady's husband?"

Jack nodded.

"I'm Bob Ludder. I'm a deputy. If you could clear the area, I'll have a look."

Jack stood up very slowly, like an old man, and eased himself out of the linen closet, clutching at the shelves of sheets and towels and pillowcases as he did so.

Deputy Ludder bent close to Claudia, placed one finger gently at her carotid artery, dislodging a lock of her fair hair. "Has anyone touched her?" he said.

"No," said Jack. "Have you called an ambulance?"

"Ambulance is on its way," said Ludder. "It'll take her to the hospital in Long Beach, but I have to tell you that the lady appears to be dead."

"Long Beach is miles down the Peninsula," Laura said. "Isn't there anything closer?" When you went on holiday, the last thing you thought of—if you were relatively young and in good health—was the proximity of a hospital.

"No, ma'am," said Ludder. "Was your wife suffering from any particular condition? A medical condition?" he asked Jack.

"Not that I know of," said Jack. "She was in good health." His voice indicated that he was on automatic pilot, resolved to answer meaningless questions in a spirit of cooperation.

"To your knowledge, did she use drugs of any kind?"

"No."

"Did she have a drinking problem?"

"No."

"Was she despondent, depressed?"

"No," said Jack, and his voice began to break.

"If you'd follow me downstairs," said Ludder in his expressionless voice.

The downstairs of the hotel was packed as full as it was ever likely to be. Everyone sat on the sofas and chairs, or on the hearth of the fireplace. Those who couldn't fit into the room crowded in the dining room. In her state of shock, Laura calmly observed Teddy eating a sandwich, even as he looked concerned and solemn. The child who had cut her knee on the crushed oyster shells lay asleep near the frog doorstop. Ralph Henderson stood near the piano, his hands folded over his chest.

Deputy Ludder strode into their midst and began to speak. "Folks," he said, "there's been an accident upstairs. It involves Mrs. Arnold, the new owner of this hotel. An ambulance is on the way. Can anybody shed some light on how this accident occurred?"

Before he'd even finished his sentence, there was a great commotion from the long couch on the bay-facing side of the living room. There were shrieks and rumbles, and when the air cleared Laura saw that Dot had slithered off her perch into a little heap on the floor. It seemed she had fainted. Wayne made ineffectual motions to help her, and seemed on the verge of tears. In the end it was Ralph Henderson who lifted her in his arms and carried her out to her car as easily as he might carry a kitten. Wayne retrieved her bag.

"Oh, I'm so sorry," he was saying, "so sorry about this. How badly was that darling girl hurt?" he asked. "What happened?"

"We're not sure," Laura said, "but it's very serious."

Everyone was asking the same question, and the noise level was very high, but Bob Ludder held up his hand and instantly they fell silent.

"As I was saying, can anyone explain how Mrs. Arnold got injured? Did any of you see anything on your trips upstairs?"

"There's that door to nowhere," a young woman in shorts volunteered. "That could be pretty dangerous."

The door she referred to was kept locked. It was a clear-paned door which had once led to a balcony no longer there. Since if Claudia had stepped through the door to nowhere and fallen to the ground she'd be on clear view out the window, no one bothered to take the woman's words seriously.

Jack was standing in the doorway to the dining room, despite a chair which had been placed for him. His face was polite and alert looking, and Laura thought he must be in shock.

"How many of you went to the upper story this afternoon?" Ludder asked. Nearly everyone raised a hand. Teddy was one of the exceptions.

"How many of you went upstairs between five and five forty-five?" No hands went up and then, reluctantly, Althea raised hers. "I did, around five-thirty I think, although I can't be sure. I didn't see Claudia, though. I just went because the bathrooms downstairs were occupied."

It was Grace Best who'd found Claudia, but when Laura looked around the room for her Grace appeared to be missing.

"I think it would be best if you all left now," Ludder told them. "You know where to reach me if you remember anything about this incident."

Incident! Laura threaded her way through the departing guests until she found Jesse in the pantry. He was bowed over, elbows on the counter, and seemed to be in pain. "This shouldn't have happened," he said. "This should never have happened."

"Jesse!" Laura spoke in a sort of desperation. "What's wrong with this Ludder? The way he's handling it, Claudia might be lying up there with a sprained ankle. For Christ's sake, Jesse, she's *dead!* My friend is dead, and I know she's been murdered, and Ludder is letting everyone go home."

"Maybe," said Jesse, "he has a method."

"A method? What's that supposed to mean?"

"What if he thinks it best to let them think she's only been hurt? That could flush out whoever knew he'd finished her off, couldn't it?"

His words hung stale in the little pantry, like something from a third-rate detective drama on television. He shrugged in apology and said only, "Poor Jack."

The ambulance arrived soon after the last vehicle had left, and Laura sat at one of the dining room tables with Jesse and Jack while the men were upstairs, trying to ignore the sounds of the grim task being performed above them. They carried her down on a stretcher, and when Jack saw the bag zipped up over her face he gave a soft grunt, the impotent noise of a man who has been hit in the stomach and can't gather enough wind to howl in protest. Laura reached for his hand, but he was oblivious.

Deputy Ludder rejoined them, and asked more questions. Had Jack and Claudia been quarreling recently? Was the proposal to reopen this old hotel a sore spot in their marriage? It seemed he wanted it both ways: to suggest either that Claudia had died and it was somehow her own fault, or that she had been killed by her husband.

"This is preposterous," Laura said. "What the hell are you getting at, Mr. Ludder? Claudia and Jack were extremely happy, and he backed her to the hilt in her aim to run the Grey Whale."

Instead of seeming grateful, Jack shot her a warning look.

"Does your wife have a will?" Ludder asked.

"Not that I know of. She may."

"But she's a woman of great wealth."

"Not great wealth," Jack said. "Medium wealth. Only medium."

A flicker of disgust appeared in Ludder's eyes. It seemed to say that wealth was wealth, and it was always great by his standards.

"Have you taken out an insurance policy on your wife?"

"No," said Jack. "Nothing like that."

"Do you know of any enemies she might have made on the Peninsula?"

"Ralph Henderson," Laura said, unable to restrain herself. "He's sure Claudia planned to ruin the oyster industry with her hotel."

Curious how Deputy Ludder treated every revelation with equal interest. Carefully, he took down notes about the peculiar phone calls, the sounds of gunfire, and the slain deer on the doorstep as zealously as he did the bulletin that she and Claudia had been friends for many years.

"Well thanks, folks," he said as he prepared to leave. "I had to ask these questions. None of it will matter, because I suspect the verdict will be death by misadventure."

"What does that mean?" Laura said, feeling murderous.

"It amounts to an accident," Ludder said. "Mrs. Arnold was wearing high-heeled shoes. The floor of that old linen closet ought to be condemned. It's uneven because of dry rot. I think the poor lady had too much to drink and just brained herself on the edge of a shelf."

He smiled, and then, as if aware of the fact that his smile was an insult, he rearranged his mouth into a tight line.

"Sorry, Mr. Arnold," he said, touching Jack's shoulder. "It's a terrible loss for you."

Laura hoped that her friend had died quickly, and not, as she feared, in a state of terrible bewilderment.

While Jack was off conferring with the doctor who had examined Claudia in death, she and Jesse conducted an experiment with the flask. It still contained the half inch or so of vodka that Laura had left after her second and last drink.

"Fill it up to how it was before anyone had a drink," she said.

Jesse smiled as he poured bottled water into the larger than average flask. "Aren't we suppressing evidence or something?" he said.

Laura laughed. She was nearing that stage in the endless day, now turned to night, where she felt she might easily laugh hysterically in a state of exhaustion and grief. "Nobody hit her with the flask," she said. "It's only mock evidence, the kind they'd like to show she was drunk. Since the vodka is inside her, the evidence is gone."

Jesse cast a worried look in her direction. "Don't worry," she said. "I knew what I meant, even if I didn't put it very well."

"It's full," Jesse said. "Now what?"

"How many nips did you have?"

"One, a very small one. It's not my tipple."

"Pour the amount you had into a glass." She selected one of the plastic glasses from the towering bag of rubbish they'd rounded up.

He poured what amounted to no more than a mouthful. "That's it," he said. "Now you."

Laura poured two larger lots in. "It wasn't a very nice mixture," she said. "I tossed the first one out after a sip or two, and I never got to finish the second." She thought of something. "I don't think Jack had any of it, but I can't be sure."

"I can. He told me he wanted to be stone sober to watch the interplay. That's what he said, 'interplay.'"

"Right." Laura heard herself sounding like a mad scientist, but she did feel a point had to be made. "We'll pour all the rest into another glass, leaving the same amount at the bottom we found."

The first glass was full to overflowing when they'd poured, and the flask was far from empty. They got a second glass from the garbage and when Jesse stopped pouring it was over half full. "That was what Claudia had," he said. "A not so small amount of booze."

"These are small glasses," Laura said. "And it was spread out over an afternoon."

"But for someone who wasn't a drinker—"

"Nobody said she didn't drink. Only that she didn't have a problem."

Jesse gave one of his eloquent shrugs.

"Oh, I know what you're thinking," Laura said. "You're imagining Claudia was a heavy drinker, but not quite an alcoholic. Well, you're wrong. She wasn't even in shouting distance of being an alcoholic. She wasn't a problem that way, not ever."

"Maybe she was unusually nervous about the outcome of the open house. It could be she didn't realize how much Dutch courage she was tossing back."

Laura was overpowered by the memory of Claudia coming in to her room and saying that it was going to be a wonderful day. She thought for a moment that she would dissolve in tears, but another memory was keeping her from a surrender to sentiment. Claudia *had* seemed unusually nervous when they'd all rendezvoused downstairs. The plan of the secret flask had surprised her.

"How's this for a theory?" she asked. "What if Claudia felt the need to drink *just because it was forbidden?*"

"You'd know best about that. Was that a part of her psychological makeup?"

Laura thought back to freshman psych courses and the concept of individuals who had "authority problems." No, Claudie was exceptionally good at accepting authority. Look at the way she had weathered her almost Victorian upbringing in Michigan. "No," she admitted. "It's more likely she felt on trial, nervous, and didn't realize how much she'd had to drink."

Jesse spread his hands slowly, and she realized that he'd abandoned his smart tweed jacket and reverted to a workshirt at some point.

"Don't give me that smug, pacifying gesture, Jesse," she said. "Even if she drank all this"—pointing to the two pathetic plastic glasses before them—"it wasn't enough to make her lurch around in the linen closet and fall with enough force to kill herself, was it?"

"Freak accidents have been known to happen, Laura."

She stood abruptly and tossed the water in the glasses into the sink. In each hand she smashed a plastic glass, feeling joy at the shattering between her fingers. She felt supremely angry, but she didn't know how to chart her anger so it could flow at the proper target. Ideally, it would be Deputy Ludder, whose dull, respectful, uninflected voice made her want to scream. Even more ideally, the target of Ralph Henderson popped up, but Ralph was too much the stock villain to fit the bill. She saw his melodramatic posturings as silly rather than menacing, and her final picture of him, carrying the hapless Dot in his arms, served to redeem him.

She was facing away from Jesse, looking into the blackness beyond the windows. "Freak accidents do happen," she said. "I'll grant you that. But how often do they happen hours after a dead deer has been deposited, like a calling card, on your doorstep?"

Jesse was silent, but she heard him light a cigarette and inhale deeply. An instant later she heard the tiny ping of his match as it hit the ashtray.

"You don't really believe Claudia died by accident?" she said.

It seemed an eternity before he answered.

"No," he said. "I don't."

She slept as if drugged, and then, just as suddenly, she was terribly and fully awake. It was still dark, and very silent. No surf sounds tonight, no thrum from the cannery. She went to stand near the window and saw, with surprise, that lights were still on down below, turning the lawn, where they shone out the windows, into a strangely unfamiliar terrain. It was past four.

It seemed intensely cold to her, as if the thermometer had plunged many degrees, but perhaps it was just her own exhaustion, the shock of Claudia's awful death. She pulled on thick socks and wrapped a blanket around her shoulders. She knew she would find Jack downstairs, and although she didn't want to force her presence on him, it was possible he might be in need of company. Jack was an amiable man, but he had always been a trifle guarded with most people; it was as if his kind instincts were always at war with a natural reserve. Only Claudia had been able to know him, and only Claudia could coax him into a state of unself-conscious pleasure.

She began to inch down the stairs, considering all the delicate ramifications of the situation. When Jack had returned from the hospital, he had said, "There was a fairly high alcohol level in her blood. They figure she fractured her skull when she fell. She might have lived for ten minutes or so, but she would have been unconscious. She wouldn't have suffered."

He repeated these words, she felt, exactly as they'd been told to him. He seemed to experience no curiosity about the things Laura was endlessly pondering. Why had Claudia been in the linen closet at all? Why, if she had fallen and struck her head, was the wound visible? Surely if one took a violent fall, the part of the head that had received the injury would be flush with the floor?

She understood that Jack would find it more bearable to believe that his wife had died by accident, and she wanted to encourage him in this belief if it would help him, but privately she boiled with indignation and wild incredulity. She had begun to see the locals as a sealed community, a group of outlaws who would expend time and curiosity only on behalf of one of their own.

Midway down the stairs, she saw Jack, seated on the antler couch.

The room was blazing with light. He held the flask in his hands as he would hold an open book, studying it with fascination. She continued down to the bottom and paused, unable to tell if he was aware of her presence. Seen at closer range, he looked half dead himself. His normally sleek hair stood up in little spikes as if he had been dragging his hands over his head, and his color was very like that of the culls she had seen Jesse fling aside on the flats.

"Jack," she said, moving toward him. "Jack?"

He looked up from his contemplation of the flask very slowly. "Oh, hello, Laura," he said. His voice sounded like something floating up from the seabed, deep and slow.

Laura sat beside him on the couch, as far away as possible. She didn't want to crowd in on his suffering. "It's so late," she said. "Shouldn't you try to sleep?"

"Soon," he said. "Not yet."

It was, she thought, as if his very self-consciousness had invaded her mind. Everything she thought to say seemed stale and shopworn. *I know what you're feeling. I loved her too.* The silence stretched on, miserable and full of pain. She couldn't even reach over and take his hand, since both hands were clasped tight on the flask.

After what seemed hours, Jack turned to her, shifting his body slightly, and in the manner of a very old man.

"The thing is," he said, "the thing is, this stupid flask was the first present I ever bought for her. It was at the Yale-Columbia game, when we were both students."

Tears, which he didn't seem to notice, were sliding down his cheeks. In a moment he would be sobbing.

"I didn't even know she still had it," he said, cuffing his cheeks. "I haven't seen it in years. She must have *packed* it before we flew here."

"Yes," said Laura.

"But I didn't know," said Jack. "Isn't that terrible, Laura?"

"No," she said, catching him as he seemed about to fall into her lap. "What's terrible is life."

SIX

Dear Nick, Wayne wrote on a sheet of tablet paper. *It has been some time since you've written to your Mother. She is not well enough at present to make the trip to Walla Walla, even if you had asked. Don't you think*—No —*Couldn't you see your way to drop her a line?*

Wayne studied what he had written, pulled at his bangs in vexation, and balled the paper up and threw it in the wastebasket. On second thought, he retrieved the paper, smoothed it out, folded it, and placed it in his cardigan pocket. Mustn't have Dot, in one of her curious moods, discovering it. Not that she seemed up to being curious these days—that was the trouble. She would do nothing but lie in the darkened bedroom with a tepid washcloth over her eyes.

He began a new letter, but he found himself falling into the same trap with phrases like "it would do her a world of good to hear from you" and "you can't imagine how happy it used to make her when she got a letter." You didn't appeal to Nick's better nature, which was what he had been doing. Nick, Wayne was sorry to admit, simply had no better nature. It would only annoy him to be reminded of obligations he did not recognize or acknowledge.

Wayne had only met his stepson once, soon after he and Dot had been married. He would never forget the sheer terror he'd felt at finding himself, even as a visitor, inside a high-security penitentiary. Merely to enter such a place was to feel suddenly guilty, himself a criminal, deprived of the rights he had always taken for granted. What bothered him most—more than the clanging doors and bursts from the guards' walkie-talkies—was the awe-inspiring noise he could sense rising up from the core of the prison. It seemed to him he could hear it the way you sometimes heard the surf on the Peninsula, and it wasn't such a bad analogy, because when the surf took him by surprise he always thought of the terrible power of the ocean. Just as the ocean's might made him think of ships splintered like kindling by a force that was not so much malevolent as indifferent, so the howling, baying, nonstop chorus of the inmates reminded him that he was now in the company of human tigers. Men who cared as little for the lives of others as the ocean did.

And then there was Nicholas himself. The moment he'd seen him in the visiting room, he'd known Dot's son was a jackal. Nick had come swaggering in, grinning in a loose-lipped, haphazard way intended to win his mother over. As if Dot had ever needed winning! Nick's arms were thickly muscled, and Wayne could see an elaborate tattoo on his right bicep, a tattoo that vanished in the sleeve of his prison jumpsuit.

He was tall, like his mother, but there the resemblance ended. Nick, unlike Dorothy, seemed radiantly healthy. His hair shone, his skin was blooming, and only his eyes seemed dead. They were bright and lustrous, dark, like hers, but when you looked into them your glance was repelled, sent back to you like a piece of junk mail, a thing of no importance.

"So you married a *hairdresser*," Nick said. "Great choice, Mom."

Just to remember the malice in Nick's voice was enough to make Wayne burn with shame. What had he ever done to be treated as Nick had treated him? Dot's response was merely to release a high, hysterical peal of laughter, as if Nick were a naughty dear who said the cleverest things. Most of what he could recall of the distasteful visit revolved around various injustices Nick claimed to have suffered at the hands of the ignorant and vengeful guards. One stupid black screw, he had maintained, had denied him his shower, but since Nick was a member of the Aryan Nation, a brotherhood of white inmates, the screw would very soon be taught a lesson.

He spoke for all the world as if he were a member of some noble clan of freedom fighters, deprived of their rights because a repressive State wanted to break them, strip them of their ideals, and make them useless when, and if, they were ever let free and returned to what passed for civilization.

The worst thing was that Wayne found himself sympathizing, until he remembered that Dot's darling boy was no oppressed guerrilla fighter, but merely a man who had raped and strangled a young girl.

He gnawed at his pen, trying to formulate the only acceptable plea which might make Nick write to his mother. Filial duty wouldn't turn the trick, that was for sure, and neither would simple emotional blackmail.

From upstairs he heard a piteous cry. It seemed wrung from her. That was what frightened him. In the past, Dot's many ailments had been displayed with a careful orchestration and offered up with a sort of pride at the craftsmanship which had fashioned them. Ever since the death of that Arnold girl, Dot's anguish seemed real. It was constant and listless, and lacked that *drama* which in the past he could take with the proverbial grain of salt.

He entered her room with great trepidation. Dot lay supine beneath her tepid cloth. He could see that she didn't care whether her bangs were ruined or not. A silvery trail let him know that she had been weeping. She was covered by a quilt, but he could see the toes of one foot, which had worked free, flexing in distress.

"Shall I bring you some juice?" he said.

The swathed head shook sideways.

"Would you like a back rub, dear?"

Again the dismissing movement of her head against the pillow.

"What can I do for you?"

Beneath the washcloth, an extraordinary effort was being made. Dot's nostrils fluted outward, as if a bellows had pumped them back to life, and her dark eyes seemed to bore through the cloth.

"Nick," she said. "I want Nick."

"As soon as you feel better, I'll take you up for a visit."

"That's not what I meant, and you know it." Her face screwed itself up and she resumed her weeping. "Oh, oh, oh," she gasped, "if only I could turn the clock back."

Wayne left her to her sorrow, knowing that he was powerless to comfort her now. The trouble Nick had brought upon himself and on his mother and, above all, to the luckless girl he'd killed, was something Dot seemed firmly to believe might not have happened if she had warned him never to pick up a female hitchhiker. He had been stunned the first time she advanced her theory. "If I'd told Nicholas the evil young girls can get up to," Dot had said, "he might have thought twice before stopping his car for one of them. There's an expression for that kind of girl, and I'm not going to lower myself by using it, but I'm sure you know what I mean. They dress in provocative clothing and get into a stranger's car—what do they expect? A boy like Nick, brought up well and used to decent behavior, is likely to lose control of himself."

He'd seen the futility of arguing with her on the subject of Nicholas. The only concession to sanity he made was not to agree with her, to sit in silence until she'd finished. In Dot's view, her boy—who'd been twenty-eight when he strangled the girl—was the victim of a lewd teenager, and then a victim again at the hands of the media. Because of the tireless reporting of a particular journalist on the *Intelligencer* in Seattle, Dot believed her son's sentence had been harsher than it might have been if the trial had been allowed to proceed quietly. The sentence was thirty years, and the judge had recommended no parole. Nick was now pushing forty and remained unrepentant, sullen and troublesome.

From her meager savings, Dot sent money to the prison to be paid into Nick's account, so he could buy, as she thought, candy bars and cigarettes.

Wayne, in sudden inspiration, saw the way to persuade Nick to write a filial letter. His salon was doing well enough, and his expenses were few. He withdrew another sheet from his tablet and began to write. It was quite a short note, and when he was finished he reread it and thought he'd struck exactly the right note. He told Nick that his mom was feeling extra poorly on account of the untimely death of an acquaintance of hers. She wasn't well enough to make the trip to Walla Walla. He suggested Nick might write to her, and asked him to make it a long letter, full of the sorts of things likely to make Dorothy happy. His masterstroke came at the end, where he had written: *I am prepared to pay you the sum of fifty dollars for every letter you write. I don't know how much of this you'll be allowed to have every week. That's for you and the prison authority to work out. I would suggest a letter a week, and I want you to sign them with love. Love, Nick, would do, or Your Loving Son, Nicholas. Payment will be forthcoming as soon as your mother receives her first letter.*

He signed it, impersonally, *W. F. Cotton.*

He addressed and stamped the envelope, and then—because he didn't want to mail it where Grace Best might see it—he drove to the larger post office in Ocean Park and posted it in anonymity.

"I just saw Wayne Cotton leaving the post office in Ocean Park," Martin Best said to his mother.

"So what?" said Grace, who had been frying potatoes and felt irritation at her son's blustery entrance into the kitchen.

Martin went to the fridge and popped open a beer. "Nothin'," he said.

"You wouldn't have commented if there was nothing in it," Grace said.

"Only he looked like he'd just won the Irish Sweepstakes," Martin said. "But beneath that he looked like death warmed over."

"What he goes through with Dot," said Grace. "They say she's really making the most of Mrs. Arnold's death."

"You found the body," Martin said in a vaguely accusing way. "Where were you when Bob Ludder was asking us all those questions?"

Grace sighed and reached for a tin of black pepper. "I went through the dining room and straight out the back door," she admitted. "I didn't want to hang around."

"It looks funny, your not being there," Martin said. "I mean, nobody cares, but if this was one of those murder mysteries, it would seem like you were a suspect."

"I don't like death," said Grace. "It's not natural."

Three days after the house party, Jack flew back East with Claudia's body. He tried to persuade Laura to cut short her stay on the Peninsula and return with him, but he made it very clear that there was nothing personal, nothing *needy* in his request. There was to be no memorial, only a small, private funeral. He would be quite all right, and intended to put the hotel on the market in time. He wanted nothing further to do with it.

His concern was for her safety. He didn't think it advisable for her to remain alone in such a place.

There was very little she could say. She could not point out that since he was apparently accepting his wife's death as a freak accident, danger didn't come into it. Even if he had acknowledged suspicions of murder, how would that place her at risk? She was not the new owner—even Ralph Henderson knew that now—but just a visitor, a temporary guest, of no possible interest to anyone bent on keeping the Grey Whale obscure and derelict. She politely told Jack Arnold that she would stay, adding that Dan would soon be joining her, and he seemed to accept her decision.

Privately, she had begun to doubt that Dan would ever materialize in the Pacific Northwest. It wasn't that he hadn't meant to join her on this strange holiday, it was more a matter of his total subservience to the corporation that sent him to Düsseldorf or Dublin, Cologne or Kyoto, with the bland assumption that Dan was pleased to serve them in whatever way he was able. Perhaps he was, she no longer knew.

"Do you know," she told Jesse when they were once more alone in the hotel, "Jack only gave up when I mentioned Dan. It's as if they need a password, a male password."

"Are these the words of a feminist?" Jesse asked the question seriously, but his voice was playful.

"Certainly not," said Laura. "I don't trust anything that has an 'ist' tacked on to it."

"Fascist, feminist, communist, environmentalist, survivalist, rapist," Jesse intoned. "These are not, under the circumstances, people we want to meet at present."

"Also no stylists, psychiatrists, or optimists," she said. "I wouldn't mind a few pathologists or forensic scientists, though."

"Guess we have to be our own," Jesse said.

She remembered the oh-so-scientific experiment they had performed with the flask and smiled sadly. "I'm afraid we're not exactly qualified."

"I meant we can be our own investigative team, if it will make you any happier." He looked out the window at the sodden, rain-soaked lawn. Today was the first utterly charmless day Laura had witnessed in her westward trek, as she secretly thought of it. The weather was being uncooperative, and from early morning until this latish afternoon hour, there had been a steady downpour of the rain for which the Pacific Northwest was so famous. "It would help to pass the time," he suggested.

They went upstairs and switched on the few old lamps in the huge hall that circled round the stairwell. Even so, it was gloomy.

"Okay," Jesse said. "First question?"

"What was Claudia doing in the linen closet?"

"We'll check the bathrooms, see if there was some crisis we didn't know about."

As if there really were some meaning to the MEN and LADIES loos, so designated in the two bathrooms intended for guests whose room had no facilities, Jesse went into the men's room and Laura to the ladies'. She found the towels had been used, but were by no means in a disgusting condition, and there were two rolls of toilet paper standing at the ready as backup for the one on the roll. She came out, feeling silly.

"Nothing there," she said.

"Nothing in the men's, either," said Jesse.

Laura sat on a sagging old couch on the landing. "If this were a film, there'd be one of those yellow tapes around the linen closet to mark a crime scene," she said. "Maybe even one of those outlines in chalk to show how she'd fallen."

"Yes, but the place would also be sealed off, with a cop to guard it. We couldn't poke around like this."

"Are you suggesting it's a better system here? Do you think police indifference is a good thing because it means *we* can bungle around and try to figure things out? I've heard of benign neglect, but this is malicious neglect."

Jesse looked at her in what appeared to be astonishment. "I don't make judgments," he said flatly. It reminded her of Althea's terse "I don't like cities." It was spoken in a tone of voice that hinted at terrible finality.

"Good for you," she said in her best flippant, drop-dead manner. "What's next on this brilliant experiment at detection?"

Undaunted, Jesse said, "I think we should check every room, every bathroom and every bedroom. There might be something that required a trip to the linen closet."

They divided the rooms up in such a way that Jesse would be checking her own. In room number six she found a collapsed mattress, and imagined a boisterous child bouncing on it until the ancient springs gave way. There was nothing in the linen closet to remedy broken bedsprings, so she continued on through the connecting bathroom, where nothing seemed amiss, into room number seven. It was a room with twin beds, and the blue chenille spreads were drawn taut over each bed, the closets were bare and swept, and nothing gave offense except for a spider building its web on the arch of the door near the washstand.

"Eureka!" she heard Jesse shout. "Room number four!"

When she found him, he was bending over a darkly stained pillowcase on the floor. It appeared to have been hastily stripped from the pillow. Jesse picked up the case and sniffed. "Cranberry juice," he said.

Laura sat on the edge of the bed and looked at the Trapper—or was he the Tracker?—as he hunkered on his haunches and passed his noble nose over the dark stain like a Geiger counter.

"What's the scenario?" she said. "Claudia finds that a guest has spilled cranberry juice on a pillowcase, and goes in a fit of housewifely zeal to the linen closet to get a fresh pillowcase?"

"Can you think of anything better?" Jesse turned widened eyes on her, as if he really wanted to know. "She strips the pillow, wanting her hotel to look as clean and respectable as possible, and goes to the closet to find a replacement."

"Why did she leave it in the middle of the floor?"

"She didn't *plan* to die in the linen closet," Jesse said. "She thought she'd dispose of it after she recovered the pillow."

"Maybe," said Laura.

"It's the only thing we have so far that gives her any motive for being in the closet at all," Jesse said.

Laura thought of her friend as she'd last seen her, slipping up the stairs after a final visit to the flask. Would Claudia, in her unaccustomed afternoon vodka glow, really make a tour of all the rooms to see if her hotel was looking its best? Or had she, at the end of an emotionally exhausting party, merely wandered about the upper floor in the happy expectation of one day seeing the unwieldy place as a going concern?

Jesse coughed politely. "Wait," she told him, holding up one hand. She closed her eyes and planted Claudia on a somewhat tipsy course. Almost through with the onerous duty of convincing her guests she is not a greedy developer from the East, Claudia is stealing a few moments to stroll through her new domain. She is happily picturing the improvements she will make, ordering up the fat quilts that will repose at the bottom of each bed, decorating the barren walls with amusing prints. Perhaps she plans little wicker baskets filled with pastel soaps in the shapes of seashells for each bathroom. By the time the hotel is open, the water will charge through the pipes diamond-bright and colorless.

In her scenario, Claudia trails her way into room number four and spends a few happy moments picturing it as it will be. She sees the bright, clean curtains that will flutter at the window, and the fresh coat of Wedgwood blue that will be applied to the walls. The blankets on the bed should mirror this blue, and the quilt could be a delicious shade of violet or mauve, backed by deep purple. Claudia's fastidious eyes are drawn by something jarring on the bed. The large stain on the pillowcase reminds her of old blood. It's depressing, totally out of character for the brave new room she has been creating in her imagination. Stained pillowcases will not be a feature of the Grey Whale she plans to bring back to life.

The question was, would Claudia ignore the pillowcase, seeing it as an example of the imperfect present, or would she pull it off and look for a replacement, needing to introduce a facsimile of perfection into the here and now?

This time, Jesse only cleared his throat. Laura kept her eyes closed. It seemed important to retrace Claudia's last moments as scrupulously as she could. Here was Claudia, purchasing lemons in a supermarket. They were intended, as she later explained to Laura, to keep her hair yellow for as long as they could. Laura was annoyed at herself for entertaining this memory when she'd meant to concentrate on the end of her friend's life. When she opened her eyes, Jesse was gone.

She found him in the linen closet. "I thought you might be meditating," he said.

"Not me. Althea or Fran might meditate, and I'm sure Teddy does, but I can't seem to even concentrate. I just tried to put all my consciousness into imagining how it was just before Claudia died, and all I could think was that she used to squeeze lemon juice on her hair."

"Don't knock it," said Jesse. "Your mind might have chosen to remember that for a very pertinent reason."

"I doubt it." It occurred to her that Jesse could become an author with Crowther and Hull, writing pop-psych books with titles like *Everything I Learned I Learned by Accident.*

"How tall are you?" Jesse asked.

"Five seven."

"Was Claudia about the same?"

"About a half inch shorter." Jesse was about the same, she thought, but like most men he probably liked to think he was taller.

"She was wearing flats, like the ones you have on, only a different color."

"How observant you are," said Laura, wondering if he had admired Claudia. Most men she knew never noticed women's shoes. Then the importance of Claudia's shoes made her draw in air so sharply it sounded as if she had developed the hiccups. "Ludder!" she cried. "I've just remembered. When he was reconstructing his version of Claudia's death he said she was wearing high heels."

Jesse nodded as if it were a thing of no importance.

"I guess I was too stunned at the time to realize what he said. Jack too." She snapped on the light in the linen closet, then turned it off again. It was too depressing, knowing what had happened here—if not precisely how—to look at the neatly folded stacks of threadbare sheets and worn towels. "That lying bastard," she said. "He was so sure of himself he didn't even bother to pretend."

"Who?" Jesse said, his dark eyes quickening.

"Who what?"

"Which lying bastard?"

"Am I losing my mind here? Who did you think I meant? Ludder, of course."

Jesse smiled one of his most cryptic smiles. "Oh," he said, "the shoes. Bob wasn't lying, Laura. By the time he got downstairs he assumed she'd been wearing high heels. Women like you and Claudia, women who are—*stylish*, I guess you could say—always seem to be wearing high heels. He was weaving this picture of how she died, and that just fit into the picture."

Laura sank down on her heels. "Let me get this straight. Bob Ludder is not only incompetent, he approaches police work according to some mental image of what certain women wear. As if poor Claudie and I were aliens."

"Something like that. You're"—he spread his hands—"high-heeled kind of women."

She wondered what Jesse would do if she threw back her head and howled with exasperation. High-heeled women!

"Let's try an experiment," Jesse was saying, switching the light on again. "Let's see which shelf corresponds to the side of Claudia's head that was injured. If you'd just stand up, with your back to the shelves?"

For the next quarter hour they acted out Claudia's possibly fatal blow, with Jesse as director, always keeping in mind the direction in which she had fallen. The shelves started at knee height, and stretched up to almost beyond her reach. The fourth shelf would have to have been the culprit, since its edge, when she stood back to back with it, touched the approximate area of her skull. Each time she pantomimed a tipsy lurch, culminating with a fall, she felt that Claudia would have slid down, kneeling from the blow, and fallen in a crumpled position quite near the source of her inanimate killer, but Claudia had sprawled out the full length of the closet floor, and her arms had been flung forward.

"It doesn't work," she said triumphantly, after the fifth re-creation. "It won't wash."

But Jesse was full of surprises. "Have you ever noticed how drunks walk down the street?" he asked, stepping out of the closet. "They have an instinct, even dead gone, to protect themselves from falling. They overbalance. They counterbalance."

Walking in his stealthy, usual tread some little distance up the hall, he turned and executed a perfect imitation of a wino's progress. The overcareful, exaggerated tread, broken by a violent lurch toward the pavement, prevented by an equally violent backward-leaning motion to prevent calamity. Yes. She had seen it, all too often in New York, and wondered if Jesse had put in some time as a drunk, or was merely showing his observant qualities. The performance could not be faulted, but it seemed he wanted to be called back for encores.

Stepping once more into the closet, he showed her how Claudia might have reeled forward, corrected herself with a violent backward motion, and struck her head a violent blow against the shelf. The phantom Claudia rocked forward, unaware of her terrible injury, and was momentarily steady on her feet before she found herself plumeting, face downward, to the floor. Jesse stretched out his arms to break the fall, and managed to land in almost the exact position in which Claudia had been discovered.

The artistry of it took her breath away momentarily, and when she could speak again she said only: "It's true she could have died like that."

"But?" said Jesse, his face still pressed against the musty carpet.

"She hadn't had that much to drink."

He bounded to his feet in one supple movement, banishing the illusion of a golden-haired woman's death on the floor of the linen closet. "How do you know?" he said.

"We did the flask experiment," Laura said. "It wasn't enough for her to do what you just acted out. I saw her run upstairs just a little time before she died. She wasn't lurching and weaving."

"Booze is funny stuff," Jesse said. "It can catch up to you when you least expect it. Claudia could have been nipping away for hours before the party started. She could have thought she was fine, and then —wham!—it might have felled her like a sledgehammer."

"It doesn't fit," said Laura. "Not the Claudia I know." She heard what she had said. "Knew."

"Maybe the person you knew had changed," Jesse said. "It happens."

Laura wanted to be away from the gloomy linen closet, the morbid reenactments of her friend's death. Jesse, who had said just days ago that he didn't think her death an accident, now seemed to be the enemy.

It was with some apprehension that she heard her own voice say, in a winsome and pleading manner, "Let's go downstairs now, shall we?"

"Of course," Jesse said. "Teddy mentioned that he might bring over some more salmon."

"Is that a code word for you-know-what?"

"Relax, Laura. It's really salmon. I'd like to grill it outdoors on the barbecue, but the weather's too miserable. Maybe tomorrow."

Downstairs, Laura poured herself a glass of wine and went to lie on the long couch overlooking the bay. She felt listless and curious at the same time. It was a bad combination. Her mind swarmed with unanswered questions, but was operating at too low a level to do anything about it.

Mist had obscured the tree line on the other side of the bay, and she might as well be staring at a gray sea. From far away, she heard Jesse greeting someone, presumably Teddy. He had explained that Teddy occasionally bartered fresh produce from his garden for salmon down in Ocean Park. The screen door slammed and she could hear a female voice laughing. Fran. Tomorrow they would grill the salmon and have a Grey Whale dinner party. Lots of companionable stirring of vegetables at the big restaurant stove. Edible flowers in the salad. Plenty of wine. Life would go on here as if Claudia had never existed, which was as it should be, but did everybody have to be so cheerful about it?

It wasn't until much later, when she was courting sleep in her bedroom, that the significance of the lemons made itself known to her. She heard Claudia's voice, that voice of rectitude and years of a personal code of honor formulated in lonely Michigan.

"I will never color my hair," Claudia had said, explaining away the lemon-juice beauty aid. "I won't ever be one of those women with improbable-looking hair. My grandmother had one of those awful blue rinses. You only have to look at Mrs. Jacoby to see what I mean."

Estelle Jacoby was the wife of one of their favorite professors, a man who taught Victorian Literature in Transition. She sported hair of a deep, dull, lusterless black. It was Claudia's opinion that Estelle Jacoby had once possessed vibrant, raven hair, and was deceiving herself in thinking that she could duplicate her once crowning glory through chemicals.

"It's the deception that's so cruel," Claudia had said. "People should know they can never remain the same. Why do they even try?"

Easy enough to say at the age of nineteen, yet Laura had never doubted the fierceness of her friend's position. She had credited Claudia with more moral fiber than anyone could possibly have. She'd been in her late twenties—a houseguest at the Arnolds' for a weekend—when she discovered a box of Lady Clairol in the medicine cabinet.

As if she knew her guilty secret had been sniffed out, Claudia had delivered a little sermon on truth and illusion during Laura's stay. "You know how I used to be against artifice?" Claudia said, mixing a pitcher of Bloody Marys for their brunch, resplendent in a Japanese kimono Jack had bought her at some opulent store.

"Lemons would do the trick," said Laura.

"I'm still as strict as ever," said Claudia, shaking Tabasco into her pitcher, "but the rules have changed. I lighten it *just to its original shade—never lighter.*" Laura remembered how surprised she had been at the tone of Claudia's voice. It wasn't like her to sound so self-righteous and defensive. "As long as I live, I will never pretend to be something I'm not."

It wasn't a serious moral lapse to color one's hair, of course, but something in Claudia's long-ago speech bothered her. Had Claudie protested too much? In the strictest sense, returning her hair to the sunny hue she had enjoyed in childhood and very young womanhood was completely understandable—Laura lightened her own hair tastefully, operating on the same principle. It looked completely natural, as Claudia's had done, because they were both natural blondes. Just as the flaxen hair of babies turns a bit darker as they grow up, so the honey hair of the teens and early twenties is likely to become sand-colored with the passing of time. Why had Claudia made such a high-minded flap over her small artifice? Why had she said, so dramatically, that she would never pretend to be something she was not?

Laura sat up in bed, feeling that she had hold of something of great importance. In her mind, she selected a sheet of white paper and wrote: *Why C. so self-important when explaining about hair?* The sort of mental posturing Claudie had indulged in could be explained away by only two things, in Laura's experience. The first was a kind of arrogant stupidity, a belief that everything one did or thought of doing was of great interest to the world at large. She had encountered it often in would-be authors, and was encountering it with a depressing frequency in published authors at Crowther and Hull. She crossed this motive, if you could call it a motive, off the list.

The second was guilt and its by-product, denial. She wrote *Because C. contrary to all appearance, was pretending to be something she wasn't.* It was cold in her room, but unpleasant expectations made her feel warm and jittery.

What, if C. was pretending, did she pretend to be? That was easy. *Loving wife. Adored wife. Well-adjusted member of community. Affluent, fortunate, educated. Adventurous, public-spirited. The survivor of an unhappy childhood. Childless by choice.*

Laura felt itchy and on the verge of discovering something she didn't want to know. *Conclusion: C. was not what she appeared to be in recent years, or maybe for a very long time.*

She lay back in one swift movement, hurtling against the mattress with much the same force as Jesse had reenacted Claudia's fatal fall.

She saw clearly, now, how Claudia might have become a secret drinker, turning to an anesthetic to dull the lingering pain of her early bereavement. So proud of her ability to overcome the lonely childhood, Claudia could never have borne to show her oldest friend certain proof that she had failed, after all.

Sad as it was, the theory brought her a certain peace. At least it banished the bogeymen of cunning locals—people who smiled at you while eating free brownies and used your hotel as a sort of soup kitchen, when all along they were phoning you with threatening regularity in the night and depositing dead deer on your doorstep.

For the second time she was lulled toward sleep, but grotesque images swam up to force her awake again. She saw a bird flap up from the reeds, one of the gray herons, but then it took on a human face, and the face was that of Grace Best, who melted and became Ralph Henderson. Next the deer on the doorstep got up and revealed himself as Jesse, but just as Jesse was pulling on long boots he smiled at her and was instantly revealed to be Jack.

It was Jack's face that banished sleep that night. Of course—Jack! She'd never for a moment put his quick handling of the situation, his seeming willingness to let idiots like Ludder call it what it was not, to reasons of guilt. She'd assumed that grief and his dislike of revealing himself had propelled him away as soon as possible. She honestly believed he was the sort of man who would say, "Since nothing can bring her back, what's the use of stirring things up?"

All that long and mostly sleepless night, Laura tried to picture a very different Jack Arnold, one who found his once-beloved wife increasingly a burden, one who had no desire to become involved in the messy business of running a hotel, one who shrewdly foresaw that her death could be conveniently ignored in such an isolated place. Could she believe in this new, menacing Jack Arnold?

She found that just barely, she could.

SEVEN

There was only one car parked outside of Luby's place, a rusted-out Ford, and Laura judged it would be a good time to beard Mrs. Geiger in her den. Ever since she'd heard Dorrie shout at Ralph Henderson, the woman had come to represent the very embodiment of common sense and rationality, qualities she had found missing in so many of the others.

It was dark and cool in Luby's, even though the sun had returned and was dazzlingly bright today. Luby's, in fact, seemed a sort of underground bunker. As her eyes adjusted to the gloom, she took in the pool tables, the shovelboard, and the two men drinking Ranier beer far up the bar. Each of them sported shoulder-length hair which was matted and unclean. One wore a baseball cap pulled backward, and the other was bareheaded. Both wore flannel shirts with the arms ripped out, the better to feature huge muscles. They never spoke, but since they sat on adjoining stools she supposed they were together and had come to Luby's in the sad-looking Ford. Dorrie was nowhere in evidence.

Laura advanced a little farther into the long room, and now she saw the poster advising spotted owls as a superior form of toilet paper. The men took no notice of her, which was gratifying, and she chose a stool midway between them and the door.

She should have been feeling hollow-eyed and sullen after her long night, but she had gone on to sleep until nearly noon, and was experiencing the need to make use of the remainder of the day. She felt alert and full of nervous energy. It had been so many years since she had slept until noon she failed to recognize the very frame of mind she'd once known so intimately on Sundays, when she was a student.

Dorrie suddenly popped up, like a genie from a bottle. She had been crouching behind the bar doing whatever it was that bartenders did, but the abrupt manifestation was both alarming and awe-inspiring. Laura thought even more of Dorrie Geiger as someone with the power to make order out of chaos.

The men made indolent hand gestures, passing a few words she could not quite hear, and Dorrie refilled their glasses. She seemed somewhat remote, as if she disapproved of these customers, but she gave them a thin smile. Then she caught sight of Laura and came striding down the walkway behind the bar.

"Hey," she said, "Laura, isn't it?"

Laura nodded her head, smiling, feeling idiotic.

"What brings you here?" The question was bald and not diplomatic, but in the next instant Dorrie was bending her head over the bar and saying, out of the side of her mouth, "I'm really sorry about what happened to your friend."

"I was hoping I could talk to you," Laura said. And then, mindful that Luby's was a place of business, she said, "Do you think I could have a Bloody Mary?"

Dorrie blew her cheeks out in a defeated manner, then shook her head. "Afraid not," she said. "This is a tavern, honey, and we're only licensed to sell wine or beer. It's the state law. You want a mixed cocktail, you have to go to a pub."

Laura wanted neither beer nor wine, but felt she'd seem snobbish and difficult if she said as much. "I'll have a glass of white wine," she decided.

Dorrie plodded off and filled a small tumbler with tavern wine. When she brought it back and slid it over the counter, Laura saw the glass was full to brimming. When she lifted it to her lips she had an odd sense of *déjà vu*. She could have been at an opening at an art gallery in New York, where the same wine was passed out in little crushable, plastic glasses. At least her tumbler was sturdy and wouldn't splinter if she involuntarily tightened her grip.

Dorrie folded her substantial arms on the bar and cradled her chin in her hands. "What did you want to talk about?" she said.

"You said you were sorry about what happened to my friend." Laura sipped at her wine and tried to feel secure and worldly. "I'm sorry, too. What bothers me is how quickly everybody accepted it as an accident."

Dorrie withdrew a pack of cigarettes from her hip pocket and lit one with elaborately careful gestures. "You don't think it was an accident?" she said, expelling smoke vigorously. "Is that what you want to talk about?"

"I have my doubts," Laura said. And then quickly, before her companion could lose interest, she told her about the shoes, which in fact had been flat-heeled, about the relatively small amount of vodka Claudia had consumed, and about how Claudia had been lying with the injured part of her head facing up. Of her new slant on Jack's possible feelings about his wife, she said nothing. Dorrie listened to it all, smoking steadily and deeply, revealing nothing in her expression.

"You won't like what I'm going to say." Dorrie looked sad, not combative. "In my experience, when something awful happens, people look at it in the way that makes them feel best. When I was living in the city, Portland, there was a woman whose husband ran out on her. Left with a young thing half her age, and was never heard from again."

"But what does that have to do with?—"

Dorrie held up one large hand. "Just let me finish, please. This woman—Shelly was her name—took to saying her old man left because she nagged him and wasn't a good wife. She'd say it to anyone who'd listen. Hear her tell it, she'd been pretty near a monster to him. Shelly would corner women and tell them not to behave the way she'd done or they'd live to regret it."

Dorrie paused in her narrative as the two men shoved away from the bar and made to leave. "Keep your nose clean," she said to the one in the baseball cap.

"Will do," he answered. " 'Bye, Mom."

"My son," said Dorrie to Laura. "Now the fact about Shelly is she was no better or worse than most wives. Old Vince took off because a pretty girl who was barely old enough to be legal was willing to go with him. Shelly couldn't face that, of course, so she invented this terrible Shelly who had made her man's life a misery and driven him away. That way he didn't leave her—*she* drove *him* off. She had the upper hand, even though it didn't result in any happiness for her."

Laura sipped her wine, absorbing Dorrie's story. She knew a Shelly-like woman in Manhattan who was dealing with reality exactly as the Portland Shelly had done, but she didn't want to complicate the issue by mentioning her.

"I agree with what you've said, Dorrie." Her words, spoken in the now empty tavern, had to be chosen very carefully. Dorrie was proving to be every bit as sensible as she had imagined her to be, but she couldn't imagine what it all had to do with Claudia.

"You're probably wondering how Mrs. Arnold fits into my theory," Dorrie said.

Laura nodded.

"Years ago there was a little boy got killed in a riptide over by Cape Disappointment. His father claimed the boy would never go wading in the ocean when he knew how dangerous it could be there. He swore up and down some tourists for the Kite Festival had forced that poor kid into the water. The truth was, there wasn't any tourists up there—they were all checked into motels at Long Beach, but his daddy couldn't stand to think the boy had just ignored his common sense. He couldn't stand to think the boy had been careless, and the tide just swept him out."

Laura shivered briefly, feeling the cold water sweeping her out to sea. She tried to imagine the father's grief and guilt. Much better to imagine indifferent tourists luring his son to his death than thinking his warnings had not been strong or effective enough to keep the boy from harm. She could understand, but it still had no bearing on her relationship with Claudia. She was not her dead friend's custodian, had no special responsibility for Claudia's safety, and wondered how to wring an answer from Dorrie Geiger without appearing to condescend.

"I know it looks bad, with Ralph Henderson making threats," Dorrie said, "but things aren't always the way they seem. Ralph wouldn't hurt a flea, but he'd die rather than advertise it."

"I don't know if I can believe he's so harmless," Laura said.

"I never said he was harmless. He's capable of getting up to all kinds of harm. I'd say he's a very dangerous man. All I meant was Ralph would never harm a person *physically*. He's kind of—*squeamish,* I guess you'd say."

Laura wondered if Dorrie might not be pulling her leg, but she was looking as sincere as ever. Leaving aside the image of fastidious, meek Ralph Henderson, she asked Laura what was really on her mind.

"Why do you think I'd rather believe Claudia was murdered? Is that what we want for our best friends?"

Dorrie smiled broadly. "Maybe so, specially if they can go quick and painless. It's better than thinking of her all tanked up and out of control, stumbling around a closet." There was no malice in her voice, and Laura believed she meant it. Time to go. She took her wallet out of her handbag, ready to hear Mrs. Geiger say the drink was on the house, but Dorrie said, "That'll be a dollar fifty, please."

When she stood blinking in the sun outside Luby's, Laura saw the humor of it. She had just paid the absurdly low price of a dollar and a half for a session with the best shrink on the Peninsula, and drunk a complimentary glass of wine.

She drove on down to Long Beach, where hundreds of colorful wind socks punched at the air like demented squid. The huge chain-saw sculptures that were the town's centerpieces seemed oppressive today, and even as she watched, a small boy tried to scramble up into the lap of the heavy-breasted mermaid, fell back, and knocked his head on the pavement beneath. Quickly, she went into the bookstore she had seen on the drive in. She wanted a copy of *The Atlantic*, because one of her authors had a short story in the new issue.

Inside, the store was clean and well stocked. The requisite bestsellers were prominently displayed—one of them a Crowther and Hull, not hers—but there were also fine books, literary books, and a substantial section devoted to works of regional interest. *The Art of the Chinook* and *Oyster Cookery* took pride of place, with *Our Vanishing Rain Forests* a close runner-up.

She asked the proprietor, a neat man wearing a dove-gray cardigan sweater, if he carried *The Atlantic*.

"Best place for that is Oregon," he said apologetically. "There's a shop in Astoria."

Laura thanked him and returned to her rented car. The man had given her instructions for the store in Oregon, and it was, after all, just over the long bridge connecting the two states. She had driven through its outward limits on her way from the airport. An afternoon trip to Oregon might do her good.

The child who had fallen from the chain-saw mermaid's haunches was being comforted with ice cream. As she drove past the mermaid, past an antic Lewis and Clark tableau, and out of the environs of the

Peninsula's party place, she saw the finger of land as if from the air. At either end it was beautiful, nearly untouched, heavily wooded and as mysterious as the misty forests in which the Indians had once lived, crafting the haunting masks now on display in the pages of *The Art of the Chinook.* In the middle was a little wasteland of chain-saw sculptures and kiddie rides, motels with signs featuring badly drawn Indian chiefs or flirtatious Disney whales. Tourists in the middle, elk at the base of the finger's joint, and bear at the fingertip.

Jack and Claudia had chosen the only place on the Peninsula where life had been compromised. Nahcotta was neither tourist trap nor unspoiled hamlet, neither wilderness nor town. It was a place where almost anything might happen, because the people who lived there only pretended to know what they wanted. Nearly all of them acted as if they were protecting some huge secret—they repelled visitors as surely as Long Beach courted them. Doubtless the Potlatch Hotel, if asked, could provide guest books filled with the names of a far-flung clientele.

The Grey Whale had had no guest book for many years.

"This feast is for you, Laura," Fran said, lifting her wineglass. She spoke shyly, her cheeks pinking up even more than usual. "We know you're upset about the terrible thing that happened here, and we want you to feel better."

Everyone made confirming sounds, and Teddy nodded his head, beaming at her. Jesse and Grace Best smiled, too. The only person at the table who didn't seem to take a visible part in the festivities was a friend the Vines had brought along. She was a woman in her late twenties or early thirties, impossible to tell, who had been presented as a traveling folk dancer.

Her name was Holly, and she had announced immediately that she was a vegetarian, and that her vegetarianism prohibited even the eating of fish. She was lean, yet bulky, with sturdy calves and powerful shoulders. She wore her dark hair scraped high in a topknot, and her eyes seemed slanted as a result.

Holly would not go hungry tonight, despite her ban on fish. Her plate was heaped with lightly fried potatoes and squash, creamed Walla Walla Sweets, and Jesse's famous egg and tomato dish. At her elbow was a plate of salad, embellished with the edible flowers from

Teddy's garden and glistening with balsamic vinegar. In the kitchen a blueberry pie waited its turn, the gift of Althea, who had baked it and sent it over while Laura was rummaging about in an Oregon bookshop. Althea, it seemed, could not be present, but wanted to contribute to the feast.

The salmon, stuffed with scallions and bread crumbs, had been sewed up by Fran and grilled by Jesse and Teddy, and now made its appearance as the *pièce de résistance* of a celebration Laura could only view as morbid.

Even so, she raised her glass and thanked them, tucking in. Salmon again! It was not one of her favorite foods. She had a cowardly aversion to eating any fish except for shrimp or scallops or lobsters. Their bland, white meat had always seemed as reassuring as a chicken's breast; to feel daring about it, she had only to dip them into zesty sauces. The salmon was something else again. She didn't mind its taste, but she felt she had to blend it with forkfuls of potato and squash to get it down properly.

"Yummy," said Fran.

"Really great," said Grace.

"The best," said Teddy.

"I noticed that you eat oysters," Jesse said politely to the vegetarian. "Where do you draw the line?"

"I draw it at anything that feels pain. I don't believe an oyster feels anything."

Earlier, she had asked if the eggs in Jesse's tomato salad came from free-range or battery hens. Laura wondered now if Holly might be an animal rights activist. They had become very vocal recently, freeing animals from experimental laboratories and holding large marches. They had taken to staging pickets in front of fur stores in Manhattan, and spraying the coats of women who chose to wear fur with paint. Laura owned a fur coat which she seldom wore. It had been a gift from Dan on their fifth anniversary, a splashy, full-length silver fox, and even then the coat had made her uneasy. Her philosophy, never realized until that day, was that wearing fur was fine for people who lived in extremely cold climates. Let the Eskimos wear as much fur as they could, and also the Canadians and Russians and Scandinavians, not to mention people from Minnesota and Montana. But New York City? It was so rarely really cold anymore, she reckoned she'd be lucky to get two days a year frigid enough to make her fox fur practical. She had always despised the sight of women swathed in fur when the mercury hovered between forty and fifty; it could mean only that they had poor circulation or were determined to parade their affluence even if it made them sweat with discomfort.

"What are you thinking about, Laura?" Grace Best leaned forward, her kind face looking troubled. "You seem so far away."

She decided to be honest. "About women who wear fur coats when there's no need," she said.

"There's never a need," said Holly.

"I disagree," said Laura. "What about Eskimos?"

"They are the sole group I'd make an exception for." Holly popped a tomato into her mouth and chewed with vigor. Teddy used the momentary silence to slip another fillet of salmon on Laura's plate. "Traditionally," said Holly, "the Innuit, existing in the harshest climate known to colonized man, have been forced to depend on animals for their sole source of food, fuel, and clothing. It's their culture, a culture which respects the life it is taking even as it takes it. Much like the American Indians, in fact. Now that the Alaskan pipeline has done to them what alcohol and disease-ridden blankets did to the Native American, I expect to see them converting to warm polyesters and wool blends."

"Holly used to teach anthropology at the University of Colorado," said Teddy.

"A static life. Now I travel and gather information about dance, and it's much more rewarding."

"Holly was in Bali last year," said Fran, her eyes shining. "I'd love to go to Bali."

"On Teddy's bicycle?" asked Grace Best, winking at Laura.

Fran leapt up, nearly knocking her glass of wine into Jesse's lap. "Blueberry pie," she cried. "Time to whip the cream!"

Laura helped to clear away the plates while Jesse made the coffee and Fran whipped the cream with Claudia's brand-new electric mixer, purchased in Seattle. At least, she thought, these brave people did not seem to care about cholesterol. A great bowl of whipped cream was carried in to accompany Althea's pie, and sighs of satisfaction rose up all round.

"Yummy," said Fran.

The rest of the evening passed in quick time for Laura. At some point Holly performed a Balinese temple dance, using teaspoons to simulate temple bells. At another Laura helped to dry the first batch of dishes Jesse was washing and return them to their place on the shelves. Later, she could remember how they all filed out the back door and took up positions on the lawn, looking for shooting stars.

The only part of the evening that remained clear and undefiled, in retrospect, was the one in which Holly sidled up beside her and said, "You're feeling pain because your friend died. You're asking yourself a million questions, aren't you."

She had nodded, incapable of speech.

"Stop it, right now," said Holly. "You're never going to get the answer. Spare yourself a lot of useless grief." Holly put her arm around Laura's shoulder in a gesture that seemed unfamiliar, yet all too rehearsed. "She was never meant to come here. This place is sacred ground, named for a chief. She was never meant to come here, and now nature has acted. Understand?"

"No," said Laura. "I don't understand."

"Give it time," Holly said. "You will."

"That's the stupidest theory I've ever heard," Laura said to Jesse later, when the guests had gone.

"She's a flake, forget her," said Jesse.

"It's not even a *good* stupid theory. Nobody here is *from* here, except for Grace and poor old Dot. And Dorrie Geiger. Why aren't we all killed, then?"

Jesse continued to wash dishes and bowls. She wiped, he washed—they were like an old married couple. Her question had been rhetorical, and she was surprised when he chose to answer it.

"I think her point was not that strangers couldn't come and settle here," he said. "That is, if they're like Teddy and Fran, or Althea, or me."

"No high-heeled women?" She scrubbed furiously at a plate which was already dry.

He cut her one of his sly, amused looks, the kind that seemed to say they were coconspirators. "High-heeled women are quite acceptable, as long as they don't open up hotels."

Laura dried three more plates in silence. It shocked her that someone like Holly had formulated an idiotic theory to explain Claudia's death. People like Holly wanted to think that everything happened for a reason. It was like believing in justice, which at its best was a form of naïveté, at worst a way of assuring yourself nothing bad would happen to you if you played things right, and a way of feeling complacent in the face of others' misfortunes. She felt surprisingly angry. "It's monstrous, Jesse. That fool babbling about Indian chiefs and sacred ground like something from a kids' horror movie. Who the hell does she think she is?"

He took the dishcloth from her hands. "That was just the wine," he said. "She was embellishing. People do when they've had too much to drink." He smiled as adults do when humoring tired children. He made her a cup of coffee, stirring the last of the whipped cream into it. The coffee was the palest tan, and tasted like a child's treat instead of a stimulant. She sat at the kitchen table and let him continue with the dishes. His movements were all so neat and economical, and she suspected that he had once worked as a short-order cook. Something to do with the way he had tipped the contents of a frying pan into a large bowl in one fluid motion.

"Tell me something," she said. "Do you want this hotel to open?"

"I did," he said. "Now it looks like it never will."

"If you were a part of Claudia's venture, why didn't the locals hate you, too?"

Jesse sponged the remnants of whipped cream from the mixer blades. "I'm just the caretaker. Someone they can recognize. If everything had gone according to Claudia's plans, and the Grey Whale became a going concern in eighteen months, who knows if I'd be here?" Satisfied with the beaters, he attacked the heavy skillet that had housed the potatoes and squash. "This is just a stopgap for me."

She suddenly felt that she was hovering over the hotel, seeing it from the air. Everything was now in darkness but the kitchen, and in the little square of light two tiny figures nodded and bobbed and talked, unaware of the blackness pressing against the windows. She felt very lonely.

"What do you do in the real world?" she asked.

"I'm a caretaker in a spooky old hotel. Before that I drove a radio cab in Seattle. Before that I worked on a shrimp boat up in the Aleutian Islands. Before that I was a ranch manager in Idaho. Shall I go on?"

"Yes, please. It sounds like the résumés authors want us to put on their books. 'Mr. Twaddle has worked as a circus acrobat, coal miner, and epidemiologist.' "

There was an offended silence from the steamy region of the sink, and Laura felt she could bite her tongue off. "I didn't mean to be nasty," she said. "I've been in New York for so long—it's like a standard joke, Jesse. The truth is, we're all jealous of anyone who really has done all those things."

Jesse did not reply. All of his attention seemed to be concentrated on the skillet.

"It's only that most of our authors haven't really done all the things they claim, or if they have, it was only for a week. They're usually fakes, self-important fakes. I guess I don't know how to act when I'm presented with the real thing."

"I may not be the real thing," Jesse said. He said it so quietly, and with so much humility, that Laura wanted to believe in his honesty. At the same time, she thought he might be offering her a veiled message. She consulted her watch and found that it was a minute short of eleven. She needed other voices around her, the impression of movement and hilarity.

"I'm going down to Ocean Park," she said. "Do you want to come?"

"Nothing doing there," Jesse said, "unless you want to shoot pool at Luby's."

"How about we play a little eight ball?"

He popped the skillet into the drainer and turned to face her. "The tide's out tomorrow," he said. "I have to be out on the flats."

"Fine," said Laura. "See you tomorrow, then."

She gunned the motor childishly and roared off down the drive in the expectation of finding all her enemies at Luby's. She planted Ralph on a stool and stuck Bob Ludder at the shovelboard game for good measure. Dorrie would preside over the mayhem and she, Laura, would stride in and show them they couldn't frighten her.

The reality was infinitely less challenging than her fantasy. There were only half a dozen men and two women at the tavern. One of the women was playing rotation pool with her husband, and the other was Dorrie's daughter-in-law. Dorrie herself was cordial in a formal way, and the low point of her evening came when one of the single men approached her at the jukebox. He was an older man, almost totally bald, dressed in jeans and a T-shirt with polyester words blazoned across the chest: DIVERS DO IT DEEPER.

"What you gonna play?" he asked her.

She didn't think she recognized him from the open house, but he spoke so familiarly she couldn't be sure. He asked again what she wanted to hear on the jukebox.

"I don't know yet," she said. "I don't know what's on it. I'm checking."

He was staring at her and she wondered if he was very drunk. He spoke in such a loud voice, as if he wanted everyone in Luby's to hear their conversation. He moved in beside her, studying the titles on the jukebox, and then he lowered his voice and said, "What do you want?"

It was not, she supposed, an existential question. She was about to tell him to clear off when he said, "I've got speed."

She wanted to laugh. To travel three thousand miles to hear the self-same blandishment that had failed to excite her in college! "Why tell me?" she said.

"Anything you want," he said.

She turned and walked away, but it occurred to her there was nowhere to go in Luby's, except maybe the ladies', where she would be forced to think of the spotted owl sign. Oh, well. She drank the last of her wine and set the thick tumbler on the bar, calling good night to Dorrie. The man had not followed her.

On the short drive home she was forced to brake for a scruffy-looking hound who was slinking past her headlights, oblivious to danger. She remembered the ominous labs Jesse said existed in the woods, labs where the deadly, home-brewed speed was manufactured. She had pictured the manufacturers as looking like Hell's Angels, like Dorrie's son, in fact, but it was entirely possible that bald men in tacky T-shirts could be involved.

The hotel was dark except for the little twinkling lights in the kitchen. The kitchen itself was immaculate. No signs of the salmon dinner party remained. On the first step of the staircase she found a scrap of paper weighed down by a sand dollar, placed where she could not miss it. On it was printed a terse note from Jesse.

Your husband called at 11:21, it said. *He will call at same time tomorrow.*

She woke to an awful feeling of unreality. Her head seemed to be halfway across the room, heavy, but weightless, like a helium balloon, while her limbs felt unbearably substantial. Her right leg ached as if an iron cast were encasing it, and when she moved the other leg, it, too, felt painful and unwieldy. Sun streamed into her room through the curtains, and when she felt strong enough to look at her bedside clock, she found that it was again nearly noon.

A vast sense of self pity invaded her. She had not had much to drink last night; why, then, did she feel as if the worst hangover of her life had come to visit her?

Fragile. Breakable. Depressed. Her discomfort was such that she wondered if she might be dying. She wanted to weep, but it seemed too energetic an idea. She lay for a long time, plotting her course of action. She could opt for a brown bath, hoping to find it refreshing, or she could ignore her symptoms and leap from the bed in one heroic motion—like Jesse's transferring of the skillet's contents—and dress herself and make her way downstairs.

Neither option seemed reasonable, so she lay, beginning to feel that only utter immobility would restore her to herself. In this forlorn state, she reeled back into sleep, and found herself swimming, underwater, in a sea of oatmeal. Each forward motion of her arms hurt her as much as her kicking legs did, but the pain was not sufficient to wake her, or not fully.

Some time later she awakened to ferocious chills. Her body seemed to have been packed in ice, yet her hands, frantically making a survey of her body, told her she was burning with fever. She shivered and burned, too feeble to do anything about it, and tried to imagine what was wrong. Flashes of her bout with the measles, at age ten, illuminated her consciousness, and they were followed by intimations of the time she had been hit with a really bad flu, soon after she and Dan were married. This was worse, far worse.

The first time she convulsed and had to run to the bathroom to vomit she rolled out of bed, injuring her arm, and crawled to the toilet. Might as well stay, since the violent evacuation seemed destined to be repeated until she was too weak to protest.

Back in bed, she could find no position that was comfortable. She'd heard of no harsh strain of flu sweeping the country, but that was what it had to be—a new, horrid flu no one had yet identified and labeled. She cocked her knees up beneath the covers to relieve the ache, then lowered them again. The light in the window hurt her eyes; perversely, the sun shone so fiercely on the bay that the water, if the tide had been in, would have been lovely to see. She groaned, and wondered if she should ask Jesse if he had aspirin. She should totter on down the stairs and inquire, but the thought of so much effort defeated her. Besides, what if she upchucked in front of him? It was all beyond her, and she pulled the pillow over her head and slept some more.

It was not a soothing sleep, but the kind where fever dreams flit in and out of the restless mind of the sleeper. Discomfort penetrated into her slumber, so she imagined she was on a seesaw in some childhood playground, and each movement of the seesaw brought nausea and cramps in her legs. Her mother appeared at one point to tell her she was neglecting her homework, and then to add that she'd have no time to see to the oysters if she stayed on at the playground.

When she awoke again it was late in the afternoon, and her stomach was trying to rid itself of whatever could possibly be left inside her. She vomited again, but this time it was a thin bile, and she hoped it would be the last time. Her chills seemed to have passed, and also her fever, but her body ached as insistently as ever, and she was dizzy and weaker than she had been for a very long time. She splashed water on her face and risked a look in the mirror, then quickly looked away. She was progressing, in an elderly way, back to bed when she heard the tapping at her door.

Jesse looked as terrible as she did. His face was the color of faded blotting paper, and he stood, diminished, in the doorway, grasping at the frames for support.

"We have food poisoning," he said.

"Flu," she said, flopping back onto the bed. "Isn't it flu?" And then, "You too?"

"Me too," said Jesse. "It's food poisoning. Probably ptomaine. Don't worry, I've had it before. It's not like botulism. There's not much to do for it, but it'll be over in twenty-four hours."

Laura tried to assimilate this new information. She was not the victim of a rare and vicious new strain of flu, but rather someone who was suffering from ptomaine poisoning. Well, what good luck!

"Are you sure we'll be all right?" she whimpered, disapproving of the sound of her voice.

"Pretty sure," the old tracker, or trapper, said, losing his grip on the door frame and weaving a bit. "I came upstairs to ask if you wanted me to phone for a doctor. I would have come earlier, but I've been pretty sick."

"Were you sick out on the flats?" She was intrigued by the idea of Jesse falling to his knees at the oyster beds, but her own misery informed her that it was no laughing matter.

"No," said Jesse, "but I felt weird. I didn't get sick until after."

"Me, too," Laura said, sensing that her train of thought was seriously off course. "It was that salmon we ate. Teddy's salmon."

"Should I call a doctor?"

"What could a doctor do?"

"Well," said Jesse, having the good grace to train his eyes downward, "I imagine he'd administer an enema."

"No," said Laura. "No doctor."

"Okay," said Jesse, bringing one hand up to shield his mouth. "No doctor." He disappeared from the doorway, and Laura heard a door slam down the hall.

Enemas aside, she didn't trust any doctor the Peninsula could produce. She had witnessed the efficiency of the police, and the thought of one of their doctors at her bedside produced terror. She would tough it out, and if Jesse was right, be herself by tomorrow.

The thought that Jesse might have been pretending to be ill didn't appear until much later, when she learned that of the five who had partaken of the salmon, only she and Jesse had become poisoned.

She rode out the second night, between bouts of troubled sleep, thinking that perhaps Holly had something, after all, in eschewing flesh.

If Dan called, as he had promised, no one was awake to hear the phone.

EIGHT

Grace couldn't help but notice the envelope from the penitentiary in Walla Walla. It pleased her to stow the letter in Dot and Wayne's box. It had been an age since Nick had dropped so much as a postcard to his poor mother, and it could prove to be the shot in the arm Dorothy so badly needed by all accounts.

Even as she felt cheered for Dot, she disliked handling paper upon which Nick had written. It made her feel contaminated. No matter that he was miles away, behind bars, and not likely to emerge from prison until he was too old to be a menace. Grace had an uneasy feeling that some people would always be dangerous until they were safely tucked into their graves.

She remembered Nick as clearly as if he had come into her post office last week, and the memory was one that could still make her shiver. It wasn't as if Nick had been your stock villain, the kind of guy whose eyes shone with madness as he laughed in shrill, soprano cadences of out-of-control ecstasy. He wasn't the kind of boy who lay awake at night plotting new ways to make life miserable for those around him. Such a master plan would have been outside Nick's scope. He was more the sort of boy who felt himself to be a god whose every wish should be instantly gratified. When things did not go Nick's way, he punished as surely and swiftly as the deity of the Old Testament. He did it in a way that was both hard and dull, and the dullness came from his certain feeling that every being or creature who opposed him was in the wrong.

Grace had seen a movie called *The Bad Seed* on television. It was an old movie when she happened to see it, but it had been disturbing, precisely because it forced her to think of Nick. Like the Bad Seed girl in the film, Nick had always been unfailingly courteous to adults, earning their praise for his charming manners. How could you tell your mother, who believed in Nick's innocence, that the boy with the chestnut pompadour liked to trap stray cats, introduce a kerosene-soaked twist of paper into their anuses, and then light it?

He wasn't the only boy she remembered who had displayed a penchant for torturing animals, but he was the only one who seemed to do it without emotion. The others giggled and whooped, half guilty at their terrible actions, but Nick watched with somber, dark eyes, as if seeing a vision vindicated.

Grace blamed some of it on Dot, who would never hear a word spoken against her boy, but wasn't it natural for a mother to defend her son? From the age of three, Nick had been raised by his mother alone, and wasn't that a heavy onus to lay on any woman who'd grown up to expect the help of a man? He played up to her, and then, behind her back, made fun of his mother.

Stop thinking about Nick, she instructed herself, and, as if to help her, the door opened and Althea came in. The first words she spoke were mystifying. "Well, *you* look all right," she said. "I guess I'm lucky I couldn't make it for dinner two days ago."

"Why? It was a lovely dinner."

"For some," Althea said. "How are Teddy and Fran?"

"Fine, of course. They've gone cycling all the way down to Chinook to pick up some fertilizer."

Althea braced her arms against the sides of the post office window and gave a low whistle. "I don't suppose you've seen Jesse?"

"No," said Grace. "I called when he didn't get his mail, but he sounded terrible. Said he had a touch of flu, nothing to worry about, and he'd be in in a few days. Pity to be missing this weather."

It was in the low seventies today, and Grace would, if possible, be spending every minute outside, turning her face to the sun.

"Foo," said Althea, "it's too hot. Anytime the thermometer goes over sixty-eight I'm not a happy woman." She gave a little grin, quite aware that she was being eccentric in Grace's eyes, and said, "I just dropped in at the hotel to get my pie pan, and Jesse was there looking like death. His face was all gaunt and sickly beige, and when he got the pan for me he had to hold on to the counters, like an old man."

"Well, flu does weaken a person—"

"Flu, my butt, Grace. It was food poisoning. Laura had it, too. They'd both been sick as dogs."

"Whyever didn't he say so?" Grace felt wounded. "Why didn't he tell me what he had?"

"Maybe he didn't know when you called. He told me he felt awful the morning after the dinner, but he had to go out on the flats. He said he fell over when one of the herons flapped up, and nearly drowned in mud. It wasn't 'til later he knew he had ptomaine."

"Lord," said Grace. "I had that salmon and I'm my same old self. Everyone had it, except for that friend of the Vines who was a vegetarian."

"How convenient," said Althea.

"What's that supposed to mean?"

Althea leaned down until her forehead was pressed against the window. "Teddy and Fran brought the fish, and their guest just happened to be a *vegetarian*. It was a setup. More harassment."

"I don't get it," said Grace, feeling that the glorious day was being poisoned for her as surely as Jesse and Laura had been poisoned at the festive dinner. "I saw Teddy and Fran eating salmon. *I* ate the salmon. What's your point?"

"The point," said Althea, "is that Teddy and Fran knew which parts to eat. You they didn't care about, and their friend didn't eat fish anyway."

Althea's dark eyes gleamed with a fanatic's righteousness, and Grace was reminded again of Nick. It was the look Nick wore when he thought he'd been thwarted.

"Did you see Laura?" she asked.

"She was still up in her room," said Althea, as if Laura's absence proved her theory. Then she wheeled out of the post office without even checking her window.

Grace came in from the garden at the time when Wayne Cotton habitually came to collect his mail. She needed to see the happy look his face would assume when he saw that Dot's son had, at last, written to his mother. She was puttering about, pretending to attack her postmistress's desk with a duster, when he came in, went to his box, and extracted the letter from Walla Walla. Instead of the joyful look she had been expecting, Wayne's face crumpled alarmingly. He grabbed the envelope out with a bitter manner, and thrust it into his coat pocket as if it had been a thing of no account.

He had aged since she'd last seen him, and the boyish face, beneath the bangs, seemed pinched and fearful.

She returned to her little garden, feeling heavy-hearted in spite of the fact that the sun was still shining at the end of the afternoon. It was warm enough so that she didn't need a cardigan sweater, and she should have been able to sit in her lawn chair, contemplating the restful view of the blue bay, safe in the knowledge of—what? Of a quiet life in the town where she'd been born, a now-vanished marriage to a good man, which had been fine as marriages seemed to go; of a son who, while far from perfect, was not a monster. Martin's greatest failing, so far as she knew, was a fondness for marijuana, a sin positively benign in the world they had all come to know.

Martin had gone out on the flats yesterday, the same day Jesse had begun to feel "weird," and when he'd returned it was to ask if they couldn't purchase the Arnold oyster beds, now that the lady was dead. He was sure her husband wanted nothing further to do with the Grey Whale, Martin said, so why not buy the stake the hotel had started?

"But Martin," she had observed in the mildest possible manner, "surely whoever buys the hotel will want to own the oyster beds?"

He had crinkled his eyes shut and smiled in the way all mothers come to know—the smile that proclaims an infinite patience when dealing with people who are hopelessly out of touch with reality.

"Jeez, Ma," Martin had said. "That old place is never going to be bought by anybody now. It was a miracle those Arnolds ever stumbled on it in the first place. How often can *that* happen?"

"The Grey Whale was quite a place at one time. Even while you were just a little boy." As she'd spoken she could feel how antique her memories of the hotel must seem to him.

Martin had taken a little time before he delivered his answer. "Nobody wants to buy a place where there's been a murder," he said.

Grace had heard it, his use of the word "murder," and now she would never know if she let it pass on purpose, or if the ringing of the phone had cut their conversation short. In any case, she hadn't reintroduced the topic.

Everything was silent from the Vines' rented patch of ground. She remembered they'd gone to Chinook and wouldn't be returning for several hours more. If she strained her ears, she could almost imagine hearing the rabbits hopping down their long, chicken-wired pens, but that was silly, of course, because you couldn't really hear the movement of rabbits from this distance. Fran called them bunnies, and that was her first mistake. Once you gave them a cute name you were finished. You had to maintain a certain attitude toward animals that were kept for slaughter, or else you would begin to sentimentalize them, think of them as cuddly creatures from a Walt Disney movie, like *Bambi*.

Her own father had been a hunter of both ducks and deer, and she'd never found any fault in it, except for the buckshot you found between your teeth when you were eating venison. Still, she sympathized with Fran's anguish over the strangling of the rabbits. Instead of seeing them as edible vermin, Fran saw them as little, furry things she'd helped to feed and keep alive.

Your head is like a mop. I could chop it off and use it for a mop.

She'd been proud of her new perm, administered at the Beauty Nook long before Wayne Cotton had come to the Peninsula. Why was the memory so terrible? Nick had been a mere child, many years younger than she, and his words had been mere bravado. In fact, if he hadn't been carrying the sharply honed ax he used to split logs for his mother's fireplace, the threat might have seemed laughable.

Chop your head off, and use it for a mop.

She'd encountered him out by the cranberry bog, where she was waiting for her father to come by and pick her up. It was one of her Girl Scout afternoons, and suddenly Nick had come into it, far from home and out of place. She wanted to taunt him for his impertinence, make him seem powerless and stupid, but the ax had silenced her. That, and his assurance that what he said was correct. Nick Brown—as he had been—seemed to think it was entirely appropriate to threaten Grace Jorgenson—as she had been—with mutilation and death.

"My father's coming to get me any minute" was what she'd finally said to him.

"Naw, don't think so."

"You know he is. Why do you think I'm waiting here?"

"Waiting to have your head chopped off."

She could still get that metallic fear-taste in her mouth when she remembered what happened next. Slinging the ax over his shoulder, he'd begun to walk slowly toward her. Since they were only twenty or so feet apart, Grace had been forced to consider running. She was older, taller, longer-legged, it was true, but where would she run *to?* She was seven miles from her town, and the closest houses were on the Bay Road, at least two miles away. He would be bound to catch up with her after such a distance; she was fast on her feet, but not known for marathon running, and even lugging the heavy ax, Nick would be able to catch up eventually. The cranberry bog seemed to stretch on forever, as if she and Nick were alone in a flat landscape, as if she had only imagined a town where they both once lived. Now he was only ten feet away, his eyes grave, his hands clenched on the ax handle with great determination.

Grace remembered how quiet it had been. They were in one of the widest parts of the Peninsula, far enough from the ocean to obliterate the sounds she could hear in her own bed at night, safely at home. It was this very quiet that changed the course of events, because both of them heard the approach of Mr. Jorgenson's Dodge pickup, even though her father—at that fragile moment in time—must still have been more than a mile away.

"Here he comes," she had shouted. "Here he comes!"

Without any change of expression, Nick had nodded, once, acknowledging the truth of what she'd said, and then turned and walked off in the opposite direction.

By the time she found herself scrambling up into the high seat beside her father, Grace was trembling. She felt larger than life, like a soldier who has lived through monstrous combat and emerged, alive.

When her father asked her why she seemed so fidgety and troubled, Grace Jorgenson could only say she'd run into little Nicky Brown, who had tried to terrorize her. "It was so dumb," she said. "He said he wanted to chop my head off." She didn't mention the ax, and joined in her father's disgusted laughter. "Watch out for that boy when he grows up," her father had said. "He'll be a *real* terror."

On that drive back home, she had convinced herself that her jokey version of Nick's behavior had been the correct one. She felt obscurely ashamed that Nick had made her think of running for her life. After all, what was he but a wild, peculiar kid who liked making himself seem more important than he was? She even told her friends about it, editing out her paralytic fear, passing it off as a ridiculous aftermath to an afternoon spent at Girl Scouts. Gradually, the story reemerged as "the time Nick made fun of Grace's perm." In the most refined version, Dorrie maintained that Nick had threatened to trim her new haircut with an ax, because even an ax could have done a better job.

Grace followed the trial some years later, and was glad when Nick was convicted of the rape and murder of the hitchhiker at Chehalis. Even though her father was dead and could never make the connection, she felt vindicated. Her fear had been authentic, because whatever demons had inhabited him then were still doing their work, and Nick was still an instrument of purest evil. Nothing could shake her conviction that their confrontation in the cranberry bog had been a manifestation of that evil, and nothing could persuade her to think of him without a sense of dread.

Her sympathy for his mother evaporated in those moments in the lawn chair by the Bay, and she had an awful feeling that Nick, so safely tucked away behind bars, could still exert his influence.

Wayne mounted the stairs, the letter in his hand, trying not to hope for too much. Nothing seemed capable of pulling Dot out of the state of misery she was in, and had been in, ever since the unfortunate business at the hotel. None of the little tricks he'd perfected over the years of marriage seemed to work anymore. She rejected shampoos and back rubs, and had eaten only a tiny portion of the cream cheese and green pepper omelette he'd made for her. The omelette, more than anything else, informed him that Dot's suffering was now endured on a level formerly unknown to him. Once she would have protested as he set the tray on a TV table or on the specially constructed invalid's tray she used in bed. She would have said, "Oh, I couldn't possibly! Cream cheese, Wayne! And the peppers will play merry hell with my digestion."

All the same, if he left the room for a little space, he would return to find the thing devoured. This time she had made no excuses, no complaints, but simply collapsed against her pillows after two bites.

"I'm not hungry" is what she had said. There'd been none of the exquisite pretense which was so much her style. The very fact that she no longer complained or regaled him with the various failings of her nervous system was alarming to him. It was as if the bedrock their marriage was built on was crumbling, and Dot no longer cared to remember it, or shore it up with her antics.

He felt badly frightened as he came to the top of the stairs and made his way toward the closed door of the bedroom. The letter from Nick, so promptly written after his bribe as to embarrass Wayne, represented what once would have been the pinnacle of any happiness Dot might know. If it failed to shake her out of her trance, he didn't know what he would do.

He tapped at the door and, hearing no answer, opened it. Dot lay, a lump beneath the covers, breathing stertorously. Her eyes were at half-mast, and the ever-present tears, which came from a well too deep for him to comprehend, shone weakly on her cheeks from the light on the landing.

"A letter, dear," he said. "From Nick."

Once she would have seized it from him jealously, ripping open the envelope and digesting whatever was inside with pathetic greed. Now she sighed painfully and tried to hitch her way up to a sitting position against the many pillows. "Read it to me," said Dot in her new, defeated voice.

Wayne slit the envelope open and withdrew a single sheet of cheap paper.

Dear Mom, he read. *Please forgive me for not corresponding with you for so long, but I was in the hole. That's solitary confinement to you. The screws said I started a fight, but I didn't. I guess they've never had an innocent man to deal with before, and this is how they handle it. Makes great sense, huh???*

There was more, about how he'd had some great talks with the chaplain—Wayne doubted that very much—and was attending Sunday services regularly. He got a little carried away on this subject, hinting that in a better life he might have become a minister and done good. There was no mention of being "born again," because Dot wouldn't tolerate that sort of thing, but Wayne had to make his voice free of any hint of doubt as he read about Nick's good deeds for fellow prisoners, his natural qualities of leadership, which even in a prison, came to the fore.

For a few moments Dorothy's eyes glowed with pride and mother-love, and she nodded her agreement with her son's assessment of his many fine instincts. Wayne, who had felt himself wanting to spit on the letter, was softened by this seeming ease it brought to her. He knew Nick was simply working hard for his fifty bucks, but if it brought her a measure of comfort, what did it matter? He tried to put some emotion into his reading. *You know I love you, Mom. You were everything to me. You stood up for me when the whole world was against me, and I'll never forget it. I look forward to your next visit. Hi to Wayne. All my love, Nick, your son.*

Wayne was nervous about the "when you're feeling better" bit, since it could tip her to the fact that he'd written to Nick behind her back, but his anxiety quickly faded. Dot, after all, was never feeling well, would never, since he had met her, feel better. She wouldn't find the phrase suspicious.

He glanced over, and found the light had gone out of her eyes. "The hole," she moaned. "What terrible things are they doing to my boy?"

"It's not like in the old movies, pet," he told her. "It's just the term for what they call, I believe, administrative detention. It's not a pit with rats."

"Why should he be detained at all, when he's trying to do so much good? Do you think it's true that they persecute the innocent? It's so wicked, Wayne."

Tears were sliding down her cheeks again, and as he watched, wondering what to do to comfort her, an amazing transformation took place. The tears which he'd witnessed in the past few days had always seemed to him to come from her physical weakness. They collected in a pool and then slid any which way with a kind of lackadaisical pattern. She had always kept the old grief well in check, but now it threatened to drown them both in a tidal wave of epic proportions. He saw the shift take place, the second when the tears of sheer sentiment, liberated by her real fragility, collided with something new and elemental.

"Oh, God," she cried. "What will I ever do? What can I do now?"

He discarded Nick's letter on the bedside table and knelt beside her. He attempted to take one of her hands, clenched on her chest, and was repelled by the clawing, febrile tactics she used to avoid prolonged contact with his flesh. Her head tossed back and forth on the pillow, as if she were trying to dash her brains out.

Wayne scrambled down the stairs to the kitchen, where she kept a list of often-called numbers. Trembling, he picked out the digits which would connect him to her doctor.

For the first time in his marriage, he felt the call was a matter of life or death.

Laura picked the phone up expecting to hear the voice of anyone but Dan, her husband. Therefore, she nearly dropped the phone when he said, "Laura! Where the hell have you been?" Not a pretty beginning to a conversation, but she had to admit Dan had cause for alarm. The illness had made her forget all about his call on the night she'd been at Luby's. "I'm sorry," she said, "but I've had food poisoning. I'm better now." She still felt weak and *crumbly,* somehow, but the sickness had run its course.

"That man who answered the phone didn't say anything about it," Dan said. "Who is he, anyway?"

"He's the caretaker. The reason he didn't say anything was because I wasn't sick when you called. He got it too, actually, and we were both sick for twenty-four hours." She realized she'd made it sound as if she and Jesse had been kneeling side by side, vomiting together. "Don't worry," she said. "Where are you?"

"London. But listen, do you mean to say you're all alone with some caretaker?"

"It's not like that," she said. "It's a big old place and people visit all the time." She knew the way Dan's mind worked. Once he'd eliminated the caretaker as a possible cause for anxiety, he would want to know what kind of terrible food she'd been eating to get food poisoning. The one thing she hoped he wouldn't say was "Did Claudia come yet?"

"How old is this caretaker?"

"A few years younger than I am. I don't know exactly. Look, Dan, he's a very nice man. Very capable. He reminds me of some character from an old Western. He's the guy the U.S. Cavalry hires as a tracker when they ride into Indian country."

"What kind of food have you been eating out there?"

"We had salmon some friends brought over. Apparently it was tainted." She felt queasy just saying it.

"Jesus," said Dan, "that makes me feel just great. My wife is six thousand miles away in an old hotel with an Indian tracker, eating poisoned salmon."

"I know it sounds awful," she said, "but it's really quite lovely here. We're on the Bay, and I can walk to the ocean in ten minutes. The day I came there was a deer eating berries out in back."

Dan make a dismissing sound, a combination sniff and grunt, quite subtle, but intimately known to her. "Did Claudia come yet?" he asked.

She had planned to say no, avoiding the turmoil that would follow a truthful answer, but when it came to it, she couldn't lie to him quite so blatantly. "Dan, something terrible happened," she said. She realized how prodigally she and everyone she knew used the word "terrible." It was called up for slow service and long lines at the supermarket, computer failures that rendered money machines temporarily useless, disappointing sales of a Crowther and Hull book, botched haircuts, badly hung wallpaper, long waits at airports on international flights. She had heard Dan pronounce a breakfast meeting terrible because the participants were not sufficiently informed to function well in the business community.

A dense silence told her that he was not prepared to ask about the terrible happening, but was waiting to be informed.

"Claudia's dead," she said, rather harshly. "There was an accident, and she struck her head."

"No!" Dan shouted, so loudly she had to hold the phone away for a moment. "I'm shocked," he said. "How could such a thing happen?"

As if she had been the laconic deputy sheriff, Laura relayed Ludder's version of Claudia's death, relying on the freak accident angle.

"Oh, Laura honey, you must be so upset. I wish I could be with you."

"How is your trip going?" Laura asked, switching the conversation into a new track.

"The thing is, they'd like me to stay on another week, run up to Holland and Belgium." He spoke apologetically, and for once Laura was sincere when she assured him she didn't mind. She couldn't quite picture Dan at the Grey Whale, and she would have to tell him the truth about Claudia's death if he were to stay here.

"Remember, you're there for a real rest. Any work is strictly forbidden," Dan said in a gruff voice meant to be both humorous and affectionate.

"No work," she said. If he knew! If Dan knew she was living at a crime scene, a murder site, he would be enraged. He was quite capable of ordering her to come back East immediately. Since he only issued orders on matters he felt were "for her own good," she did not feel oppressed by him, only sadly amused.

"Love you," he said.

"Yes—oh, there's someone at the door. I'd better go." She replaced the receiver, wondering why she couldn't have spared him an endearment. The someone at the door was only Jesse, coming in with the mail.

"That was my husband, calling from London," she said. "I'd totally forgotten that he called before."

Jesse smiled cryptically, sorting through the envelopes, and then he handed her one. It was a Crowther and Hull envelope, and she winced thinking how quickly Dan's command to do no work was likely to be ignored.

Inside was a clipped review from the *New York Times*, sent by her assistant, Paula. It was a short review, and from the title blurb, MORE BARK THAN BITE, apparently a dismissive one. Laura sighed, and laid it aside to read later. She liked the young author of the book in question, and knew how wounded he would be if the review proved to be really snide. His was a "midlist" book, the kind you had to fight for because everybody knew it couldn't earn big bucks, and she had faith in its originality and insight. The man who had written the review was famous for savaging young writers; since he had not, himself, won attention until he was in his forties, he bitterly resented the efforts of anyone, say, thirty-seven.

"Bad news?" said Jesse, uncharacteristically invading her privacy.

She explained about the young writer's certain anguish over the review.

"But you haven't even read it," he said. "How do you know it's bad?"

Laura picked the review up and handed it to him. "Read it to me," she said. "I guarantee some viciousness."

Jesse held the scrap of newspaper in both hands, taking his duty very seriously. He sat down on the stairs and began. *"Armadillos,"* he read, "by Peter Lloyd. Crowther and Hull. 230 pages. $17.95. In this engaging first novel, Mr. Lloyd's abundant talents reach us from a remove, as flickering images on the wall of a cave. Plucky Jake Porfirio, the novel's protagonist, is on his way to Mexico for all the wrong reasons."

Jesse looked up. "So far, so good," he said. "He said it was engaging."

"Read on," said Laura.

"We're in all too familiar territory, but we suppress our judgment in the hopes that Mr. Lloyd will wring something disturbing and fresh from Jake's odyssey. Alas, he does not."

"Told you," Laura said.

Jesse read on, his voice hopeful as he delineated Jake's adventures, but wary as he neared the end of the review.

"There is nothing very wrong with *Armadillos,* but neither is there anything very right. Should trees have died so that *Armadillos* could see the light? I think not."

He passed the review back to Laura and lit one of his Marlboros. "Was it a good novel?" he asked.

"I thought so," said Laura.

"That part where the reviewer says he substitutes bark for bite was really mean," said Jesse.

"That particular reviewer exists to be mean. That's his main distinction in life."

"How come?" said Jesse. "I don't understand."

She shrugged. "Some people just aren't very nice to begin with," she said. "This man's the Ralph Henderson of the publishing world."

Jesse continued to ask her questions about the ethics, or lack of them, in that world. Had it been someone's decision to give the new novel to the unpleasant reviewer in the hopes of harming Peter Lloyd's career, or had it simply been an accident? Would Laura now be in trouble because she had bought the Lloyd book in the first place?

"Oh, no," she said. "Crowther and Hull doesn't care about reviews, unless you can get a celebrity to endorse a book. I'd only be in trouble if a big book I bought for lots of money didn't earn its keep. Nobody at C and H cared about *Armadillos* but me and Paula."

Jesse was regarding her keenly. His eyes shone with sympathy, and she realized she must have been speaking in tragic tones, as if they were discussing political prisoners rather than novels. Her melodramatic air must be a lingering effect of the food poisoning. She still felt she might burst into tears if someone jumped out of a shadowy recess and shouted "boo" at her.

Later, while Jesse was writing at one of the tables in the dining room, she called Peter Lloyd in New York. The time difference was such that Peter, who liked to work at night, had just risen from his bed in Chelsea. It was three in the afternoon in New York, and Peter sounded sleepy and a trifle unsure of himself. When he understood that it was his editor, Laura McAuley, calling from the other coast, his voice vibrated with pleasure. She hoped he wouldn't think she was out here making a movie deal for *Armadillos*.

"Peter," she said, "I've just received a copy of the review by that nasty piece of work in the *Times*. I do hope you're not taking it too hard, because he's dumped on more good writers than I can count."

"Yeah." An only slightly bitter chuckle came down the line. "That's what they all say. You honestly think it won't hurt the book, Laura?"

"It's a good book, Peter. I have faith in it. You should be getting some nice reviews from all over the country, so don't let this one get engraved in your memory."

"He did say I was engaging," Peter said in that hopeful way authors had that always broke her heart.

"And so you are," she said. "So you are."

They spoke for a few more minutes, she feeling unequal to a task which was usually such a breeze, and when she put down the phone she felt depressed. She reentered the dining room in a sort of trance, and was surprised to find Ralph Henderson at one of the tables. How could she have failed to hear the wheels of his truck on the drive, his voice in conversation with Jesse?

"Howdy," said Ralph, baring his teeth like a dog. "I understand you folks have had a spot of trouble."

"We've had food poisoning," Laura said cooly. Ralph was wearing a T-shirt that said JAZZ AND OYSTERS on it in huge, turquoise letters.

"Are you aware that every case of food poisoning has to be traced?" he asked. "It's like one of them sexual diseases. We have to know how many people ate the sucker, where it was caught, and who caught it. It's Department of Fisheries law, very important."

Ignoring Jesse's subtle look of complicity, Laura gave him the answers he required.

"Teddy Vine brought the salmon," she said. "I have no idea where he got it."

"Interesting," said Ralph, trying to invest the word with nuances he only dimly understood.

Jesse kept shaking his head at her whenever Ralph wasn't looking. Was it to say she shouldn't have given Teddy's name as the supplier of the fish? "That's all I can tell you," she said as coldly as she could. "I hope you'll be pursuing this with the same vigor that Ludder used in pursuing Claudia's killer." Jesse winced violently.

"Killer! We all know who her killer was, don't we? Old devil rum, although in her case it was some other kind of booze—gin? vodka?" He shook his head, ponderously, as if in awe of the damage alcohol perpetrated.

"That's *ludicrous,*" she said, spitting the word out. "And you know it."

Jesse leaped to his feet and worked his way around in back of Ralph. He put a finger over his lips and then said, "Speaking of booze, Ralph, care for a drink?"

Dully, a moment too late, Laura realized that Jesse was acting out a little charade, and she had nearly ruined it. "Well, yes, Ralph," she said, "do have a drink."

But Henderson got to his feet, kneading his chest and frowning. "No," he said, "I don't believe I will. Too much to do. You folks take care, now." He walked the length of the dining room with a steady, measured, self-conscious tread, and Laura thought that men like Ralph tried to imitate the walk that was Jesse's naturally, and failed. Ralph looked like nothing so much as an overgrown schoolyard bully strutting away when the teacher came to intervene.

At the door in the kitchen he turned, and faced them. It was growing misty again, and she couldn't make out his features at such a distance, but the melodramatic voice carried to her perfectly. "What you said, Mrs. McAuley, about your friend being killed. I wouldn't go around saying that if I was you. Those are very serious allegations."

Laura and Jesse sat in silence until the sounds of Ralph's pickup had receded in the distance. "Allegations," she said finally. "Where do you suppose he learned a word like that?"

"TV cop shows," said Jesse, sounding mournful.

"I'm sorry I didn't catch on soon enough. Why did you want him to stay?"

Jesse leaned forward and spoke in a low voice, as if they still ran the risk of being overheard. It made her feel frightened.

"All that stuff about tracing food poisoning cases is a crock," he said. "Ralph just assumes we'll fall for it, being outsiders."

Laura could see how she might be considered an outsider, indeed had to be considered one, but it still amazed her that Jesse could share her status. "Why did he come here, then?" she asked.

"You're the editor," he said. "You tell me."

This seemed unfair, and Laura was afraid she was actually pouting before she straightened up and told herself that she was really at a conference at C and H, imperious and fully informed on all the issues.

"All right," she said briskly. "He could have come to retrieve something he left here on the day of the open house. Something incriminating, or of personal value to him. Possibly he only just remembered it, and thought he could conduct some sort of subtle search."

Jesse smiled and nodded. She was doing well.

"Or," said Laura, "he could have come to see if we knew where Teddy got the salmon. There's a possibility that Ralph poaches undersized salmon and wanted to protect his interests. There's not much future in fencing salmon if it gives people ptomaine poisoning."

"Good," said Jesse. "Any other possibilities?"

"To annoy us."

"That's your basically outer-directed activity. Ralph is very much an inner-directed man. He wouldn't spend a minute with us if it didn't fit into some plan."

"You tell me," said Laura. "I don't feel really great."

"What I think," Jesse said, "is that Ralph did leave something here, but not on the day of the open house. I think it goes way beyond the time you came here. I think it even goes beyond the time I came here from Seattle. We had the bad luck to wander into his plan."

Her view of herself as a cool professional evaporated with astonishing speed, and she was only Laura, sitting in a dining room, stunned by unexpressed grief and further felled by illness, listening to the theories of a man she barely knew. "What was his plan?" she asked in all humility.

"This place is a drop," Jesse said. "I'm not sure for what, but I think the Grey Whale has been a drop for ages, long before we arrived."

"What does that mean?"

"It means," said Jesse, "we're in the way. Claudia was in the way, and so was Jack. Their lawyers are in the way."

"And now, you and I are in the way?"

"Yes," said Jesse. "Definitely."

NINE

"Oh lord, I'm just so sorry," Fran was saying for the fifth time. She literally wrung her hands. "I would've come over to help you, but I only just found out."

"Relax," Laura told her, trying to be genial. "It wasn't your fault."

She was sitting on a blanket out in back of the hotel. She had brought a paperback novel by Ella Leffland—one that she had read so long ago it would seem like new—together with a tall glass of tomato juice out to her resting place. She beckoned for Fran to join her, and after looking anguished, Fran collapsed on the blanket in one rag-doll motion.

"I feel so guilty," Fran said. "Usually salmon is such a treat, and we had no reason to think—especially since nobody else got sick—"

"I wondered about that too, but it seems the taint can be confined to one area while the rest of the fish is fine."

"Holly left in a hurry," Fran said, "after she found out about the rabbits. I tried to tell her that raising meat for food isn't like wearing fur coats or torturing lab rats, but she wouldn't listen. She said I was a weak-willed person who let myself be dominated by a murderer."

"A murderer!" Laura's voice emerged more sharply than she'd intended. It was a part of her convalescence, she thought, that she wasn't quite in control yet of her body. Her depth perception seemed at times a bit skewed, and her own voice sounded odd to her. She felt she had screamed at poor Fran, but when she looked up Fran was biting her lip apologetically. "I'm sorry," she said, "I shouldn't have used that word, under the circumstances, but it's what Holly said. She meant the bunnies, of course. I wouldn't want you to think—"

"Of course not," said Laura. It was so obvious what Fran had meant she was astounded that the first image of murder had been not that of Teddy and his long-eared dinners-to-be, but of Teddy in the linen closet.

She had tried so often to remember who had been in her line of vision while Claudia was being killed, but in the end it didn't matter. She hadn't watched all the time, and because there'd been no proper investigation, nobody knew just when Claudia had died. If Teddy Vine had been glimpsed toking in the woodshed at a certain time, what was to have prevented him from leaving the shed and mounting the stairs ten minutes later, when she wasn't paying attention? She shut her eyes and saw his hand, serving her an unwanted second helping of salmon.

"Teddy wouldn't hurt anything he couldn't eat," Fran said.

"I'm sure he wouldn't." Laura stretched out on her stomach and buried her face in her crooked-up arms. "If you'd like a drink, please go in and help yourself," she said. "You know where everything is."

"Maybe just some water," Fran said. "I'll be right back."

Jesse had gone up to the recycling center out along the bay road, piling the trunk of her rented car with the hotel's used cans and plastics. "You're sure you'll be all right?" he had asked anxiously. "Wouldn't you like to come along?" At that point she'd felt only one desire, to lie on a blanket on the springy lawn, looking down to the landing where the herons played. No sooner had he left than she began to feel ill at ease, almost afraid to be alone. What could harm her on a bright afternoon, out in the open? What, indeed—who had come to disturb her solitude but kindly, pink-cheeked Fran. She heard Fran's sandals on the oyster shell path at the back door and turned to watch her approach.

Solemnly bearing her glass of water, Fran made her way on sturdy legs down the incline of the grass. The sun wrapped her golden plaits in fiery glory, so that Fran appeared to be a goddess entrusted with some momentous duty. This time Fran sank more gracefully to the blanket, tucking her knees under her and sitting with her back militarily erect. Unlike most women Laura knew, Fran had no mannerisms, nervous or otherwise. It would never have occurred to her to play with the ends of her thick, corn-maiden braids or sweep them back over her shoulders. However they landed when she changed position was how they stayed. This seemed, somehow, admirable.

"I've been thinking," Fran said. "There's something that happened when I was a little girl, growing up in Vermont. I've been asking myself if I should tell you about it." She took a deep swallow of her water, fortifying herself. "On the one hand, you might find it upsetting, and I wouldn't want that. On the other hand, I sense that you're confused about what happened to your friend, and my story could be *useful* to you. It illustrates a kind of frame of mind that's only found in isolated places. Places where people keep pretty much to themselves."

"Go on," said Laura, feeling excited and fearful. "I want to hear, even if it's upsetting."

Fran removed her glasses, which was disconcerting. She had seen many people put on or take off glasses as they prepared to read a story, but never one who removed them to tell a story orally.

"I can't see you now," Fran said, "but I can sense you're confused."

"I only wondered why you took your glasses off. I've never seen you with them off before."

"Oh, right," Fran said. "I do it when I try to reconstruct the past. That way nothing can distract me, nothing in the present, visually."

Laura said nothing, merely waiting in much the same spirit she had waited for Althea to read her Tarot cards.

"People think New England is so beautiful," Fran said at last, "and it is, but what people don't realize is that there are pockets of poverty in New England as bad as anything you'll find in Appalachia. It's a mean, grinding kind of poverty, and it doesn't seem to result in folk songs or religion or any of the compensations folks might have in the

South. We weren't specially poor, but I went to school with some girls who didn't even have bathtubs in their houses."

Laura thought of a Vermont, or was it Maine, writer who'd made quite a splash with a first novel several years ago. The author had boasted she could now afford to have a bathtub installed in her house.

"There were some pretty wild boys, the ones who went jacklighting, you know, poaching deer, and I always thought they were capable of anything, anything at all."

"Like Dot Cotton's son," Laura found herself saying.

"I wouldn't know about him, but I don't think he's a good example. I'm sure Dot was all over him, unsuccessful as she might have been at controlling him. These boys seemed to have no authority to answer to. They were like a pack of feral dogs who'd banded together, as if their parents had turned them loose. They had last names we all recognized, as if they belonged to local families, but we came to find out their connections were so loose you could never place them anywhere exactly."

Laura took a long draft of her tomato juice and then wished she hadn't. It had watered down from the ice, and tasted unpleasant. She had the feeling she'd drunk from someone's leftover glass rather than her own.

"Otherwise," Fran was saying, "it was the kind of place where everyone knew everyone else, like on the Peninsula. I know now that the grown-ups knew exactly who those boys were. They had everything all filed away neatly in secret parts of their minds we kids never knew existed." Fran's naked face registered a look of betrayal, or perhaps it was only impatience for her youthful naïveté.

"One day," she continued, "in the middle of the winter, there was a terrible discovery. A man was found hanging out in Mullen's Wood, hanging from a tree limb. He was dressed for deer hunting, so they reckoned he was a hunter who'd come up to Vermont for the season. That meant he'd probably been hanging there for two months before they found him, but it was very cold, so he was well preserved."

"A stranger?" Laura asked.

"Yes," said Fran. "Nobody had ever seen him, and there was no identification on him. Also no gun to be found." Fran smiled. "What's a hunter without his gun?"

"Probably one of the wild boys came along and found him and stole his rifle," Laura said. "Wasn't that what happened?"

"That's what they said, of course. It was ruled a suicide at the inquest, and that was that. I don't know if anyone came looking for news of him, because I was too young to know things like that. I would have believed in that suicide. Why not? A disturbed hunter hanging himself in a remote Vermont woods?"

Not for the first time, Laura had the unpleasant impression that someone was pitching a book to her at an editorial meeting. She knew it was unfair to suspect Fran of ulterior motives, and in fact ulterior motives were the very least of it. Her editor's mind was demanding to know where the story was leading, how it would develop, what inconsistencies in the seemingly straightforward tale could be blended in to make it marketable.

Fran proved to have a fine sense of drama, because she paused before she said, "If my brother hadn't been one of the kids who found him, I would have accepted the suicide without another thought."

"Let me understand this," said Laura. "Your brother and the others who found the man saw something that made the verdict of suicide misleading?"

"More like impossible," said Fran. "He'd been shot in the back." Her hands scrabbled for the discarded glasses, found them, and popped them back on smartly. She was back in the present, her need to remember the past in minute detail at an end. "You see?" she said, smiling.

Laura nodded yes, and Fran looked out over the bay to conceal her embarrassment. They were saved by the sound of wheels on the drive. They rose to greet Jesse, and staggered up the uneven lawn in mute complicity.

Fran had come to tell her how justice was ignored in remote communities, and also to ask for forgiveness for the tainted salmon. She had offered the tale from her childhood as atonement. For her part, Laura did not know whether Fran was urging her to keep silence or exhorting her to get to the bottom of Claudia's death.

Jesse got out of the rented car and approached them with his head hung down in sorrow. He drew even with them and looked up, his fine eyes full of ambiguity.

"I just heard it up at the center," he said. "Dot Cotton's had a stroke."

"Oh Jesus," Wayne prayed at the wheel of his car, "forgive me for all the times I thought she was a hypochondriac. Let her not die." Unaccustomed as he had been to praying for so many years, he still slid back into the cadences of prayer as he had known it in his youth. Instead of saying "don't let her die" when you talked to Our Lord, you phrased it in old-fashioned language, used the archaic phrase. If anyone had asked him why this should be so, Wayne would have replied that he supposed it was a courtesy to Jesus to speak to him the way he was used to.

"Keep her safe in thy bosom," he continued, "and restore her to me. I knew not the injustice I committed when I suspected her of being a hypochondriac." He brushed away the tears that kept forming in his eyes, thought "Amen," and turned the key in the ignition.

As he maneuvered out of the tiny parking lot at the Peninsula's only hospital, in Long Beach, he tried to take comfort in Dr. Hemingson's assurances that the stroke was relatively mild, that Dot should recover with few ill effects, but the doctor's words did not reassure him that much. For one thing, the doctor was assuming that Dorothy's low spirits and listlessness were by-products of the stroke. Wayne could have told him she'd been like that for days before it happened. The doctor assumed, also, that she would be willing to follow his instructions when she was released from the hospital, and since one of the things she was forbidden was cigarettes, Wayne knew the prescribed regimen would go right out the window. It was true she had smoked far less since the beginning of her decline, but she was still a great puffer. Whenever she'd remembered to light up a ciggie, she'd smoked by habit, dragging deeply, deeply on the damned thing just as she'd done before the black cloud came to envelop her.

It was dark as Wayne headed up the Peninsula at the end of the evening visiting hours. Dot had been taken around noon the day before, and Dr. Hemingson said she should be able to come home in one more day. The dark forests swept by him as he left the precincts of gaudy Long Beach and headed for home, his hands gripped so tightly on the wheel that an answering ache in his shoulders was beginning to trouble him. He felt epoxy-bonded to the wheel of the car, and thought he might have no volition in the matter of where, and when, the vehicle would turn onto the cross-peninsula road that would take him to his house.

Sure enough, he sped past the turnoff and found himself rocketing up the road, toward Ocean Park. The blackness of the night suited him. He didn't want to arrive at his house and enter a dark and silent place which had been deprived of its mistress. What good was the little house to him now, without the heaping ashtrays, the querulous complaints, the sheer negative energy Dot had always invested in their lives? Once, she would have been pleased at having a certifiable illness, a stroke. She might have whined and protested, but beneath it all he would have been able to discern her joy at having been proven right after all these years of vague complaints. It might have been a victory for her, the first.

Instead of feeling victorious, Dot was that most bewildering patient —the one who didn't seem to care what was happening to her. She accepted the stroke in a dull and unadventurous way, as something she merited, an affliction for which she was long overdue. She didn't even seem to care.

He could see the little oasis of lights which was Ocean Park a few miles ahead. There would be people crowding the taverns, milling about on the streets, maybe even some folks night-flying kites on the beach, gearing up for the festival later this month. Wayne did not want to hear music drifting out of tavern doors or see kids, arms around each other, slinking into the dark, away from the lighted pavement. He did not think he could bear to watch his fellow creatures enjoying themselves on a night when he was feeling such pain. He made a precipitate turn onto a cross-peninsula road that ran through the cranberry bogs. "Back into the darkness," he said out loud, and somehow that was satisfying, so he said it again. "Back into the darkness." Some more tears slid down his face and dripped onto his collar, making it damp and uncomfortable. He acknowledged that what he was feeling, even more than grief, was fear. He was so afraid, and there was no one to whom he could confide his fears. It seemed perfectly obvious to him that it was best to keep to himself, to the dark, because then he couldn't make any mistakes.

But it wasn't to be. He saw trouble lights flashing from the back of a vehicle parked up ahead, and a tall figure with a flashlight looming up beside it. From habit, he slowed the car, since he would ordinarily stop and see if there was any way he might help a distressed motorist. The figure with the flashlight waved impatiently for him to continue on, but in his beleaguered state, Wayne slowed to a crawl. The vehicle was one of those big vans with blackened windows, and the man with the flashlight was Bob Ludder.

"Move on, Cotton," Ludder said loudly. "Situation's under control." He peered in at Wayne, frowning. "What the hell's the matter with you?" he said.

Wayne merely shook his head, incapable of answering a man he despised and feared.

"She didn't pass on, did she?" Ludder asked, not so much, it seemed, in sympathy as from the desire to be the first to know.

Again, Wayne shook his head.

"Then get the hell out of here," Ludder said, making a violent, arcing motion with his flashlight.

On any other night he might have asked himself what the sheriff's car and the black van were doing in the middle of a cranberry bog, but he drove off swiftly. He was sorry the road was so straight, because he could see Ludder's flashlight, like a will-o'-the-wisp, in his rearview mirror for a very long time. When he emerged at last on the bay road, he turned and headed back toward his house, which he had passed by a good five miles on his grief-stricken joyride.

Joyride. Why had he thought of that word? A man who weeps and drives at excessive speeds in his own car cannot be said to be joyriding. Joyriding, in fact, was the one crime Dot had ascribed to the youthful Nick. "It wasn't so wicked," she said, smiling. "Nick and some of the other young boys used to borrow people's cars and nip around in them 'til all hours. It wasn't right, of course, but do you take away a boy's whole life for borrowing a car?"

It sometimes seemed Dot believed Nick had been sentenced so harshly for joyriding, as if she was able to magically forget the murdered hitchhiker. Terry Baker.

No! Wayne smacked the steering wheel. He had trained himself to keep the girl's name, still more her photograph, from his mind. Whenever, in those early years with Dot, Teresa Baker's smiling, supremely young and innocent face had swum into his consciousness, he had always banished her by dwelling on the last three women whose hair he had styled. He would walk himself through the process, seeing each head as it had been when its owner entered the shop, then going through the task of shampooing, wet-cutting, blow-drying —or perming and streaking as the case might be—until he was able to visualize her as she walked out the door, beaming her gratitude for his mastery, his ability to change and alter her for the better.

He tried to summon up his last three clients, but he had been away from the shop on account of Dot's stroke, and had to burrow back in his memory. Just before she'd been taken, he was working on Alma Bloomquist, a sister of Luby's. Alma was an unadventurous customer who had worn her hair the same way for thirty years. She favored teasing, a practice Wayne had disapproved almost since the beginning of his career. Mrs. Bloomquist said she required the teasing at the crown of her short, permed hair to give it that natural look. Alma Bloomquist wanted it both ways. She wanted the sort of style that was impervious to wind and weather, but she thought a little artful teasing would make the do seem more natural.

Reliving his battles with Mrs. B., his failures at convincing her of the futility of looking "natural," Wayne forgot that he was driving a car down a dark, twisting country road. Images of Alma looking like an angry hen, the plastic cape rising and falling with indignation over her bosom, were with him when he took a bend in the road too sharply, felt the car skitter out of control, and gave a little cry as he hurtled into a ditch.

He was glad he'd been wearing his seat belt. Unhurt, he climbed out of the car and tried to see how deeply he was stuck and whether it was possible to get out of the ditch without help. The darkness he had wanted earlier was here in such abundance it was difficult to tell. The headlights weren't much help, either, pressed as they were against the far side of the ditch. There weren't many houses on this stretch of the road, and it was too late to awaken strangers in any case. There wasn't much to be done until morning.

Feeling oddly relieved, he got back in the car, switched the ignition off, and curled up in the front seat. Within minutes he was asleep.

Long after Jesse had turned in, Laura found herself descending the stairs in the hotel. She had not been able to sleep after her lazy day, and told herself she would take a long hike tomorrow, perhaps drive out to the nature preserve at the point and walk one of the trails. Tonight she felt restless and unsettled.

Jesse had left one light burning, as always, at the foot of the stairs. Normally she would have switched on some other lamps in the sitting room, but the uncurtained windows would make her feel, at night, like a fish in a bowl, or like, admit it, a target.

She made her way to the larder and opened the second fridge. Although she wasn't hungry, she surveyed the contents, paying special attention to the new items Jack and Claudia had brought, not for the party, but for an anticipated stay of several days. Here was a jar of the jalapeño peppers Claudia so loved, and there an unopened pot of shallot mustard. Claudia favored hot and exotic tastes, always crediting her craving to the bland, meat-and-potatoes meals she had been served in the days of her growing up.

Laura bent her head against the top shelf of the fridge and saw another of Claudia's favorites wedged between some cheeses: a deli container of rolled grape leaves, probably purchased at the covered market in Seattle. What a sybarite her friend had been! Claudia never traveled anywhere without providing herself with sensuous treats. To sum her up in such terms, however, was unfair. She was not a fool who refused to travel without her own Porthault sheets or demanded heated towel rails in a cold climate. Her niceties were quite personal. They were small comforts, unique to her, and not the trappings of a great lady who would not stir without assurances of a guaranteed environment, the kind that made being in Naples no different from being in New York. If she'd been that kind of woman, she would never have wished to purchase, and make a going venture of, the Grey Whale Hotel.

Sadly, Laura shut the larder fridge and walked through the kitchen, lit by the little twinkling lights, and on into the dining room. The dining room was dim and vast, and she was all too aware of the blackness pressing at the windows. She wove her way between the tables and lit the dimmest lamp on the sideboard. She sat down at a table for four and realized she was directly across from Jesse's research center, as she secretly called it. His books and papers were neatly aligned, the large notebook closed and weighted down by an ashtray. She was sorely tempted to lift the ashtray and read what it was he so compulsively transcribed in the book's pages each day.

After all, he never made the slightest attempt to conceal his work. Day after day it lay on the table, open to inspection. Did he operate on the honor system?

She decided what prevented her from snooping, apart from her loathing of people who did so, was an awful, if unfounded, suspicion, that Jesse might be writing a novel. She had seen far too many of those, and she feared that her liking and respect of Jesse might be utterly shattered if she were to lift the corner of his notebook and find the beginnings of a manuscript.

Nothing, however, dictated that she could not examine the topmost book in the tall pile. Guiltily, she snaked over to the table and sat in his chair. She plucked the heavy book up and opened at random to a page containing maps. They were the sort that seemed to have been taken from a satellite. Each mountain ridge and valley was picked out in a kind of visual bas-relief. It was obviously an atlas, the deluxe kind only an enthusiast could justify possessing. A quick look at the front of the book showed her it was from the Ocean Park branch of the public library. It was, in fact, a week overdue. Enough. She was about to vacate Jesse's seat when the wide sleeve of her robe knocked a small pile of letters from the table, sending them spinning out over the floor.

Kneeling, she retrieved the envelopes. Most of them seemed to be bills, but she made a very real effort to not notice them. One envelope was addressed in a real hand, and she quickly shoved it into the pile, out of her line of vision. She was about to replace the letters in their accustomed place when she saw a pale shape on the floor just at her feet. She picked it up and would have shuffled it in with the others, but was arrested by the ugly, misshapen nature of the script. It was a tortured, backward-slanting, unnatural sample of handwriting, the sort a disturbed ten-year-old might produce. It was an eyesore.

It was addressed to "Laura McCaulley"—misspelling her name— and it had been opened and filed away in Jesse's little heap of letters. Her indignation hardly knew where to take root first.

With suddenly unsteady fingers she pried the thin piece of paper out. In the same insane hand someone had penned: GO HOME! IT HAS NOTHING TO DO WITH YOU!

She was tempted to wake Jesse now, just stride into his room, turn on a bright light, and brandish the note in his startled face. How dare he open, and then conceal, a message that had been intended for her? Not a very nice message, in fact a piece of outright hate mail, but still hers. She knew exactly what he would say in his defense: that he had been able to tell from the disguised writing what kind of message lay inside the envelope, and when it proved to be what he'd expected he had hidden it from her. He didn't want her to be any more upset than she already was. But why save it instead of simply destroying it? She was less clear in imagining his probable responses to that question. Could he be saving it as evidence for some future investigation into the sad events at the hotel?

She almost laughed out loud at the very idea. From the level of police work she'd glimpsed here, they were hardly likely to provide distinguished handwriting analysts to show that only Ralph Henderson, say, could have produced such an ugly script by way of disguising his own hand. Or that Deputy Ludder was trying to hasten her on her way so he could mark the case well and truly closed, instead of closed in Peninsula fashion. Or that—not to leave the ladies out—Althea or Grace or even Fran had resorted to that most feminine of tricks, the poison-pen letter.

She turned the envelope over and studied it. It was the cheapest, lightest paper, and available everywhere. She thought they sold packets of such envelopes at the supermarket in town. The paper was equally untraceable. It had been mailed the day before from Ocean Park, and the address and message were both rendered in black felt-tip marker of the sort one could buy everywhere.

She contemplated returning the envelope to Jesse's pile minus the paper, or, better still, writing a little note to him beneath the spiteful words, just so he'd know she wasn't to be fooled so easily. In the end, though, she knew she would do none of these things. If she did, he would know she had gone through his mail. He might suspect her of much greater curiosity than she'd allowed herself to satisfy. "We're both guilty," she thought, and set about trying to restore his working surface to the exact state she'd found it in.

Laura's legs began to ache when she'd gone no farther than the equivalent of two city blocks in the wildlife preserve. It perplexed and annoyed her, since she was a great walker at home, sometimes walking to or from Crowther and Hull when the prospect of boarding a slow, grunting city bus seemed too daunting. The ache in her legs wasn't at all like that she'd known during her food poisoning, but rather an insistent, unpleasant feeling that her legs were working overtime. She came to a fallen log and sat down gratefully.

Of course! She remembered the time she and Dan had taken the ferry to visit friends on Fire Island. They had managed to take the wrong one, which deposited them at a community fully two miles from Saltaire, where they had wished to be. There was nothing for it but to walk by way of the beach, and neither of them had thought to remove their shoes. By the time they had reached the dune where their friends' house was located, she had been cross and exhausted, for all the world as if she and her husband had just completed the Bataan Death March. The beauty of the rolling sea, the rare fresh, bracing air, the faultless blue of sky and water—all had failed to make it up to her. Walking on sand was extremely tiring, unless you were just mooching about in a bathing suit, sidling a little this way and that, free to plunge into the ocean at any time.

The trailways at the wildlife preserve were mainly sand, and there were quite a few little hills. It was a beautiful place, she had to admit, not unlike Fire Island, but a Fire Island when nobody else was around. She had driven through timber-guarded back roads, endlessly, to arrive at her destination. She had passed through the hamlet of Oysterville, which seemed a ghost town now, lined with pretty, eccentric houses built by oystermen for brides who had died early. She saw handbills at the Oysterville church advertising chamber music concerts that would take place long after she had left. She saw other handbills that proclaimed the soon-to-be celebrated *Jazz and Oysters* event she had seen touted on Ralph Henderson's T-shirt. It seemed that every year people traveled from all points to listen to jazz in the now-deserted school yard and eat oysters while they snapped their fingers and bobbed to the beat.

Outside Oysterville she saw many side roads with rural mailboxes, so she supposed most of the village's inhabitants lived in the depths of these secret lanes, away from what had once been the capital of this part of Washington. She had a sense of the Peninsula narrowing, drawing in, before it expanded to the crooked-finger bit that formed the habitat for wildlife.

When she had bumped over the interminable road that led to the preserve, she saw an enormous recreational vehicle parked in the designated lot, and two other cars, but no human form was in sight. When she studied on a cedarwood board, the possible walks a person might take, she saw why. One could, if the tide was right, hike in a long, looping march which would take one to the open sea on the east side, and return along the bay to the starting point. It was a walk of approximately two miles. She thought she would plunge in and wander wherever her will took her.

Sitting on her log, Laura had to admit that the air was superb. She breathed in the smell of bracken and something she vaguely associated with a holiday in Northern Wisconsin she'd once enjoyed with her parents. All around her were the scrubby but pungent bushes that seemed to grow near the sea, and on the higher rises above her, pine trees. These were not the giants of the rain forest, but tallish pines that exuded a heavenly odor. The light-colored, sandy trails diverged in a bewildering number of directions. If she ever rose from her fallen log, she could pursue one that led directly upward, or plunge down through a veritable thicket of berry bushes. All the time, the sound of the sea was in her ears, much closer than it ever came to her in her bedroom at the hotel.

So far, she had seen no animals, only an army of small bugs that seemed like miniature butterflies. They swooped and darted everywhere, their tiny wings working double-time, and she supposed they were mildly interesting. She had never seen them anywhere else. Far above her she could hear the sound of a woodpecker boring into a tree, but every time she looked up the sound ceased. Bears, according to her book, were plentiful here, sucking honey and eating berries. She remembered that first day at the Grey Whale Hotel, when she had wondered how the bears could have the delicacy to eat berries.

As comfortable as her log was, something told her it would be even more comfortable to slide off it and squat in the warm heaps of sand beside it. She rested her head against the log, but found it ungiving and scratchy. She removed the cotton sweater knotted around her neck and formed it into a pillow to shield her from the harshness of the bark. She removed her shoes—new, unbroken sneakers purchased especially for her holiday—and then her cotton socks. She paddled her toes in the warm sand and felt almost blissfully uninhibited.

She knew she had come to this place to take a bracing walk, but she wanted to stay in this comfortable position, nestled against the hospitable log, for as long as possible. Perhaps, she thought, she had been deceiving herself for all these years; it was quite possible she was meant to be lazy, had a talent for it. She flexed her toes in the sand and watched, through half-shut eyes, the industrious little insects she had never seen before. She was floating in this Nirvana-like state when she was startled to hear the sound of footsteps in the under-growth, quite near. They were the steps of a rather large animal, she thought, and they brought her out of her trance immediately.

She got to her knees and tried to determine from which direction the animal was approaching. All her fantasies about bears seemed to have become frighteningly alive. She crawled on hands and knees behind the sheltering log, toward the sounds as it turned out. Now she could hear a grunting sound, as if the animal was pacing so heavily the air was periodically forced from its body. Crash. Crash. Grunt. Crash. It was maddening.

She inched forward, remembering that she was on a little rise, and found that another path lay directly beneath her, the long loop path that made a circle. Directly below, a boy of about eight was jumping in the low bushes as hard as he could, trampling them quite viciously, and in utter silence if you didn't count those little grunts that escaped him when he jumped too hard.

Around a bend in the path came three adults, two very large, a man and woman, and a tiny, weathered senior citizen wearing hiking shorts.

"Daniel!" shouted the heavy woman, who appeared to be the boy's mother. "What do you think you're doing?"

Daniel stopped his demented jumping and trampling and turned to confront the grown-ups. He didn't seem to have much to fear. His mother's tone had been curious rather than disapproving.

"He's just working off all that spare energy," the old lady said, answering for her grandson.

"Get out here on the path," said the father. "That's where you're supposed to be, on the path. Why do you think they made all these paths?"

The boy shrugged and did as he was told, and the party moved on while Laura withdrew out of sight, glad nobody had noticed her. She

decided she'd tell Jesse about her silly fear of bears and let him laugh
at her. She continued along her own path, carrying her shoes. It was a
series of hills, and at the crest of each she expected to see the Pacific
on the horizon, but it never appeared. She seemed hermetically sealed
in this green and sand-colored world where you could hear the sea
without glimpsing it. She decided Daniel and his entourage were the
passengers of the huge R.V. she'd seen in the lot, and wondered how
they had come to this deserted place, and where they would go next.

She became aware that she had been foolish to think herself alone
out at the tip of the Peninsula. She passed a couple who said hello to
her in loud, hearty voices, and then a party of three elderly women
who merely nodded. One of them was sketching in a book while she
walked along. Naturalists, Laura thought. Amateur scientists who
made wonderful drawings of plants and ferns and insects for their
own pleasure.

How could she have been stupid enough to think she was alone,
even here?

As she walked, her tendons adjusting to the soft material of the
path, the tranquil mood slipped away and her mind became as invigo-
rated as she had intended her body to be. She even branched out
onto a side path that led upward to no destination she could imagine.
The sounds of woodpeckers filled the air as she went steadily up, and
although the trees along this stretch were tall and shut out much of
the light, they proved, on close inspection, to be frail and crumbling.
Their roots in the sandy soil could not have a very good chance at
settling for longevity, and she supposed the salt air did its part in
eroding them.

The farther she came from her point of embarkation, the more her
senses refused to be drugged and demanded her to think rationally
about Claudia's death. She found another fallen log, not nearly as
homey as the one below, and sat down on it. This time she made no
attempt to get comfortable. The bark irritated her thighs through the
fabric of her jeans, and the sand beneath her feet was not warm. The
thick plantation of trees made this spot cool, and her toes, encountering only a dank, granular substance, were not encouraged to dance
and play.

Who killed Claudia? Now was as good a time as any to ask herself
the question and try to answer it. The problem was that any good list

of suspects ought to have a head and a tail, ranging from the person most likely to the suspect who could just barely fit in the picture. Laura's list was not vertical, but horizontal. The person most likely, Ralph Henderson, was too obvious, too pat, and thus he went to one side of her list instead of the top of it. His motive was impeccable, but he was too much the stock villain to take seriously.

She reminded herself that she was trying to analyze real life rather than fiction. In real life, the most obvious suspect was generally the guilty party. It was only in novels that the author had to plant a red herring or two and then pin the murder on the least likely subject. She reevaluated her list and planted Ralph at the top. She felt a modest surge of achievement, but it was overwhelmed when she calculated that all the other suspects still fanned out along a horizontal line.

Teddy Vine? She had no reason to suspect him except for his zeal in plying her with tainted salmon. Bob Ludder she suspected not of murder, but of laziness and the general desire to cover up the mayhem that Fran had tried to explain happened in out-of-the-way places.

Grace was someone she would never have thought of, if it weren't for the fact that Grace was the one to discover Claudia's body, and the only one to disappear when the questioning began. There was a tension between Grace and her son, Martin, and Laura wondered if Grace's mother's instinct could go so far as to cover up a crime?

The two people she wanted least implicated in the affair were Jack and Jesse. She could hardly afford to ignore Jack's influence in Claudia's death. It was he who had managed to hush it up and ensure that nobody would inquire why a capable woman like Claudia could meet violent death on the day of her open house.

Jesse was the true dark horse. What possible motive could she impute to him? As far as she knew, Jesse only hoped to survive for a time as the Grey Whale's caretaker. He, more than anyone else, was presumably motivated by a sense of honor. His secretive ways, his manner of having seen it all before, were the only reason she placed him on her list of suspects.

What, after all, did she know about any of them?

She cataloged the reasons why the hotel might upset the delicate superstructure of the Peninsula. Oysters, as always, came first. That took care of Ralph, Grace—and by extension Grace's son, Martin. It might also include Jesse, the outsider from Seattle, if Jesse had signed on as caretaker with the express purpose of making the Grey Whale seem a threat.

Second came drugs, in the shape of the terrifying ice labs Jesse had told her about. Almost all of the suspects could, conceivably, be involved in the manufacture of this new, home-brewed, commercial venture. Come to think of it, a new culprit, Deputy Ludder, could be incorporated into the fold. Mightn't his refusal to investigate the death at the hotel mask a quite different concern? Wasn't it likely that Ludder was taking large bribes to insure that his patch of the Peninsula remained clean and obscure, so that drugs could be manufactured in the woods?

So many possibilities were dizzying, and the morose aspects of her resting place were beginning to depress her. She pushed up and off the log, continued on up through the unhealthy forest toward a high point that seemed sunnier. She felt the presence of someone quite close, but when she peered down on the sandy path where she had been, it was empty. So was the path below it, the one where Daniel had performed his furious pantomime.

She chided herself for this unsupported feeling that she was not alone, putting it down to nerves, and then nerves made her think of poor Dot, who was coming home from the hospital, and Dot's stroke made her think of how frail and vulnerable human beings were. Claudia in the linen closet, her parents who had been killed in a crash, Grace Best's husband, the hitchhiker Nick Cotton had murdered, the unknown man found shot and hanged in the Mullen's Wood of Fran's youth, all seemed to be trudging with her toward an elusive, sunny place they could never reach.

When she had reached the point where the sun had seemed to shine through a clearing in the trees, she found it dark and cheerless after all. Perhaps it had been an illusion. From her vantage point she could see the lower trails, bathed in sun and seeming to represent safety, quite close in fact, but impossible to reach unless she turned and went back the way she had come. It was like being in a darkened movie theater on a bright afternoon, when someone opens an exit door and the real, hectic world intrudes for a moment. She needed the exit.

Turning back, she felt more than ever that she was not alone, but it was a feeling only, and could not be borne out by any fact. No twigs snapped sharply under a misplaced foot. She didn't glimpse an improbable color, one not natural to the forest, between the trees. It was only a feeling, but it was enough to make her want to run in panic. Running was an activity not open to her at the moment. Even if she stopped to put her sneakers on, the path she was on was littered with the sort of roots that snagged at feet and sent the runner sprawling, and once she had reached the lower trails she would encounter the sun-warmed, friable ordeal by sand that made walking a chore, much less running. She would simply walk firmly on, suppressing her too-vivid faculties of imagination, and somehow manage to gain the safety of the parking area. It seemed very far away, but she knew she could have come no more than three quarters of a mile at most.

When she emerged at the bottom of the splinter trail, she allowed herself to think she had completed the first lap. The second would be when she passed the first fallen log, and the last would be the distance between it and the car park. The presence seemed to have altered, and as best she could judge was now viewing her from above instead of on a parallel route. She longed to see a party of tourists so she could attach herself to them, no matter how intrusive and obnoxious she might seem.

The wind had sprung up strongly, and she wasn't sure if the movement in the bushes was the natural tossing of thick undergrowth or the progress of her unseen companion. She was midway between the fallen log of lap three and her destination when a figure appeared, seemingly from thin air, and came toward her with a relentless, slow, measured gait. The sun was in her eyes, and he appeared as a black shape. A terrible, rushing noise filled her ears, like the beating of huge wings, and she thought: *This is it.*

"Mosquitos!" a deep, dreamlike voice cried in anguish.

Laura's vision sharpened and she saw a tall old woman, her hair done up in a crown of white braids, standing in the path before her. She was slapping at her arms in an ecstasy of revulsion. "They're like vampires," the woman said. "Nobody warned me." She made the sound of disgust Laura had mistaken for her death knell. It was a deep, sonorous exhalation of her breath that sounded like Doomsday.

The woman grinned and struck off in the opposite direction, and

Laura felt sanity had been restored. She had mistaken the sounds of real life for something prophetic and doomed. No one was stalking her, no evil had singled out Laura McAuley for a violent end. She was reacting to her recent illness in an inappropriate but predictable way.

When she reached the parking lot she heard a car leaving the sanctuary at very high speed, considering the roughness of the road. Apparently there was someone else who was eager to put the place behind him. A troubling thought was trying to surface, but she pushed it down ruthlessly. She had had enough trouble.

TEN

Althea sat in her pickup as giant buffers rolled and thrummed against it at the drive-thru car wash in Long Beach. Poor truck looked like it had come to Washington from the Dust Bowl, so she was indulging in the small extravagance despite her alarming bank balance.

She prided herself on being a self-sufficient woman, one who had never asked for help, but she was beginning to be alarmed. When she'd first come to the Peninsula, her modest savings intact, her children grown and thriving, it had seemed she would be able to survive quite well. She had immediately been hired as a part-time librarian at Ocean Park, and she was a free-lance accountant, picking up small jobs here and there as she became known to the locals. No one could have foreseen the cutbacks in her first days here; the mean little nips and tucks at folks' ability to survive had made themselves felt so gradually that when the full extent of the calamity hit home, nobody was prepared.

First the library was forced to reduce the hours it could remain open, and as the most recently hired employee, it had been Althea who had lost her job. Some of her clients had had to make do with managing their own accounts. None of it would have been so frightening if not for the fact that she had sunk a good portion of her savings into buying the little house in the woods a mile up from Grace's post office. She loved the house, but she should have been more conversant with the availability of water on the Peninsula. Currently she was negotiating with the owner of the lot in back of her house, hoping the stubborn woman would sell her the acre and a half so she could dig a well. Her own acre would not accommodate a well, and the process of hooking up to the town's water supply was so costly it would wipe her out financially.

Claudia and Jack had arrived on the scene like saviors, buying the old hotel and opening up the possibility of all sorts of lines of gainful employment in the near future. They would need a chef, possibly two, and chambermaids and waitresses, and—most importantly—a local accountant. It had been all but agreed that Althea would be the local bookkeeper for the Grey Whale when it opened, and she had held that future position up as a token of certain salvation. She knew she could keep things going as long as she had a time plan, but now all that was, if not gone, in jeopardy.

Claudia's death had changed everything. The moment Althea heard that Claudia had met with a fatal accident, she saw her modest game plan swept down and under beneath a cruel wave of indifferent, hit-or-miss destiny. She was sorry Claudia had met with such an untimely end, but she was dead and nothing more could be done for her. She, Althea, was still obliged to survive, and Claudia's death had made that survival less certain. If Jack had been a different sort of man, the kind who vowed that his wife's last wish should be honored, the hotel might yet become a going concern, but Jack had turned out to be one who cut his losses and ran. She felt quite sure he wanted nothing further to do with the hotel where his wife had died.

She and the pickup emerged at the end of the cleaning process, and Althea slid out of the car wash, making a U-turn, and headed back toward her little house in the woods.

The road was lined with the kite enthusiasts who were checking in for the festival. On the horizon she could see a dozen kites making trial runs in the air over the beach. There were two fighter kites, swooping and darting, and one so large and beautifully colored— mauves and blues outlined in black and daringly scored with slashes of crimson—that her attention was dangerously diverted from the road.

More than anything, she wanted Laura McAuley to leave the Peninsula and return to New York. Laura was a reminder of all that could have been, but there was something worse. Something that had caused Althea to avoid her ever since she'd laid out the Tarots. She had never seen a preliminary reading so full of destruction and death. To tell Laura what she saw in her cards would have been an act of hostility, and she had nothing against Laura at all. Aside from the fact that Laura, like Claudia, seemed to prefer to live in a city, Laura seemed a decent sort.

She had even wondered if she'd managed to confuse the two Easterners when she laid out Laura's cards. It was Claudia who had attracted death. She didn't see how it was possible to mix the fates of two entirely different women, but Claudia and Laura had been friends for years. It could be that they had entered into the ritual on some plane she wasn't aware of, diluting the meaning of the Tarot's message.

She had experimented with the cards every day since Claudia met her fate in the linen closet, and everything she could divine from her experiments told her that Laura was still in terrible danger. Death and mayhem swirled around Laura's psychic core as surely as the spectre of poverty and dependency haunted Althea.

She thought it possible that Laura could avoid her fate by going home, but what in the name of all that was sacred would turn up to rescue *her*?

At the oyster shell junction, she thought of going to the hotel and making a clean breast of it to Laura, but on reflection this seemed an unwise idea. She turned in the direction of her cabin, the home she might soon lose if things continued as they were, but she felt she was suffering from loneliness, an emotion almost unknown to her. As a curative, she drove slowly by the post office to see if Grace was anywhere in sight.

Fran hailed her from the plot of land between the P.O. and Teddy's place. Fran was straddling her bike and looked flushed. Althea stopped and leaned out the window, curious.

"They found Wayne Cotton asleep in a ditch," Fran told her, abandoning the bike and coming to stand a few feet from the window.

Confused, Althea had a picture of little Wayne curled up in a ditch, like a tramp from silent films. "Who found him?" she asked.

Fran lowered her voice. "Some people who live out along the bay road. They're elderly, retired. It seems the wife went down to her mailbox and saw this car in the ditch at the edge of the road. She thought some kids had stolen a car and left it there, but when she saw Wayne asleep in the front seat she nearly had a heart attack. She thought there'd been an accident and he was dead."

"Well, obviously there was an accident, Fran. Otherwise he wouldn't have been in the ditch."

Fran looked annoyed, her pale, furry eyebrows contracting at Althea's tone. "Not a real accident," she said. "Wayne was only sleeping. I told you that right up front. The woman went to get her husband, and by the time they returned Wayne was awake."

"Did he explain how he came to be in the ditch?"

"That's just the thing," Fran said. "He couldn't remember how he got there, and when they said they were going to phone for help he started crying." Fran came closer, leaning her elbows on the windowsill. "He seemed really disoriented, out of it."

"Where did you hear about it?"

"At the supermarket. It's all over town."

"I never hear anything interesting at the market," said Althea, disliking the petulant sound of her voice. If she never heard anything it was because she had trained herself to remain deaf in small communities. It had saved her from premature madness in Alaska.

"There's more," said Fran. "Dot's coming home tonight, and even though the car is perfectly all right, Wayne claims he can't drive it. She's coming home by ambulance."

This was the first of Fran's bulletins that truly alarmed her. Wayne asleep in his car in the ditch was peculiar, but all too understandable. The poor man had been under a terrific strain, and she could imagine the little accident easily, but a Wayne who didn't feel himself fit enough to reclaim his Dot from the hospital? He had lived to provide services for his wife, and now, when he was called upon to bring her home, he seemed to have relinquished his role as her cavalier. It didn't make sense. She said as much, and Fran nodded wisely.

"Now," she said, "there will be two invalids instead of one. We have to help them, don't you think?"

"I suppose you're right." Althea envisioned years of having to help Wayne and Dorothy, and barely restrained a visible shudder. She had not moved to the Peninsula to become an unpaid social worker or nurse's aide. Fran's evident delight at the prospect of doing so filled her with malaise. Then a cheerful thought came to dislodge the other. If the hotel never opened, she wouldn't be living here. She might migrate south to Oregon, or Northern California, blessedly unaware of the travails of the Cottons' declining years.

Just then Grace's rusted-out Cougar drew in beside the post office, and Grace got out, carrying a sack of groceries. "What's this?" she called. "A conference?"

"We were just talking about the Cottons," Fran said.

Grace nodded briskly, as if she had sorted out that problem. As she neared Althea's pickup she said, "Poor Wayne. Katha told me he's canceled all his hair appointments for the next week."

"How are they going to manage?" Althea asked. Her concern over her own financial problems seemed to make her view every problem as an economic one. "Of course," she said, "everyone's always said Wayne has money salted away."

Instantly, she was aware of her gaffe. Grace disliked gossip. She disliked it as only one who was determined not to fit a stereotype could do. Her dislike covered speculation only, so while it was perfectly all right for her to relay the news of Wayne's cancellations—a fact—it was decidedly not the thing to ponder on Wayne Cotton's possible savings. Grace's frank blue eyes looked unnaturally piercing and luminous, and Althea was afraid she was about to be chastised, but the postmistress's next words revealed distress of a different kind.

"I'm going to ask you both a very difficult question," she said. "I'm worried about Martin. It's just a vague feeling, but it's there."

"What about Martin?" Fran asked, twisting the handlebars of her bicycle and frowning. She took motherhood very seriously, Althea knew, and had decided not to have children in such an imperfect world. On more than one occasion, Fran had expressed awe at Althea's willing conspiracy to repopulate the world.

"What question?" she demanded.

Grace reddened, then plunged on. "Have either of you ever had reason to think that Martin was involved in anything illegal? I don't mean have you *heard* anything about Martin. What I mean is, have either of you seen him do anything that seemed—well—questionable?"

"Like smoking grass?" Fran asked.

"No," said Grace.

"No," said Fran. "Never."

"How about you, Althea?"

Althea had been thinking about her only view of Grace's son that might be considered worrisome. It had all the elements of gossip, being an impression, merely, but it was also something she had seen first hand.

"It's probably nothing," she said, "but one night about a month ago I passed a van on the road up from Ocean Park. I passed them because they had sort of taken control of the road, and I didn't want to drive anywhere near them. They had those dark windows you can't see into, and I thought they were up to no good. It was just a feeling, like yours, Grace—"

"Joyriding!" cried Fran. "As Dot would say, so quaint!"

"No, not joyriding. Nothing so innocent as that. The van really seemed sinister to me." She smiled at Grace to indicate that her feelings were far from impeccable.

"I know what you mean," said Grace. "But where is Martin mixed in?"

"The van slowed down and let him off at the post office," Althea said reluctantly. "I saw him in the rearview mirror."

"So what?" said Fran.

"Exactly," said Althea.

"Thank you," said Grace. "It's what I was afraid of." Her lips tightened. "Excuse me," she said, and turned to go in her house.

"What was that all about?" Fran asked.

Althea shrugged. She had, in fact, a very good idea of what it was that worried Grace, but she wasn't going to pass it on. She ended up accepting Fran's invitation to "have tea in the garden" as Fran put it, and sat, a cup of iced herbal tea in her hands, on the grass next to the vegetable patch. Teddy joined them, emerging from the rabbit hutches with a delighted smile.

"Althea!" he said in his most jovial voice. "Been avoiding us because of that bad salmon? It'll never happen again, I assure you."

"Don't be silly," she said. "I just needed to be alone for a while."

She thought it interesting that he dated her scarcity from the night of the salmon supper, when she had been avoiding everyone from the day of the open house. Strange how people rearranged time in order to make themselves the pivot from which all activity ceased or commenced. One of the nice things about being a self-sufficient woman, one who had actually lived for a long time in Alaska, was that you didn't have to talk a lot. Poor Claudia had abhorred a silence, jumping in to fill one whenever she could. To a lesser degree, Laura felt the same way. Fran could maintain a restful silence only when all was going well in her life; at present, she was still chagrined at having given the folks at the Grey Whale food poisoning, and kept up a constant barrage of little vocalized responses.

"Uh-huh," Fran said, reacting to Althea's purported need for solitude. "Mmmmm."

I guess I'm the female version of the strong and silent type, Althea thought. Aloud she said, "Anyone feel like a glass of wine?" Fran's eyebrows wriggled and Teddy grinned. They knew she seldom drank anything alcoholic. Her aversion came from the sad spectacle of Alaskan Indians ardently drinking themselves to death. She had strong opinions about liquor, but Teddy and Fran could be counted on to have some bottles of homemade dandelion wine cooling down in the mud of the bay. It was, she thought, relatively harmless stuff, and she badly wanted to paste a layer of gauze over the harsh realities.

"Sure thing," said Teddy.

The wine was splashed into her teacup and she was made to sip and pronounce on its excellence. She closed her eyes and said, "First-rate," the only words that came to mind.

Later, she would remember cocktail hour *chez Vine* as another lazy, late-afternoon vignette of life on the Peninsula. While the bay became darker by degrees, going from its earlier festive shade of powder blue to a deep tinge of mauve surrounded by a darker nimbus of navy, she listened to environmental talk. Teddy was convinced that the Hanford nuclear plant was still poisoning the oysters, and Fran agreed. Complicated tides in the Columbia River were more powerful than Acts of Congress, and always would be.

While she nodded and smiled, her mind was always full of an entirely different image—that of the van with blackened windows. It was infinitely more evil, more capable of destroying this point of land than all the nuclear facilities a cynical Congress could impose on them.

"What are you thinking of, Althea? You seem about a million miles away," Teddy said.

"I was thinking the bay is the color of a kite I saw this afternoon," she improvised. Teddy looked hurt. "It isn't that I wasn't listening to what you were saying," she said, "but we have discussed it before. We're in agreement."

"Uh-*huh!*" Fran beamed at this show of solidarity. "More wine, Althea?"

But Althea, murmuring excuses, unfolded her long limbs and got to her feet. Fran saw her to her car and stood looking anxious while Althea searched for her keys. "They're in the ignition," she said.

Althea hated to look scatterbrained, and wondered if Fran could detect her rattled state of mind.

"It's just that Teddy cares so *much,*" Fran said. "He cares about the environment in a completely different way than the rest of us."

"Which is to say he cares more."

"Oh, no, I didn't mean that. He takes it personally, as if it were his child. You have children, Althea. Think of how you felt when one of your daughters cut her finger or fell out of a tree or—"

"Nearly walked into a chain saw," said Althea.

"Good heavens—did that actually happen?"

Althea could still feel the contraction of panic after all these years. She remembered it more viscerally than the pain and indignity of childbirth itself. "*Nearly* walked into," she said. "Catastrophe averted."

"That's how Teddy feels about acid rain and water pollution," said Fran. "Come to think of it, it's how our friend Holly feels about animal rights."

"Yes," said Althea, who had killed and dressed various animals in her life, "I see what you mean." She smiled reassuringly at Fran, thanked her for the wine, and made her getaway.

For a long time she pondered the nature of motherhood. She grappled with it as she slid into the wooded driveway of her acre, and continued to dwell on it as she noticed a hornet's nest expanding beneath her kitchen window. So far, she was a lucky mother, but she had known many unlucky ones, women whose sons and daughters had succumbed to drink, or drugs, or unknowable despair. Their children were gone from the world in one way or another. There was Mickey, who had drunk prodigiously and then staggered out, one Alaskan night, under the impression that he was living in Santa Monica, and frozen to death at the age of fourteen. Another boy, Tommy, had sliced three toes off while chopping wood and quite soon died of blood poisoning. Her own Vivian had nearly walked into a chain saw at the tender and unpredictable age of three. It seemed a miracle, when you thought of it, that any of them survived.

She went inside, but the usual feeling of peace her house gave her was missing, and she knew why. Grace was a mother, too, and possessed with keen, motherly radar that let her know when her boy was in trouble, or about to be. Althea sighed, got out her bottled water to make some coffee, and then thought she'd had entirely too much tea at the Vines'. She put the water back and paced through the house, thinking of what her moral obligations did and didn't involve. The house was too small for pacing—the living room could be traversed in four steps—so she dropped into the hand-carved rocker by the fireplace. If only it were winter she could distract herself with the building of a fire, but at present a brass bowl heaped with sand dollars sat on the cold grate.

She hadn't thought twice the night she'd seen Martin Best get out of the van, but the moment Grace asked her worried question an unpleasant possibility presented itself. The meth labs moved from state to state, just ahead of the law's ability to track them with expensive new computer techniques. They had started in California, moved up through Oregon. Their next haven, once Washington acquired the equipment, would no doubt be Idaho.

It was always the same with the really illicit stuff, not the happy-family, blissed-out camaraderie once employed in the Age of Marijuana. The scouts always selected some local kid, befriending him, buying beers, flattering him with their confidence. Local kids were often thrilled to find themselves in the company of outlaws, especially when they lived in quiet backwaters where nothing ever seemed to happen. The kids knew all the information the men needed to set up an operation: which cops could be bribed, what parts of an area were genuinely isolated and safe from scrutiny, who was likely to make trouble . . .

Often, the local informant was given samples of the lab's wares, and if he proved susceptible, offered a job once the lab was set up in some remote forest. When it reached that point, the kid was as good as dead. In this case, Grace's son.

Althea rocked back and forth in a fit of moral anguish. Should she tell Grace her suspicions about the trouble Martin might be in, or was she being melodramatic? Should she contrive to warn Martin Best, a boy she scarcely knew, of the terrible danger he courted? And what if she was wrong?

It was growing dark when she heard the sound of a vehicle turning into her drive. She moved to the front door and peered out. Ralph Henderson was moving toward her door with his usual purposeful step. She cracked the door open a few inches and waited to see what the born-again oyster cowboy wanted with her.

"Althea?" he called.

"No need to shout," she said. "I'm right here, Ralph."

He halted a few feet from her doorstep. "Thing is," he said, "I've brought someone who wants her fortune read."

"I only read the cards for friends," she said. "I'm not in business, Ralph." She was trying to distinguish the features of the woman leaning against the side of Ralph's truck, but it was too dim. All she could see was a tremendous forest of ringlets, dark and wild, which seemed to dwarf the pale oval of face beneath.

"That's not anyone I know, is it?" she said.

"Well, I know her, and I could introduce you." Ralph sounded almost earnest, and she could smell the juniper aroma from five feet away. Gin. "She's just a little tourist gal," he said.

"Is it OK?" the girl shouted from the truck. She sounded like a teenager. "Why don't you take that child back to where you found her," Althea whispered furiously.

"She's of age," Ralph said. He was grinning now, and she could only imagine what stupid, misguided thought had occurred to him. "There's no harm in being friendly to tourists," he said, "long as they're really tourists. Long as they don't plan to stay and poke their noses into things that are none of their damned business."

"I'll tell your fortune right from my doorstep," she called to the girl. "If you stick around with this man, it won't be a very pleasant one."

The girl giggled, and Ralph scowled at her. "Come *on*," he said. "Don't spoil my party just because you got no party of your own."

"If you like, I'll drive you back to Long Beach, or wherever you're staying," Althea continued. More giggling, as if Althea had been delivering one-liners into the rapidly approaching night.

"I guess a woman gets bitter when she's your age and she doesn't have a man," Ralph said, seeming to speak out of a judicious and even sympathetic understanding of human nature. "Now, in spite of your meanness, I'd like you to call on me if you get lonely. I know a thing or two about mature women." For the first time he lost his footing and lurched a little. He caught himself and planted his legs wide for leverage.

"Just get off my property," said Althea. "Clear off and don't come back."

Ralph pointed at her, extending his index finger with ludicrous force, making little jabbing motions. "You may not be a tourist," he said, "but you're not one of us, either. You just remember what I said about people who poke their noses in—"

He seemed to lose track of his sentence.

"Put a sock in it, Ralph," she said, slamming the door in his self-righteous face.

Long after his truck had backed off her property, she worried about the giggling tourist. She gave the unseen face a set of features, and too often they were the features of one of her daughters. They were powerfully intelligent and reasonable young women, but at some stage they had giggled, too.

She made herself a supper of cucumber and tomato, cheese and bread, and washed her face in bottled water. She got in bed at an early hour, taking with her a copy of *Pilgrim at Tinker Creek*, a book she read over and over again, for comfort. In the distance, the canning factory had swung into motion and was trying to lull her with its rhythmic, drumlike thrums, but sleep proved elusive.

Just at the point when insomnia, a condition which had rarely plagued her, threatened to make its claim, she got out of bed and loaded her shotgun. She placed the shotgun beside her bed, where she could reach it easily in the event of a night visit. She refused to dwell on the subject of who might visit her at night, or for what reason. She knew she would be able to sleep, knowing that she could protect herself against unwanted visiters.

Just in case, she told herself. And then, sleepily, *Just in case.*

It shouldn't be sandy in the hotel. Laura was puzzled, because she had removed her sneakers and clapped them together on the oyster shell path before coming in the kitchen door. Nevertheless, there were stray grains in the kitchen and pantry, even one or two in the dining room. There was nothing quite so unpleasant as the feel of sand on floorboards beneath the sole of one's shoe.

She had changed her shoes immediately on returning, and placed the sneakers upside down on the windowsill in her room so that any stubborn particles could drift down to the ground beneath. Now, three hours later, as she and Jesse were planning to sample Willy's Pizza—dispensed from a one-story building near the library in Ocean Park—the question of the sand was still nagging at her.

"Excuse me," she said to him, "I just want to go upstairs for a minute."

She kept her dirty laundry in a pillowcase purloined from the infamous linen closet. She hadn't accumulated enough dirty laundry yet to try out the hotel's washer and dryer. Jesse had warned her that the dryer was the most temperamental of the two. It walked, he said. If it was feeling especially vigorous, it was capable of nearly juddering out the door of the raincoat room during the spin cycle. "I usually sit on it," he had told her. "Just grab something to read when it goes into Spin and hold it down."

Kneeling at the closet, she withdrew the socks she'd worn on her hike at the nature preserve. She ran her fingers over the soles and encountered a little pocket of clinging sand in the small fold near the toe end. It seemed sealed in by the fold, and she couldn't imagine a time-release method through which she had deposited sand throughout the uncarpeted first floor of the hotel. And there was something else. She'd gone straight upstairs on her return to the hotel—through the kitchen and dining room, on into the sitting room and up the stairs. She had never been in the pantry at all.

She shook the socks out her window, releasing the offending sand, and returned them to the pillowcase. She did it all very carefully, drawing the motions out, because to do otherwise would force her to think the unthinkable.

Jesse had come in a half hour after her return, looking flushed and sheepish. She'd been in the kitchen when he came sauntering up the long, curved path and onto the oyster shell walkway. "Hey," he'd said by way of greeting. "I've been over at Teddy and Fran's." As if she'd asked.

The sand under foot was not the damp sand of the bay's bottom, which was crumbly and dark. It was not the sand that Jesse ventured out upon every time the tide was out. It was the dry, crinkly sand of Fire Island, or of the sanctuary at the end of the Peninsula.

She continued to kneel in the darkening room, and then she heard him call her name. His voice sounded quite close, as if he had climbed partway up the stairs. "Laura?" Yes, he was defininitely getting closer. "Are you all right?"

The thought of seeing him in the doorway to her room was suddenly unimaginably frightening. "I'm coming right down," she cried, hearing the panic in her voice. How would she tell him she'd lost her appetite for pizza without arousing his suspicion? *Calm down, don't show him your alarm. There could be a rational explanation for that sand. He could have been walking on the beach, earlier, before visiting the Vines.*

He was waiting at the foot of the stairs. *The old tracker himself, wearing a lightweight windbreaker, is seen waiting patiently in the hall of an old hotel. He is prepared to escort an alien, high-heeled woman to a pizza place on the edge of the North American continent. Afterward, perhaps a few games of pool before he takes her home and murders her.*

"I've been sweeping up sand," Jesse said. "You must have tracked it in from the sanctuary." He spoke happily, as if sweeping up sand were something he enjoyed. There was nothing accusatory or complaining in his tone of voice. She wanted to believe in his innocence, but she could no longer deny that danger was very close. *Someone* had tracked sand in, and the possibility of a third party accompanying her, unseen, on her little hike was dizzying.

"About the pizza," she said. "I'm not sure—"

The sound of a car in the drive came to rescue her, on cue.

"Who can *that* be?" she said in a cross voice, feigning irritation.

Jesse went into the dining room and looked out. "Wayne Cotton," he announced.

They listened for the crunching sound on the oyster shells, and then moved to the kitchen to receive their guest. Wayne loomed up at the door, carrying a plastic supermarket bag. He was wearing the sort of belted trenchcoat Laura associated with war correspondents, and his normally glossy bangs seemed stiff and unkempt.

"Hello?" Wayne called, although he could see them clearly. "I can't stay but a moment. I won't take long."

It seemed so pathetic, his assertion that he would not burden them with his presence, that Laura welcomed him extravagantly. "Come in," she crowed. "How is Dot? What can I get you, Wayne dear?"

Wayne shook his head distractedly, refusing refreshment, and stood just inside the door, holding out his shopping bag. "It's only," he began, "only that Dorothy, only that she meant to give this to Claudia. She thought it was only right Claudia should have it. It belongs here, at the Grey Whale. She only took it as a memento, and then, when Claudia and Jack bought the old place, Dot said to me, 'Wayne,' she said, 'it's only right I return this to its proper place. The only question is when.' "

He seemed to choke up a bit and tried to hide it by coughing. The smile that followed was ghastly in the extreme. He was ignoring all suggestions that he come and sit down in the dining room. Wayne Cotton kept to his little space inside the door as if his life depended on it.

"When the announcement came about the open house, she said it was the perfect time. She brought it, wrapped in tissue paper, in her purse. She meant to present it to Mrs. Arnold, to Claudia. Again, you see, she was waiting for that perfect moment. And then—" Wayne's face took on a horrified look, as if it had been he, and not Grace, who had discovered Claudia's body. "And then—well, in the confusion, with what happened—she never had the chance."

Laura remembered the confusion very well. Suddenly, the whole scene after Dot fainted was as clear to her as if she were seeing it on videotape. In the wake of Ralph Henderson's heroic rescue, Wayne had turned back to retrieve Dot's handbag, which was lying on the floor, close to where its mistress had been felled. A corridor had been cleared for them, for Ralph who bore Dot in his arms, and for Wayne, who scuttled after, the handbag in his arms. He was talking about Dot in the past tense now, and she feared the worst.

"Is Dot, has Dot?" She couldn't say it. "Has she had another setback?"

Wayne mumbled something that sounded like "all setbacks now." Then he withdrew an object from his plastic bag and handed it over to Jesse. "There," he said. "Now it can be back where it belongs."

Laura couldn't make out what it was, only that it was as big as Jesse's hand and a dark gray color. A rock, perhaps?

"Thank you, Wayne," Jesse said, and passed it along for her to see. It was much heavier than she expected it to be, made of some substance like pewter. She set it down on a table and saw that it was a primitive sculpture of a whale.

"A gray whale," she said. "I see."

"It lives right on the mantelpiece in the main room," Wayne said. "That's where it always was."

"Thank Dot for us," she said, still not sure of Mrs. Cotton's viability.

Wayne nodded solemnly, like a child. "I'd better get back to her, then," he said, and without another word he turned and went out the door.

Laura took the whale sculpture into the living room and placed it on the mantel, a little to left of center. Then she stood back a few paces and judged the effect. It was consciously primitive, she decided, and not the result of poor workmanship. A person could grow fond of it. She thought she understood why Dot Cotton had decided to take it away as a memento.

"That was strange," said Jesse. Laura jumped. She had actually forgotten about him for a moment.

"I don't think so," she said. "If Dot thinks she's dying, it makes perfect sense. People like to die with a clean conscience. She doesn't want to feel she's guilty of even the smallest offense. Technically, this whale belonged to the hotel."

Jesse sighed. "Could we get that pizza now?" he asked. He sounded so plaintive, so like a hungry boy, she couldn't imagine him as menacing. Her mind knew what her emotions were rejecting, and quite possibly she'd suspect him again before the night was over, but for the time being she craved creature comfort—pizza and the sound of other voices would go a long way toward banishing the obscure fears wrapping round her.

"Pizza," she agreed.

ELEVEN

The one thing Dot had never been able to understand was why Nick's lawyer hadn't allowed Nick to take the stand in his own defense. It had seemed scandalous to her at the time, a perversion of justice. Here everybody and his cousin was allowed to say anything they liked in the newspapers, in the courts, on the TV, and Nick himself was gagged as thoroughly as if they'd stuck a huge Band-Aid over his mouth.

She remembered his words to her on those visits before the trial had begun up in Seattle. They'd changed the venue, claiming that he couldn't get a fair trial in the area. To her mind, that was the first evidence of their insincerity. They wanted to take him to the city to cut him off from all the people who had known him when he was growing up. Their strategy had been to isolate him, try him where the jurors wouldn't understand a boy from the Peninsula, a high-spirited boy with a devoted mother who had always done the best she could for him.

"I'm innocent," Nick would tell her on those pretrial visits. "I never meant to hurt her."

"Of course you are," Dot always said. "Any fool could see you are." She never fully appreciated the degree to which she could touch Nick in those pretrial days. She was free to smooth his hair back or squeeze his hands in her own, no matter how he flinched away from such motherly attentions. If she had only known! Fully expecting him to be acquitted, she had never anticipated a time in which she would address him by telephone, separated by that cruel window of glass.

Now she would never see him again. First she had been prevented from touching him—until he was an old man, if she were still alive— and now she would not see him again in life. Contrary to what the doctors said, she knew she was dying. Now that she didn't care if she ever saw Nick again, she didn't care about dying, either. Nobody understood her, nobody knew how she suffered. Wayne, bless his heart, tried as hard as he could, but sometimes trying was not enough.

"Wayne?" she called out in sudden fear. "Wayne!" Her voice emerged in its new, slightly slurred version, the one she was assured would go away with time and the proper treatment. It might have been a minute or an hour before he appeared at her bedside. Time was no longer available to her on a regular basis; she slipped in and out of it, scarcely caring if it were night or day.

"I'm here," came Wayne's voice. "I'm here, Dot dear."

"Did you return it to the hotel?"

"Yes, Dot. I told you—you remember, don't you? I gave it to Jesse and told him exactly where it should be on the mantel."

"When was that, Wayne?"

"Three days ago now. Yes, three days ago. Everything's fine, dear. You mustn't worry."

"It was wrong of me."

"God forgives," said Wayne, trying to hold her hand between his. "He forgiveth all who ask for redemption."

"Forgives, Wayne. God forgives, not *forgiveth.* It's old-fashioned to say *forgiveth.* Probably pagan."

"You made a joke," Wayne said in a wondering voice.

She opened her eyes and saw him staring at her in amazement, as if she'd grown wings or spoken in tongues. "It's not a joke, it's the simple truth," she said.

This small dialogue was so exhausting she was forced to ignore its meaning and creep back into her torpid state. It was far too late to talk of jokes and God and redemption. Far too late.

Her memory served up odd snippets of speech to torment her. Once, when she couldn't tell if she was asleep or in the twilit state that now described her every waking moment, she heard the booming voice of the prosecutor, just as she had heard it sitting in the court- room. *A crime so depraved, so vile and vicious, makes any civilized person* ask: *what punishment is great enough? What punishment can serve to recompense the grieving family of a young woman who had scarcely begun her life —when, ladies and gentlemen of the jury—when, I repeat, she had the great misfortune to cross paths with one of life's misfits. One of the human cobras or sharks that exist in our society. One who, like the defendant in this case, ought to be removed from the face of the earth, or segregated from normal society for the rest of his natural life.*

To hear such words spoken against her son! It wasn't an experience many mothers had. No matter how violently she disagreed with the prosecutor's words, she couldn't help but feel a bit special. It was her Nick he was speaking of in such dreadful terms. Nick had come from *her* body, no one else's. The prosecutor was only doing his job, and she didn't, couldn't, hate him, but the journalists were another matter. They had a whole world of events to choose from, other crimes even, as bad as the one Nick was charged for—why hadn't they left him alone?

Wayne?

Yes, dear.

Did you take it back to the hotel?

Now you know I did, Dorothy. I told you.

The journalist she always felt to be personally responsible, unlike the prosecutor, was someone Dot blamed for Nick's sorry life in jail. When that wicked hitchhiker's body turned up out Chehalis way, the journalist just wouldn't let the matter drop! Ann Dickenson. Even now the hated name could make Dot feel that dirty pennies had been placed on her tongue. Ann Dickenson, of the *Intelligencer* up in Seattle, had taken up the cause of a dead hitchhiker as if the girl had been important. To hear Ann Dickenson rave on, you'd have thought the Queen of England had met an untidy end instead of some human riffraff out for a good time. The hitchhiker might have faded from everyone's mind, in time, if damned Dickenson had just shut up and turned her busybody attention on some *real* issues, like crime carried out against the innocent elderly in the cities all over America, or drug abuse. She seemed to champion the very people who were part of the problem, writing with seeming sympathy about the depraved child prostitutes who all seemed to end up on First Street in Seattle, or mothers who bred like rabbits in order to get a bigger welfare check.

It's time for your medicine, dear.

Take it away, Wayne.
But you must—it's important.
I don't want it.

English people had an expression they used which was supposed to be very rude. It was "bloody." How this expression had come about Dot couldn't imagine, but they'd been using it for hundreds of years. Privately, she always thought of the journalist as Bloody Ann Dickenson. Dickenson had blood on her hands on account of the way she had persecuted Nick. Dot saw her as a kind of vampire, a woman who fed on other's misfortunes until her perfect, white teeth, bared so convincingly in a smile, were streaked and smeared with blood when she sat down at her typewriter to write inflammatory words which would lead to a young man's being shut away from the world.

Bloody Ann Dickenson had interviewed Dot after Nick's conviction and before the time when his appeal could be launched. She had seemed so sympathetic at the time, as if all she wanted was to convey Dot's thoughts to a waiting public.

Stupid me, Dot said, and then, hearing her words in the silent air, cringed into her pillow. Had she spoken out loud?

She'd been outwitted. She'd thought she had a chance, at last, to speak her mind about the nature of crime, but she'd been mistaken. All her brave, sensible statements about the special relationship she'd had with her son had been twisted and held up to ridicule in the *Intelligencer*'s Sunday magazine. Nick was portrayed as the product of a broken marriage, and all his little, normal faults had appeared as clear guidelines to the triumphant emergence of an angry and sociopathic personality.

She would never forget how she'd felt when the article by Bloody Ann Dickenson came out. First she'd studied the accompanying photographs, smiling at Nick's image from a happier time, approving of the picture of herself further along in the piece. She'd had her hair freshly permed so she'd look like the respectable mother she was. Her smile dimmed when she came to a picture of the dead riffraff looking innocent and fresh at her high school graduation, and became a frown of anger when she saw they'd included Nick's mug shot. So unfair. He appeared to be sneering in defiance, when probably he'd been frightened out of his wits. Anybody knew that a man looked nothing like his mug shot, so why include it?

Her displeasure at the photos was as nothing compared to the outrage she felt when she read the article. Bloody Ann Dickenson, using some conjurer's trick of her damnable trade, made Dot look a fool. She never said it, never wrote "Nick's mother is a fool," but she didn't have to. It was there for anyone to see, or read, and Dot had wanted to rip the article into tiny shreds, or burn it to death, but something told her it must be saved. It might come in handy for Nick's appeal, to show he'd been unfairly tried by the press as well as the courts. She'd put it away in a closet in her old house, and it had remained deep in closets wherever she moved. She had never looked at the thing again.

The trouble was, she didn't have to look at it to experience the humiliation and anger, because she knew it almost by heart. For example, "Nick's mother maintains that he was always a handful. 'He was always a high-spirited boy, up to all sorts of pranks,' she says fondly. 'But he never harmed anyone. That's why I believe in his innocence.'" That had followed a description of the hitchhiker's body when it had been discovered in that ditch in Chehalis. Or, "Confronted with impeccable forensic evidence linking her son to the crime, Nick's mother says science is an imperfect method for determining guilt or innocence. 'A mother always knows the truth about her child,' she said."

Nothing wrong with those statements, on their own, but to make real sense they ought to have reported everything she'd said. Where was the story about the time Nick had been accused of blacking Glenn Geiger's eye when they were in the fourth grade, only to have it come out that Glenn had been punched by a sixth-grade girl when he made a rude remark about her underpants? A boy with the reputation of a bully always got accused of everything, and it simply was not fair.

She remembered the long letter she had composed to Ann Dickenson, charging her with libel, with the more terrible crime of deepening the pain of a mother whose son had been taken from her and locked up. The reply had stunned her with its arrogance.

I am so sorry you did not like the piece, Bloody Ann had written in return. *I tried to be fair to all sides in this most painful matter.* She'd made no mention of Dot's threats of a libel suit, which was just as well, since Dot was so far in debt to Nick's lawyer any further litigation, aside from the automatic appeal, was unthinkable. If Wayne hadn't come along . . . She arched her neck against the pillows and called for him, wanting to thank him now, before it was too late. She hated the sound of her diminished voice as it wailed for him, but she needed to let him know how grateful she had always been for his support.

"Here I am," he said brightly, but his appearance was anything but bright. She was shocked at his pallor, at the unclean look of his hair. There was something she had meant to tell him, but what?

She nearly asked him if he had returned the whale to the hotel, but her guardian angel told her she had had this conversation many times before. It was like that. Occasionally some informing spirit, some vestige of her old self, appeared to set things straight. What had she?— Oh. The image of the article, deep within a closet off the kitchen, burned its way into her consciousness. It must not survive her, to be read by Wayne or anyone else.

"Get rid of it," she said.

"What? Get rid of what?"

"The article."

"What article, Dot?"

She was about to try to tell him when her guardian angel warned her. She'd been very lucky that no one on the Peninsula read the Seattle paper. They read the local paper, and on Sundays some of them got the *Astorian*. To all her neighbors, the ones who knew about the article and anxiously queried her, she said it had been canceled. "Could prejudice the appeal," she told them. "Maybe later on."

She was no more anxious to have Wayne see her as a fool than she had been for her neighbors to do so. Wayne must never read the article by Bloody Ann, who had long since moved from the area to a job on the *Chicago Tribune*.

"What article, dear?" Wayne was bending forward in distress, really wanting to know, and she could smell fear and uncertainty.

"Never mind," she said. "My mind wanders." It was clear to her now. She must do it herself. Her last strenuous act would be the descending of the stairs, the crouching position as she knelt at the kitchen closet and unearthed the old Sunday supplement of the *Intelligencer*.

Just as she had wanted to do when the article first appeared, she would, at last, rip it into tiny shreds or burn it to death.

It was the last act she could perform for her son, and for herself.

Dorrie studied the items a logger from over in South Bend had sent her to put up in Luby's. They were Campbell's soup tins, she guessed, originally, but someone had peeled off the labels and substituted white paper marked with black felt pen lettering. One said "Cream of Spotted Owl," and the other—surprise—"Spotted Owl Noodle."

She set them up on the bar, and added a few cans of real soup to make a little display. It wasn't too original, but Luby would appreciate it. The logger had included a note in which he proclaimed that good folks on the Peninsula ought to "show solidarity" with the loggers to the east. Well, what was that supposed to mean? What was *he* prepared to do to make sure the oyster beds were unharmed? Could you be dead against one ecological cause and stand behind another? Of course you could. It all came down to money. Oystermen could champion clean water and oysters, both, because they went together, but there was no way you could cut timber and also hold out for the abode of the spotted owl.

Tonight was one of those times when a modest crowd would have cheered her. She was feeling a little, well, *down,* and lots of customers would have been a distraction. True to form, though, on the night when her spirits most needed lifting, Luby's was dead as the spotted owl jokes were getting to be.

She ran her hands over her crisp hair, thinking that soon it would be time to get a new perm. Kath wanted her to try something called a "relaxed wave," but to Dorrie that sounded like a technique used for Negros. Not that she had anything against them, no, she made friends with several Negro women in Portland and came to know their families, too. She also had a lot of time for Indians—the sober ones. She just didn't see what a relaxed wave could do for a white woman, since her hair was relaxed enough already and it was on account of this fact she got it permed. Anyway, Wayne wasn't available, and she didn't trust anyone else.

The vast interior of Luby's was uninhabited tonight, and only one customer sat at the bar. He was an old man—Bob Ludder's uncle Raymond—and he rarely spoke. As a girl she'd known Ray Ludder as something of a wild one, a fisherman who worked out of Ilwaco, a man who had lost three toes to frostbite in the Korean War. Now he was just an old, seven-toed man who came into Luby's every night and kept to himself, drinking beer augmented with something he regularly poured in from a flask kept in his breast pocket. She didn't want to know what Ray spiked his drinks with and always averted her eyes whenever the flask came out. It was illegal, but she wasn't about to say anything.

Farther down the Peninsula, she knew, the taverns would be packed with Kite Festival enthusiasts. They would be crowding the taprooms in Long Beach, playing shovelboard and pool to rhythms dictated by pulsing jukeboxes, while she was stuck, like a permanent feature at Luby's, minding one customer.

It was what she wanted, what she still thought she wanted, but on this particular night in late summer, it didn't seem enough. She was rapidly going from feeling a little down to a major depression, and that was a bleak place she did not choose to inhabit. She thought of remedies, available to her when she'd locked up and gone home. A glass of brandy, but only one, sipped slowly while she lounged in a hot bath and got sleepy, followed by a little soft music on her bedside radio while she could feel her body unknotting, bit by bit.

She had the place ready for closing when Ray slid his glass down the bar in her direction, rose from his stool, nodding dreamily, and left. She washed the glass and put it up on the shelf, locked the cash register, and pocketed the dollar he had left for a tip. She doused the lights, both in and out, and walked back to the kitchen to get her jacket and handbag. She was in the act of writing a note to Luby to tell him they were nearly out of cooking oil when the man himself came through the back door.

At first all she heard was heavy footfalls and heavy breathing, and she felt unreasonably afraid. In the dim light she was confused and thought some intruder had found his way into Luby's kitchen, but the familiarity of the heavy breathing telegraphed his identity before she saw him clearly. Luby had asthma, a condition he did not take seriously.

"Luby," she said in her flat voice. "You took me by surprise."

"Who were you expecting?" Luby said, slinging the cardboard carton he carried on one shoulder to the counter. "I've been driving around all day with this stuff."

The carton contained a drum of cooking oil, four six-packs of toilet paper, a large canister of baby powder for the shovelboard table, and a box of cue chalks for the pool table.

He was a small, round man with a surprisingly delicate face mounted on a neck ringed with turkey wattles. He withdrew the last item from the carton with an air of glee. "You might like to see this," he said. "Guy in Astoria came up to me and said I might like to put it up."

Dorrie looked at the can of Cream of Spotted Owl and felt her sinking spirits sink further.

"You don't look so good," Luby said. "What's wrong?"

"Just one of those days," Dorrie said.

But Luby wasn't a man who coasted through life on platitudes. She should have remembered.

He took a seat, got serious. "What days?" he asked earnestly. "Do you mean some secret female's thing?"

"Lord, no," Said Dorrie. "I'm beyond all that." For safety, she rapped her knuckles three times against the Formica table where she'd been taken by surprise.

"Well, dammit, what then?" His small but piercing blue eyes narrowed, zeroing in on her like movie cameras.

Dorrie gave herself up to the luxury of confessing all to a superior force. "Something's not right," she began. "Something bad is happening here, and I don't know what it could be. I've asked myself over and over, and I can't come up with the right answer. It bothers me, because I was born here."

Without taking his eyes from her Luby asked, "You want a drink?"

"I don't think so, unless you have any brandy hidden away."

"So, brandy's your poison? Known you all this time and didn't even suspect."

"It's not my poison, Luby, godsake. It's just sometimes nice to have one at the end of the day." Too late, she saw that he'd been joking. Her indignant response was an indicator of her low spirits.

Luby lit a cigarette. He'd had to cut way back, with his asthma, but he never went anywhere without his pack of butts in one pocket and his Primatene inhaler in the other. "Are you referring to those drug labs, Dorrie? Because if you are, hell, they'll be gone and away to Idaho before the end of the year."

She gave him a weak smile. Like everyone else around here, it would never occur to him that she could be referring to the death at the old hotel. The girl hadn't been one of their own, so it was just like something you read about in the papers—remote, even though it happened right in the community's backyard, on the bay.

"There was a fellow in here a week or so ago, and not for the first time either. But basically a stranger, probably from Oregon." Luby flicked ash into the carton he'd brought in. "Lindy Engels told me he was trying to peddle the stuff, came up to her by the jukebox and said he had drugs. Not a young man. She pointed him out to me in Long Beach one day, and I went over and told him who I was. Said he wasn't welcome here. Not ever. He took my point."

Dorrie had an abrupt memory. She saw the McAuley woman over by the jukebox, and the way this creep in a jokey T-shirt was circling round her like a shark. He'd never been back, and she'd bet he was the one. She decided to mention it to Luby, to see if mention of someone connected to the Grey Whale would prompt him to allude to what had happened there.

"I'm sorry to hear that," he said. "Leaves a bad impression. Still, she'd be used to it, living in New York. I imagine that one can handle herself."

"The other one couldn't," Dorrie said, surprised at how angry she sounded. "The other one got herself killed."

It seemed she had managed to surprise him. Luby squinted at her through his smoke, incredulous. "Is *that* what's bothering you?" he said, as if being bothered by a murder in the hotel was on the order of sulking over a paper cut. "Everyone agreed it was an accident. Bob Ludder himself said it was just one of those tragic accidents."

"I believe I will take a drink after all." She wondered what he would offer her, and was surprised when he opened the fridge freezer, reached around behind mounds of frozen peas and carrots, and brought forth a bottle of Finnish vodka. She'd seen it advertised. Apparently it was such a high proof it could survive in a freezer without actually freezing.

"That may be too much for me," she said, but Luby poured a small amount of the vodka into a coffee cup stenciled with the words NOR-

WEGIANS ARE NICER and placed it before her. "It's just as good as brandy," he said. "If you want, I can mix it with juice, but try it."

Dorrie sipped. It had a pleasant, peppery taste, and once she had swallowed it the vodka had an instant warming effect. It swam through her bloodstream until it reached the tips of her fingers and toes, and made her feel as if she and Luby were sitting in front of a crackling wood fire. She tried another sip.

"You don't believe that business at the hotel was an accident," she found herself saying, "any more than Bob Ludder does. It was just a convenient thing to say."

"Maybe," said Luby. "What's so wrong about doing the convenient thing?" He poured himself a shot of Finnish vodka and extinguished his cigarette at the tap. His pale eyes wore an expression of genuine bewilderment. "It saves a lot of good people from grief, Dorrie. It spares them. Bob wanted to spare us all from bad publicity and endless trouble."

"It's not right," she said.

"Didn't we have enough of that when Dot's son went to Walla Walla?"

"We did, but it died down eventually. And it was better than letting Nick go free."

Luby nodded, giving her the point. "True," he said, "of course that's true, but this case is different. There would have been no stopping Nick. This person won't ever kill again."

Dorrie was so shocked by his tone of authority she took a larger sip of vodka than she'd intended. "You'd better explain that one," she said. "You talk like you know who the killer is."

Luby wandered over to the fridge and opened it, searching for something, or maybe just delaying his response. After a while he extracted a bottle of sweet bread-and-butter pickles. He unscrewed it and offered the bottle to Dorrie. When she shook her head he brought the pickles to the table and sat down, fishing with his fingers.

"You see," he said, munching, "if I know who the killer is it isn't on account of I know something you don't. It's something I can feel in my bones. I arrive at this person by a process of elimination."

Although it was cold in the kitchen, she felt a kind of prickling heat pass over her scalp. For one horrid instant she thought he was going to dip a pickle in his vodka, but it was only a cross-purpose his body arrived at while his mind was otherwise occupied.

"It's like this," he said. "I sat down and asked myself who could do such a thing. You ask yourself the same, Dorrie. We're born and bred here. Who of all these people we've always known, or known for a long time in some cases, would be capable of murdering a little gal from the East because she was going to open the old hotel, maybe stir things up? Stir them up in a way some folks might not appreciate?" He gave her a stern, inquiring look. When she didn't answer he smiled.

"See? When it comes to it, it's hard to think of anyone. Most crimes round here are on the nature of a barroom brawl. Or there's domestic violence."

"You mean Bob Ludder beats his wife," she said flatly.

"Maybe," said Luby, but he sounded uncomfortable. Bob was a good customer.

"No maybe about it, unless that poor woman walks into a door two or three times a week."

"Be that as it may—what kind of person commits the kind of crime we're looking at here? A drunk? A wife beater? Remember"—another pickle came out of the jar—"this was a cold-blooded crime, carried out in broad daylight, at an open house where there was no booze, except for the hostess and her friends."

Dorrie thought of another kind of person who could commit irrational and violent acts. It was a young person who took frightening drugs, the kind that could persuade a pacific personality to turn murderous all in a second of paranoia. Even as she was mentioning this possibility to Luby, she thought of Martin Best. Martin went in only for grass, as far as she knew, but there were rumors that he had been seen in the company of suspicious strangers, the harbingers of death from farther down the coast. The ones who were going to usher in the new Ice Age.

"There was only Martin," Luby said, "and Teddy Vine told me Martin was smoking pot with him in the shed. Martin never even went in the hotel the whole afternoon, between parking the cars and toking with Teddy."

"Well *who* then?" Her voice was impatient. She wanted Luby to leave off his old philosopher pose and deliver a satisfying theory, but the man was not to be budged before his time.

"Okay," he said. "I take it you agree with me that none of us locals is a real murderer. The last one in these parts was Nick, and he's safely locked up. Now who—think hard—is usually the first suspect when a married woman gets herself killed?"

"The husband," said Dorrie. "But why—?"

"Word gets around, you know. A man hears things. I could have told you months ago that Jack wasn't thrilled about buying the Grey Whale. It was all her idea."

"But a man doesn't murder his wife because she has a crazy impulse," Dorrie said. "Not in *their* world."

"That's where it gets interesting, Dorrie. Their world is a different one from what we know. There's money in it, lots of money, and a man could do worse than kill his wife in the sticks, no questions asked, and wait for the profit to come to him. Tragic accident out West, and who's the winner?"

She felt as if they'd been playing a board game, and Luby had rolled the dice and accumulated an easy win. It didn't feel right. Some final move had yet to be played.

"He was in plain view the whole time," she said. "I saw him, out on the lawn."

Luby ate the last of his pickles, washing it down with a huge gulp of vodka. He sat motionless, as if waiting for the combination of tastes to stabilize him, and then he leaned forward. "I don't claim to have all the answers," he said. "I told you what I believe; it's where the truth is, even if I can't prove it. Go figure it out."

They parted without another word. She left him in the kitchen and wearily made her way to her car, the unaccustomed grain alcohol investing her with artificial warmth.

Once home, she forgot her earlier plans for brandy and a hot bath, and sat on the edge of her bed, too tired to change into her nightgown, and too charged to lie down fully clothed. She didn't hear the sound of the ocean any more than she consciously heard the sound of her own blood shunting through the chambers of her heart, but Luby and his mad theories had taken total control.

Time after time she saw Jack on the lawn and tried to make some sense of what Luby had said. If a man wanted to kill his wife and make it look like an accident, if he wasn't prepared to do the actual murder himself, how would he plan it? Another party would be required, someone who would steal up and strike the fatal blow while the man himself remained, in full view of all his guests, entertaining the very people who distrusted him.

Laura McAuley hadn't been in evidence during the fatal time, but she couldn't see Laura as a murderess. That left Jesse Paget, who was, after all, an outsider, an unknown equation.

Who better than Jesse, if you really thought about it? He had been hired as caretaker, presumably by Jack and Claudia, but what were his credentials?

She had a terrible image of Jack and Jesse, having a drink in Seattle.

You're the caretaker, Jack was saying. *Take care of it.*

TWELVE

Althea dropped by the next morning, insisting that Laura drive with her to Long Beach to see the exhibition kites. They were the largest and most colorful, and it was a sight not to be missed. Dutifully, Laura packed her camera in her large bag and climbed into the pickup. She honestly wanted to see the exhibition kites—why, then, did it feel like a kind of unwelcome duty?

She supposed it had to do with not trusting anyone. Just when she'd decided this person or that was a potential friend, something would happen to make her doubt her judgment. Just as Althea had avoided her at one time, now Grace Best was acting as if Laura did not exist. Only yesterday she'd gone for the mail, and when she'd spoken to Grace, the postmistress had turned on her a look of such gloom she'd wanted to run out of the place. She wanted to ask Althea if anything was troubling Grace, but how could she describe Grace's behavior without also describing the manner Althea had manifested only days before?

"You're quiet today," Althea said as they drove down the little strip of Ocean Park.

"Sorry." She saw Dorrie Geiger standing in front of Luby's and waved, but Dorrie, too, looked solemn and troubled as she lifted her hand.

"It's no wonder, really," said Althea. "Here you come to Washington for a vacation and all hell breaks loose." She slanted a look at her passenger, and Laura felt there was something too hearty and determined in Althea's concern.

"All hell is probably breaking loose back in New York," she said. "It's a different sort of hell, though, and I'm not there to witness it." She knew she was being uncooperative, but didn't seem to care much.

"Cities," said Althea, "are always hell. We're usually pretty peaceful here."

"Maybe," said Laura, "it's because you refuse to acknowledge reality."

Althea gnawed her lower lip. Presently she said, "That's not fair. Most of us do." The pickup had left Ocean Park behind and was racing down the straight road between towering pines. It was another glorious day, belying the myth of constant rain in the Pacific Northwest. The sun beat down on the truck's white hood, the sky was the blue of a travel agent's dreams, and there was just enough sea breeze to lift the kites heavenward.

"I'm going to tell you something ugly," Althea said. "Are you ready?"

"Ready," Laura said, with a tough little smile that wasn't really *her*. She gripped the handles of her bag so tightly they twisted into a knot, cutting off the circulation in her fingers.

"Grace sent her son, Martin, off to Bainbridge Island for the rest of the summer. She has a sister living there, Martin's aunt."

Laura didn't reply. Was it Martin Best, then, who had caused Claudia's death? Her bag unwound its way from her fingers and dropped to the floor. The fact that it was Grace who had discovered Claudia's body took on a terrible significance. But Martin had been, like Jack, outside the hotel when—

"Laura! You look as if you've seen a ghost!" Althea was snatching glances at her and came perilously close to drifting into the oncoming lane. "You didn't think I meant that Martin—?" Althea laughed. "Oh, no, not *that*. Poor Grace has enough on her mind without being the second Peninsula mom who raised a murderer. No, Martin was hanging out with some bad types. It was Bob Ludder who finally warned her. Seems he stopped a van in the cranberry bogs one night and Martin was one of the passengers."

"Drug people?" Laura asked.

Althea nodded. "Scouts for likely locations, isolated spots where they could get an ice lab going. Martin's not a bad kid, really, just bored and a little confused since his father died. Bob told Grace he didn't think Martin appreciated how dangerous those men could be."

A break in the trees revealed a sudden view of the sea, and far off on the horizon they could now see kites, specks in the sky above Long Beach. The tension had fallen away, and Laura permitted herself to relax. The story was a familiar one: a mother sends her son away from potential danger, preferably to a wholesome place where he can be guarded by a loving relative. That drugs entered into the picture only made it more familiar. She was glad Martin had been removed from the clutches of the scouts, and surprised that Bob Ludder had had the decency to warn Grace. But then, she reflected, the Bests were local, one of the Peninsula's own.

"The ugly thing," Althea was saying, "is what Martin told his mother before he went away. He asked you to forgive him, said he did it before he met you."

"Forgive him? For what?" Althea was glancing over again, and since they were nearing the outer limits of Long Beach and its steady stream of traffic, she said, "Do watch the road."

"*Do* watch the road," Althea parroted. "I swear, Laura, you're lucky I can see you're a nice person beneath it all. You're the most uptight, citified woman it's ever been my pleasure to meet."

"Sorry," said Laura for the second time that morning. The kites were getting bigger now. They had almost taken on individual shapes. They drove on in an aggrieved silence, until Althea relented.

"It was that yearling," she said as they approached the first cluster of chain-saw sculptures. "Martin rowed it over in that old boat at the bottom of Teddy and Fran's garden. I'm surprised it took the weight, frankly. He was high when he did it, seemed like a good joke at the time."

"What was the punch line?"

"You have to understand that Martin looked on the opening of the hotel as the death of the oysters in the bay. He thought you were all part and parcel of a syndrome that would destroy his mother's way of life. He *hated* the oysters. He hated going out on the flats on cold mornings, but what he hated even more was his mother going out when he couldn't. The most classic guilt trip, Laura. Martin always planned to escape. The oysters were his mom's future, do you see?"

"I'm afraid not. Not quite. Run it by me once again." She sat motionless, watching the kites become larger, almost recognizable as kites, and listened while Althea explained. Martin truly believed the propaganda Ralph Henderson had been spreading about. He believed the oyster industry on the Peninsula would be ruined if the hotel opened, and it followed that his mother would have no income and he would have to stay and take care of her forever. He was at an age where the need to get away and see a bit of the world was so great he had experienced it as an almost physical pain. The yearling, almost certainly shot by Henderson on one of his "target practice" sprees, had provided him with an opportunity to warn the Easterners off; with childish enthusiasm, stoked by the marijuana he'd been smoking and the many bad movies he'd watched, he dumped the creature at the hotel's front door while the inhabitants were gathered at the back.

"I never thought anyone would get killed." Those were the words he had spoken to his mother when she'd confronted him about the drug scouts.

"For a while he believed everything would turn out fine, that no one would want to run a hotel there after what happened to Claudia." Althea made a curiously dismissive gesture, fluttering her fingers against the steering wheel. "But, have you noticed, nothing stays fine for long? Pretty soon these heavy dudes appear and start trying to make friends with him. Poor Martin was in over his head before he even realized it."

Laura was aware that she seemed cold, even hostile, but she could find nothing to say. Each new revelation seemed to anchor her in silence. How intricate, how impossibly *connected* life was here. The texture of life on the Peninsula was like a fine but very old, moldering tapestry, full of knots. Push one knot back in and it disturbed the balance and another knot appeared somewhere else. No wonder the postmistress hadn't been able to meet her eyes!

By the time Althea was maneuvering into a parking place on the strip in Long Beach, she roused herself to ask a question. "Do you think Martin will be all right?"

"Who knows?" Althea grimaced as she turned the steering wheel. "I swear," she muttered, "this truck hasn't been the same since Jesse borrowed it."

They walked up the packed pavement toward the access to the beach. Each shop was festooned with lively wind socks and posters for the festival. Someone had put a garland of flowers around the sturdy neck of the chain-saw mermaid sculpture. Music poured from the doors of taverns and everywhere came the shrilling voices of children. Laura remembered the child who had fallen from the mermaid's lap and hoped she was having a fine time today. It all felt unreal to her, and always, at the periphery of her vision, the kites hovered in the air. There were so many of them, and she resolved not to look at them until she and Althea were on the sands. There was something unsettling about so many people who were prepared to travel to the ends of the earth to launch frail scraps of silk and canvas in capricious air-streams over the Pacific Ocean. The fact that the ocean could not be seen from the thoroughfare made it even more peculiar. What if it weren't there? You had to take it on faith that the sea lay somewhere beyond Jo's Pacific Tavern, Jackson's Shell and Curio Shop, and the Dog Salmon Restaurant.

"Left here," said Althea, turning onto a swarming path that led to a huge archway.

Laura kept her eyes down, following. The sun was hot on her shoulders, and from somewhere close by she heard a voice shout, "OH, LOOK AT THE ALLIGATOR!"

She looked up, although the cry had not been addressed to her, and saw a huge green crocodile in the sky above them. It swooped about on the sea breezes, its open jaws revealing fearsome lines of teeth. Many people had chosen patriotism as their theme, and she couldn't count the star-spangled banners of different sizes. There were fish kites and dragon kites and butterfly kites. The people seemed a good-natured lot, although a few children, manipulating smaller kites, looked grim with the strain of performing.

"This is quite mad," she said, and Althea grinned at her.

"I told you you'd like it," she said.

They perched on a dune, where they could look down on the people and up at the kites. "That wouldn't be a spotted owl?" Laura asked, pointing at a whimsical bird far out over the modest, silvery waves.

"Afraid so. It's good the owl isn't a fighter kite, because someone would be sure to cut it down. The fighter kite owners are forever being tossed out of the competitions for attaching razors to their lines."

Laura wondered if a coffee-table book on spectacular kites might go over at Crowther and Hull, but she decided it had been done before. There was something wonderfully restful about sheltering in a dune and watching unnatural objects in the sky above the Pacific. Except for the automatic patriotic reflex of the people who had chosen the American flag motif, the kites were original and endearing, works of art. She was pleased to be watching the exhibition kites, and had no desire to see the fighters, with the deadly razor blades designed to cut their opponents down. She thrust Martin Best and his problems from her mind. She had already forgiven him for his grotesque action, if only because his desperation to get away from the insular world in which he'd been raised reminded her so poignantly of a similar—and equally desperate—desire felt long ago by Claudia.

"Don't look to the left," Althea was saying. "There's a big salmon kite going up. It might give you indigestion."

She was laughing when a shadow covered their little patch of sunlight. Soundlessly, someone had come up behind them and was even now kneeling down, joining them without their permission. She turned to see who the intruder might be, but before she could see him Althea said, "Hello, Jesse. I didn't see you at the hotel or I'd have asked you to come with us."

"I was just finishing up with the oysters," he said. "It was so still on the flats I could hear you drive up."

Laura noticed that he was still wearing the caked Wellington boots he normally drew off the moment he came to the hotel's back door. "How did you get here?" she asked.

"Hitched," he said. "Everything all right, Laura?"

"Why shouldn't it be?" she said. It was an inappropriate answer, and she knew it. Events had conspired to show any rational person that at any given time things were not likely to be all right. Nevertheless, his question puzzled her. He had asked her as a minder might ask an invalid—Wayne and Dot sprang to mind—and she wondered why. She also wondered if she could tell him the mystery of the yearling on the doorstep had been solved, but she thought Althea had spoken to her in confidence. Still, in such a closed community everybody was bound to know about Martin's banishment to Bainbridge Island before the day was out.

"Which kite do you vote for?" she said, more to break the atmosphere than anything else.

Jesse scanned the horizon, his dark eyes quickening, and she saw him on the bridge of a trawler in the Aleutian Islands. After a prolonged survey, he raised an arm and pointed. "That one," he said. "The kite that's just coming into view from behind the monarch butterfly."

She followed the trajectory of his arm, located the orange and black of the monarch, and saw the kite behind it sailing luminously up into the air. It was a diamond-shaped kite, blue-black in color, with a mysterious burst of light that streaked from the source and plunged downward. It was much less decorative than many of the others, but it possessed a kind of power that disturbed her.

"It's a comet," said Althea.

"Why that one, in particular?" said Laura.

"It's an omen," Jesse said. "Tonight is the night of the Perseids. It's the prime time for seeing shooting stars. The night of the shooting stars." He sounded mournful, and Laura found herself crossing her arms as if a chill had seized her. Only Jesse could make the words "night of the shooting stars" seem ominous instead of uplifting and beautiful.

"What I think," she said, "is that you all just wait until I've turned my back and then yell out 'Oh, there's one!' It's a conspiracy."

"Oh, Laura, no." Jesse looked concerned for her. Even Althea seemed concerned. Realizing how childish she had sounded, Laura wanted to laugh, but something in their tender protection of her sensibilities pleased her. "Come on," she said, "let me take you both to lunch at that fancy-looking inn down the coast. Then we can come back and watch the kites."

"I'll pay my own way," said Althea, looking prickly.

"Afraid I can't," said Jesse.

"Can't have lunch?"

"Can't pay."

"I *said* I'd pay. I want to treat you both. It would give me pleasure."

"In that case," said Jesse, "I accept."

"You only want to go there because it's the only Eastern-looking place for miles around, could have been plucked from New England," said Althea shrewdly. "It's very Ye Oldie."

In that instant, Laura felt she loved them both very much.

The night of the Perseids had finally arrived. Standing on the lawn, a wineglass in each of their hands, Jesse and Laura observed the night skies as they had done on her first evening at the Grey Whale. It seemed a lifetime ago, yet less than ten days had passed.

The night was clear and incandescent from the unusual clarity of the stars and the glow of the Milky Way, and Laura felt a deep sense of well-being. It had been her best day on the Peninsula—the kites, the sumptuous lunch at Ye Oldie, followed by more kites and a long walk along the beach, had exhausted her in a nice way. And there had been more. At some point a man she understood to be Althea's gentleman friend had joined up with them. It was, she thought sheepishly, rather like a double date. She and Jesse, Althea and Michael, had resolved to play every silly game at every tavern between Long Beach and Ocean Park.

She and Jesse had beaten their opponents at pool, but been bested at shovelboard. She had amazed herself by scoring highest in a barroom basketball game, and then it was back to pool. They'd ended up at Luby's, playing obscene songs on the jukebox and laughing at the slightest provocation. The men and Althea had drunk only beer, and Althea often ordered Coke instead. Laura had left many tumblers of wine half full, and if she felt drunk now it was more the exhilarating high brought on by vast amounts of salt air and movement.

It was cold, and it occurred to her that she might go in the hotel and get a sweater, or one of the old jackets in the mac room, but she didn't mind being cold. She told herself it would be many months, back in New York, before she ever found herself cold from natural causes, and relished the oddity of it.

"There!" cried Jesse, and Laura saw it this time. A star burned extra brightly, like a light bulb about to give out for good, and then fell in a swift arc. If she had been a child, unaware of the incomprehensibly immense nature of the universe, she might have plotted the dying star's trajectory and announced that it had plunged to earth near the cannery. In some way, the kites had been the curtain raiser for the stars. Brave, man-made kites. How very personally their owners, their makers, would take it if a kite plummeted to the sands, or into the sea. She could picture the distressed faces of the people at the other end of the string, especially if one of them happened to be a child. The child would, no doubt, mourn the death of the kite the same way people mourned the death of pets. So much had gone into their maintenance, so much invested in their futures! There was no one to grieve over the death of a star but God, and since she didn't believe in Him, she was forced to nominate herself and Jesse as chief mourners at a celestial wake.

"Oh, god," she sighed, and immediately the sky quickened in its brightness and a small company of stars slid off to oblivion. One of them streaked across the sky like a comet, leaving a quavering trail of its fall to earth. She held her breath until the trail vanished, and then expelled it in a little gasp of wonder.

"That was the finale," she told him. "A wise woman would go to bed now."

He nodded solemnly, and she could see he, too, had been moved by the light show. She turned to go back inside, but an impulse made her shake his hand, as if he had been the producer, and she the gratified customer.

"Good night, Jesse," she said, and he returned the pressure of her hand, smiling.

She went straight upstairs, removed her clothing, and fell into bed. She didn't do any of the small things she'd normally do before going to bed, not even brush her teeth, because she didn't want to break the spell the stars had cast on her; she thought perhaps she might dream of them if only she could pass from this strange and wonderful state into sleep.

Soon she was wandering down a long, sandy path, in full sunlight.

It was the path in the sanctuary at the tip of the Peninsula, but this time she moved with supreme ease—even though she was wearing high heels—almost as if she were on a conveyer belt. The bushes and trees moved by, faster and faster, and occasionally she could glimpse deer in them. The deer regarded her benevolently, she thought, and she wanted to stop and pet them. The trouble was that she couldn't seem to move in any direction but forward. She couldn't, she found, stop moving.

She was gliding uphill, and beginning to panic a little, because she could glimpse the blue band of the sea ahead. It was still some distance away, but if she couldn't stop her progress she would eventually be propelled right into the Pacific. There must be some way to find the controls, a button she could push, or some words she could utter. Even if she could learn to go backward, away from the sea, she'd be safer. She had just reached the top of the hill and was beginning her descent when she saw a man with an ax chopping away at one of the pines. The ax was over his shoulder, and now he brought it forward and cleaved into the tree, but there was no sound. She had glided past him, picking up speed again, when she heard a sharp, cracking report and understood the tree had fallen.

She woke in a state of dread, not understanding she was awake for a moment. She connected the dark with the falling of the tree, and thought she was dead, or buried under the sea. When she realized she was in her bed at the hotel she sat up, remembering from childhood that it was all too easy to slip back into the same nightmare if you simply lay there.

It was perfectly silent and peaceful. She couldn't even hear the murmur of the sea. Between the curtains at her window she saw the dark sky, feebly lit by starlight now as if the great light show had never taken place. When she was sure she wasn't likely to reenter sleep for a bit, she eased back down and asked herself what it was that made her uncomfortable.

She remembered the actual day on the path of the nature preserve, and how her ankles had ached in the sand until she took her shoes off. She'd been afraid then, too, and her fear had been shaped by the same unreal factors as her nightmare. The jumping of the little boy, which she'd mistaken for a bear crashing through the underbrush, the woman slapping at mosquitoes whom she'd mistaken for an assassin . . . The only thing she hadn't imagined was the mad haste someone had used in driving away from the preserve. Why would someone drive off so frantically? Nobody drove like that except for teenagers, and the people who hiked along the sandy trails were not, as a rule, the people who experienced power by driving eighty miles an hour up a bumpy dirt track. The only reason for making such a dramatic getaway was that the driver didn't want to be seen anywhere near the sanctuary.

This truck hasn't been the same since Jesse borrowed it, she heard Althea say.

She bounded from the bed and into the bathroom, locking the door that connected it with bedroom number two. That blocked the way from the hotel's front, but what was she to do about her own door? There were locks on the bathroom doors only. She was searching for something which could serve as a weapon when reality returned. She was behaving irrationally because of a bad dream. She, Laura McAuley, was preparing to defend herself against—what?

She shivered, became aware that she was naked, and pulled her nightgown on. Over it she pulled a sweater, and drew her socks over her feet. Her eyes never left the door. When she'd clothed herself as well as she could, she sat at the foot of her bed, alert. She needed to make sure that her night panic was unfounded before she could slip between the covers and try for sleep again. Her breath, which had accelerated with her fear, filled the room. She told herself to breathe deeply and evenly, and eventually the rasping sound went away and it was as quiet as a tomb.

Again there came a loud, cracking sound, as if someone had bumped into one of the chairs in the dining room and sent it to the floor. It was the noise she had heard in her dream, probably the noise which had wakened her in the first place. It was followed by the loud complaint of violently breaking glass.

Someone was in the hotel, on the lower floor. It could not be Jesse, the silent tracker. Someone clumsy and unused to wandering about in the night had broken in. The unwanted visitor was groping his way toward the staircase. He wanted to inspect the bedrooms, one by one, until he located the one where Laura lay, unsuspecting in her sleep, to do the same to her as he had done to Claudia. He had it in mind that she would pass from sleep to death quite peacefully. The poor, fragile head crushed against the pillow.

Her only chance was Jesse. Insane to wait in her bedroom like a sitting duck. If she could only make her way to the quarters where Jesse slept, there was a chance she might save her life.

She unlocked the bathroom door and found herself in bedroom number three. From that room she crept to the landing, trying to gauge the position of the killer. Was he on the stairs? Was he even now up here with her, doing a workmanlike check of each room? She opened the door of number five and peered out at the landing. Nothing. She ran past the next rooms and found herself at the linen closet. She hurtled into the men's room, hoping for a lock, but found that it had long since worn away. The killer, it seemed, was waiting below, aware of the noises he had made. He wanted her to go to sleep, feeling secure in the silence he was now perpetrating. Where was he hiding, she wondered? Had he hunkered down in the larder, waiting for a false sense of security to seduce her? Was he crouched among the macs and boots in the other room?

She had never known that fear could produce a sensation of nausea. The idea of creeping down the stairs in the dark was horrible, but there was no other way to get to Jesse. She prayed that he, too, had been wakened by the noise, but he was likely to be a sound sleeper. At the head of the stairs she braced herself, curling her toes hard against the carpet. It wasn't so dark that she would collide with him on the stairs—something she'd considered with revulsion. The stairs were empty, and she started down them very slowly. She heard nothing but her own shallow breathing; it was almost unnaturally silent. As she had done on her hike at the point, she told herself she had completed the first lap of her journey when she got to the bottom of the stairs. The second was the dim corridor that led to Jesse's rooms. It was such a short journey, but probably the most important of her life.

She was facing the telephone on the hall table, but it offered no salvation. Who could she call? If it had been a touch-tone she might have silently stabbed out Althea's number, or Grace's, and whispered a plea for help, but it was the old kind of dial. It would take an eternity to dial their numbers, even if she knew them, and the intruder would hear, and make his deadly assault on her.

Right, she told herself, and turned into the hall that would take her to Jesse. She passed the ladies' lavatory to her right, and then the men's, and came to Jesse's door, which was ajar. She was about to push it open when she heard the hinges of a door protest close by. Someone was coming out of the men's room. She ran into Jesse's apartment so violently that she nearly lost her momentum and would have crashed into the opposite wall if strong arms hadn't caught her. She was pinned from behind, awkwardly, because one of her captor's hands carried a hunting knife. She drew air into her lungs so she could scream out Jesse's name, but the hand not carrying the knife clapped itself over her mouth. She struggled, but it was no use, and she felt the raw despair of an animal caught in a trap.

In her terror, she was icy cold, but gradually she became aware of warmth in the region of her right ear. Warmth, and a tickling sensation. Someone's face was pressed against her neck, and the warmth came from his breath as he whispered something in her ear.

"Don't make a sound," he said. "Stay here—you'll be safest here."

He had to repeat his message three times before she understood that the voice in her ear was Jesse's.

THIRTEEN

The intruder was playing a game of cat and mouse with them. Laura had refused to wait in safety and joined Jesse on the flashlit prowl through the hotel. She allowed him to go first, but that was as much as she would concede to his maleness and tracking skills. They were in this together, she told herself. It played over and over in her head, like a maddening tune overheard in a supermarket or on a television commercial: *We're in this together.*

Jesse had already checked out the bathrooms on the ground floor, had been in the act of looking into the men's room when he became

aware of Laura's presence in the chase. Together they had recovered
the flashlight from the room where the macs and boots gave off their
companionable, rubbery aroma. Swinging the flashlight, the two-man
patrol had gone from room to room, switching on lights until the
Grey Whale could be seen to blaze for miles around.

They were deadly silent on their surveillance, alert to the sound of
closing doors or stealthy footfalls. There was no vehicle parked out in
back, so they knew the killer had arrived on foot or by water.

"Could he have sneaked upstairs while we were in the larder?"
Laura whispered.

"No," said Jesse. "From where? We would have seen him."

He seemed so sure of himself, so calm with his deadly hunting
knife. She began to think that the brilliance of the old hotel was more
alarming than the darkness she'd feared earlier. What was she doing,
walking point with an armed man in the middle of the night? What if
the intruder had been Jesse all along, and she was entrusting her life
to a maniac?

In the dining room they discovered a broken wineglass on the
floor. Hers, from last night. She had put it too near the edge of a
table on her way to bed, and their quarry had bumped with some
force into the table. Jesse kicked the shattered glass away to one side
so they would not step on it in their stockinged feet. The fact that he,
too, was hastily dressed was reassuring to her.

They moved out onto the lawn, which felt safer. Dew seeped
through Laura's socks and chilled her feet as she trailed along in the
little moon of Jesse's flashlight. There was an insignificant pain in her
right heel, and when she massaged it she felt the sticky pull of blood.
For all Jesse's care to move the shattered wineglass, she had managed
to cut her foot on the oyster shell path.

"I've cut my foot!" she wailed. The anguish in her voice had more
to do with her fear than any minor injury, but she seemed to hear an
echo from the shed. She cried out again, and again a tormented moan
answered her.

Jesse crouched at the door of the shed in a battle position. He had
thrown the flashlight to her, and she trained it with trembling hands,
but all she could see in the weak beam of light was a bundle of old
clothes. The hand in which Jesse carried his knife described circles,

made jabs and passes, and the bundle of clothes released a sobbing moan of despair.

"Don't hurt me," it said. "I've had more than I can take." The voice was so distorted she couldn't tell if it belonged to a man or a woman. Just as she was convincing herself that the stranger was an old tramp seeking shelter, the flashlight's beam shone on something that glinted. The tramp threw the object on the floor of the shed, and she could see that it was a pair of long, sharp scissors.

"Don't hurt me," the tramp cried again. "I surrender."

Jesse stood back from the door, and when he spoke his voice was soft with surprise. "Come out, Wayne," he said. "I won't hurt you."

Wayne sat at the kitchen table, blinking in the bright light, and shivering violently. He did indeed look like a tramp. His clothes had not been changed for days, his hair was filthy and matted, and the white stubble on his unshaven cheeks made him look like an old man.

"He's in a state of shock," said Jesse. "I'll make you some hot tea, Wayne." While Jesse put the water on to boil, Laura stood at the far end of the kitchen, as far from Wayne Cotton as she could get and remain in the same room. He might be a pitiful sight, but the scissors he'd been carrying had looked lethal when Jesse picked them up. She believed they had been intended for her.

When the tea was ready, Jesse set it before him. Wayne looked into the cup for a time and then, obediently, began to drink it. When he set the cup down his hand was trembling so much that some of the tea slopped over on the table. "She's gone," he said. "Dorothy's gone."

"Dead," Jesse mouthed at her. "I'm sorry," he said. "When did it happen?"

"I found her at midnight," he said. "She shouldn't have been messing with that old closet. It killed her." This seemed as much as he was prepared to say. He finished his tea, weeping, and Jesse made him another cup.

"Why did you come here, Wayne?" Jesse asked.

"In some ways," said Wayne, "it's a mercy she's gone. It's what she wanted."

"Because she was so ill?" Laura ventured.

"Because of what she did," he said. "It was the only fit punishment."

As long as they stuck to the subject of Dot, Wayne seemed capable of answering their questions, but when they asked him what he was doing in the hotel he clamped his lips together and shook his head.

"I only began to suspect when she had her first stroke," he said. "At first I thought it was the stroke or the medication, but in my heart I knew it was the truth."

"What was the truth?" Laura asked.

"That she had to be punished. I hoped the first stroke would be punishment enough, but no, it wasn't enough for what my Dorothy did."

"What did she do?" Laura asked, beginning to feel impatient.

He raised his head and looked into her eyes. "You know," he said. "The worst thing."

Laura held on to a counter for support. She was not sure she wanted him to continue.

"Your friend," he said. "Mrs. Arnold."

"That's not possible," she said in a bright, prim voice. "Dot would never have harmed Claudia. She *liked* her, everybody knew that."

"Oh yes," Wayne said. "That's why she made herself so sick. It was the remorse, the terrible remorse. If she could have given her own life to bring that innocent girl back, she would have." He seized the stiff tufts of his hair and groaned again. "*And* now she's gone and given it anyway."

"If she felt that way about Claudia, why did she kill her?" said Laura.

"She went and got the wrong one," said Wayne. "She thought Mrs. Arnold was you."

"She meant to kill—me?"

"She didn't *mean* to kill anybody," Wayne said, his voice indignant now. "She didn't come to the open house with that intention. But when it came over her the way it did, so sudden, she thought it was you in the linen closet." Wayne folded his hands and looked out the window, where the sky was lightening a bit. "I'm sorry," he said.

It was fully dawn when they were able to piece together the events of that fatal day. By the peach-colored light above the tree line, Laura slumped against the counter and considered what they had learned.

Dot had come to the open house full of goodwill, with a memento to present to Jack and Claudia deep in the folds of her large handbag. Her new glasses were troubling her, the prescription was a bit off, or perhaps it had to do with the onset of her stroke. In the end she simply took them off and saw the day's proceedings through myopic eyes.

She'd been seized by the desire to inspect the upper floor, even though she hated climbing the stairs. She had lived here, after all, and she felt a proprietary interest in the hotel's upkeep. She had approved of the guest soaps in the bathroom, but her main concern was for the contents of the linen closet. Most of the old sheets were so thin a person could put a toe through the linen if he turned over abruptly, and the towels were likewise thin and threadbare. She wanted to see if Claudia had begun the job of restocking. Deep in the dim closet, she'd seen the blond girl appear from one of the bedrooms. The girl walked past the closet, turned, and came back. "Dot?" she had said in her foreign, Eastern voice. "What are you doing in there? Come back and join the party."

She'd come into the closet, tried to take Dot's hand. She was so confident, trying to coax Dot out of the closet. It made her blood boil that one of *them*, that breed of hypocritical women who wrote terrible things about people and ruined their lives, should try to boss her around. She might have been the very reincarnation of the journalist who had ruined Nick's life.

All of the grief and pain she had suffered over the years seemed to wrap around her and make her shake with rage. And when the woman she believed to be Laura suddenly turned and squatted down to examine something on one of the shelves, at that very moment her fingers found the memento deep in her bag. She clutched it for strength, and then, Wayne said, it was out of the bag and before the woman could turn around again it was smashing into her skull under all that bright, golden hair.

She had been sure her nerves would be in a terrible state, but she felt oddly at peace, as if she had helped to right an old wrong. She had replaced the object in her bag, stepped over the body, and returned to the party.

It was crazy, she told Wayne, but those moments after she'd killed the woman she thought was Laura were the happiest she had known in years. She didn't have long to be happy, though, and when she realized she'd killed the wrong woman, she'd fainted. When she came round it was to a living hell that would never end until she died. That was the way Wayne put it. "A living hell," he repeated, and she understood that he, too, had been dwelling in that state. What she could not understand was how he hoped to make things better by plunging scissors into her sleeping body.

Jesse asked the question for her, and Wayne looked astonished. "Oh no you don't," he said. "You can't say that. I never meant to hurt her."

"Those scissors look very sharp," Laura said.

"They're my haircutting scissors," he said. "The ones I keep at home."

"Well, you weren't coming here to cut my hair, were you?"

A ghost of a smile appeared on his face. "People do funny things when they're grieving," he said. "It seemed so sad that Mrs. Arnold got killed and you were right as rain. It was like I could carry out Dot's plan, do that last thing for her. I couldn't hurt a fly, but I thought I might just—" His voice trailed off in embarrassment.

"Cut off her hair while she was sleeping?" Jesse asked.

"Something like that," Wayne said. "People do funny things when they're grieving."

Soon enough Bob Ludder arrived at the back door, surveying the trio in the kitchen with amazement. "You three have had some night," he said. "Found your car half in a ditch just up the road, Wayne. That's why I'm here. You've got to stop leaving it in ditches."

Laura could feel Wayne's terror at the presence of the law. The scissors were lying on a counter near Jesse, and might have been part of the hotel's kitchen equipment. Did one tell a hostile deputy sheriff about Wayne's nighttime activities, or about his dead wife's act of murder? She decided one did not.

"Dorothy's dead," Wayne said to Ludder. "She died last night."

Ludder removed his hat and held it over his heart. "I'm real sorry to hear that, Wayne," he said. "Come on, I'll help you get to your car. Dorothy's death has to be reported."

At her bedroom window she watched the flats where the tide had receded. She and Jesse had sat at the table in the kitchen until the sun rose fully. Neither of them had suggested moving to the living room, where they could view the sunrise from the windows facing east, and in retrospect she was glad. How frivolous it would have been.

They sat in exhausted silence. Every once in a while she would rouse herself to ask him a question, and he would answer. Then some more silence would occur while he formulated a question for her. They were sorting things out.

Laura: Why were you following me at the sanctuary that day?

Jesse: It made me nervous to think of you out there alone. I thought you needed some sort of protection. I knew there was something evil going on, but I didn't know what it was.

She had nodded, satisfied with his explanation. The crows had begun their fretful cawing in the tall trees, and a few cars passed by on the road. The day had begun for everyone, it seemed.

Jesse: Did you ever think I might be the killer?

Laura: Now and then. But I never wanted it to be you. Did you ever think it could be me?

Jesse: Never.

About then something had whispered to her that she ought to go sweep up the shattered glass in the dining room as a gesture of new beginnings, but she'd remained at her place at the table.

Laura: Remember when we thought Ralph Henderson had left something here, that the hotel was a drop?

Jesse: Sure. It seemed like a good idea at the time. But Ralph was just being Ralph.

Now, bathed and drowsy, Laura stood vigilantly at the window, waiting for Jesse's figure to appear on the landscape below, trudging out toward the oyster beds. She'd been amazed when he consulted his watch, swore softly, and went to the mac room to pull on his Wellington boots and an anorak.

Laura: You're not going to bother with the oysters, are you?

Jesse: Oysters have to be seen to. I have a contract with Jack Arnold.

Laura: Not anymore, surely?

Jesse: Until I hear otherwise.

Before he'd gone down to the flats, Jesse had asked her to step into the living room. There, in its honored place, stood the sculpture of the whale Dot had returned. The sculpture of a gray whale which she had wielded with enough force and fury to put an end to a human life.

"It's ironic," he'd said, pointing to the whale's back. "Don't you see?"

"See what?"

"Whoever presented this whale to the hotel thought it was a gray," Jesse said. "Everyone else thought so too. Dot must have imagined she was returning the very symbol of the hotel to the source."

"I imagine that's exactly what she thought."

"This isn't a gray whale," Jesse had said. "It's *Orcinus orca*. A killer whale."

The killer whale sat smugly on the mantelpiece while she wondered what to do with it. She could ask Jesse to take it with him out onto the flats and sink it in the mud, where the tides would rise to bury it forever, or she could leave it where it was.

"Let it stay," she said.

Life moved on, as people never tired of remarking. Soon she would be back in New York—reading manuscripts, going to book conferences, deciding whether or not to remain married to Dan—and this place would be only a vivid memory in the fast-running stream of her consciousness. She would think of it with pain at some times, with pleasure at others. Dorrie and Grace would soldier on at tavern and post office, and if Grace was lucky her son would mature and survive. Althea would find a way to dig a well or pull up stakes and go to live somewhere else. Even Wayne would go on to use his hair-cutting scissors in the manner in which they had been intended. Ralph and Bob Ludder would continue to bully in their separate ways, Teddy would pedal to Oregon to buy *Mother Jones,* and—with any luck—Fran would learn to think of the bunnies as rabbits.

Until Jack Arnold told him otherwise, Jesse would continue to see to the oysters Jack had claimed when he and Claudia had bought the hotel. Even as she watched from her window, his figure emerged on the flats. It was tiny and foreshortened from her viewpoint, pulling the sledge behind, planting one foot in front of the other, and steadily drawing toward its destination.

About the Author

Mary Bringle was born in Racine, Wisconsin. *Little Creatures Everywhere* is her fourth novel for the Crime Club. She lives in New York City.